Snowblind

^A Tiger Lily's Café® Mystery

By Kathleen Thompson

Kathleen Thompson

Snowblind

Volume 9

A Tiger Lily's Café® Mystery

By Kathleen Thompson

ISBN-13: 978-0-9984023-8-3

ISBN-10: 0-9984023-8-9

© Registration #TX 8-512-373

Library of Congress Control Number: 2017919082

Kathleen Thompson

A List of Tiger Lily's Café® Mystery Series Books:

This cozy mystery series has everything you seek: an eclectic cast of characters, a mystery or two, and diligent detectives on duty. The detectives just happen to be feline.

Tiger Lily's Café is set in a Midwestern town nestled into the coast of a Great Lake. The setting itself acts as a character, bringing the reader into the sights, sounds and smells of the small resort community of Chelsea.

Read the series in order, or read any book alone. While characters grown and change, each volume stands alone with a clear beginning and a clear end.

- Turtle Soup (2014)
- Boo! (2015)
- Phishing (2015)
- Holiday (2016)
- A Rock And A Hard Place (2016)
- Splash (2016)
- Chasing A Butterfly (2017)
- Pumpkin Squash (2017)
- Snowblind (2017)
- Hearts On Fire (2018)
- Morel Of The Story (2018)
- Dragon Fire (2019)
- Beach Bunnies (2020)
- Shipwreck (2020)

Kathleen Thompson

Kathleen Thompson

Cast of Characters

Humans

Annie Mack, with the help of her "kids" and a talented staff, owns and manages a bed and breakfast, a cafe and other businesses on the south side of The Avenue. She has lived in Chelsea for only a few years, but her ancestral roots to the town date to the Civil War era.

Annie's SASHET Rainbow: (sa SHAY) a model that assigns color to each core feeling. Sadness is blue; Anger red; Scare green; Happiness yellow; Excitement orange; and Tenderness purple.

For more information, visit Liberation Psychotherapy: www.libpsych.com/articles/sashet/sashet.html.

Austin and Angela live in another state. They are the parents of Chris and have not been supportive of his career in the Coast Guard or his choice of a woman. Annie.

Ben and JoJo are college students. They work part-time all over town, including most of Annie's businesses.

Boone is the person to call if you need anything: mowing, snow removal, landscaping, maintenance, preventative maintenance, and just about anything else. He is married to **Harriet (Hilly)**, who provides business cleaning services. His sons **Daryl** and **Donny** work for him. Their roots are in rural Appalachia, and they are so much more than people think.

Candice is the head waitress at Mo's Tap. A native of Chelsea, her long, thick, dark hair is the envy of most women who meet her.

Carlos is the manager and baker at Mr. Bean's Confectionary. He is a citizen of the US but was originally from Mexico. He supports his mother and younger sisters, who still live there. He is married to Isabel.

Cheryl inherited The Marina from her parents. It's a small deep water marina with basic amenities. Cheryl is married to Ray. She has known Annie since they were children.

Chris is Annie's special friend, although neither of them are ready to commit to a permanent relationship. He is the Officer in Charge of the Coast Guard Station. His stress relieving hobby is art. His sketches – in charcoal, pencil and pastel – are sold for charity.

Clara owns the flower and gift shop, Bloomin' Crazy. She is a citizen of the US, originally from Haiti, and has an ebullient personality. She keeps The Avenue decorated with fresh and silk flowers year-round.

Cookie probably has another name, but this is what he goes by. He cooks at Mo's Tap and learns what he can from Felicity at every opportunity. He's reticent at best, and he yearns to have his own restaurant. To keep him, Annie opened a fine dining restaurant, Bon Vivant Grille, on Fridays and Saturdays inside the Café.

Daniela is a former professional baker from Mexico. She has been a mother figure to Isabel, who is married to Carlos. She and her adult daughters, **Rosa** and **Valeria**, now live in Chelsea

Diana is the chief instructor at L'Socks' Virasana (Veer AHS ana). She is Mem's daughter. Diana left home right after high school and did not speak to her mother until her return ten years later. Their relationship, while tenuous, continues to grow stronger.

Felicity is the chef at Tiger Lily's Café. She is young, perky and extremely talented in the kitchen. She manages the Café, the upstairs catering facility and outside catering operations.

Frank owns an antique shop, Antiques On Main. He and Mem are in a relationship.

Gema owns Gema's Creations. There, she makes and sells unique jewelry pieces. She has space in the front corner of Antiques On Main.

George is the bartender and manager of Mo's Tap. He is a top-notch bartender and can be counted on to keep confidences. He is a volunteer with the local Coast Guard.

Georgia manages the kitchen at the Bon Vivant Grille on weekends, coordinates catering for the Café, and cooks part-time at Mo's Tap. Her father, **Fred Calendar**, comes to town on occasion to see her and her daughter Frederica **(Little Fred)**.

Geraldine was the leader of the "it" crowd in high school, and somehow, life didn't turn out quite as she expected. Everything Annie isn't – perfectly dressed, perfectly coiffed, and perfectly awful – Geraldine is more than a thorn in Annie's side. **Everett** is her on-again-off-again husband.

Ginger is the daughter of Pete, the Chief of Police, and Janet. She works part-time at L'Socks' Virasana. Because she moved to town as a teen (when her father retired from the Marine Corps), and because she is one of the few African American teens in town, she sometimes feels like an outsider.

Greg is a progressive realtor in Chelsea. His goal is to get the right property to the right owner, always moving Chelsea forward.

Gwen is Annie's accountant. A motherly figure, her financial acumen is hidden from all but those lucky enough to have her in their corner.

Hank is a former member of the Town Council. He opposes Annie in every way.

Harry is the regular driver for the rental company used almost exclusively by folks on The Avenue.

Henrie manages the KaliKo Inn in an elegant manner. He does not invite confidences and speaks little about himself. Always formal in tone, people have difficulty pegging his accent. Is it French? Cameroon? Rwandan?

Holly and Jolly, twins, own DoubleGood, an electronics and hardware store. Holly lives in a wheelchair. Natives of Chelsea, they used to hate the names given them by their parents. Now, they enjoy the novelty of it.

Ian is a childhood friend of George. He coordinates local sporting and community events. He is light-hearted and fancy-free.

Isabel is married to Carlos. She is attending classes to become a citizen. She works with Carlos in the bakery and at Bon Vivant as the hostess.

Janet is Pete's wife. She spent twenty years as a Marine officer's wife. She traveled the world and is now living in Chelsea. She is an outsider, not having grown up here like Pete. She is the ultimate community volunteer.

Jennifer and Marie, sisters and nurse practitioners, own The Drug Store and The Clinic. Folks call the sisters before calling nine-one-one. Chelsea natives, they know everyone. And their secrets.

Jenny is an attorney who focuses on family law. She enjoys taking on cases that will right an injustice. She is always ready to engage in battle with those who don't believe a woman, much less a woman of color, can dance with the big boys.

Jerry learned how to make candy in a minimum security federal prison. He was not an employee. Jerry works hard to overcome his shyness, particularly around women.

Jet is from Puerto Rico. He moved in with Holly and Jolly, taking up residence with Holly. He works at Sassy P's Wine & Cheese.

Jerry is the candy maker at Mr. Bean's Confectionary. He learned how to make candy in a minimum security federal prison. He was not an employee.

Jesus manages Sassy P's Wine & Cheese and also selects the wines. His family, famous vintners in the Napa Valley, owned, farmed and made wine for generations before California became a part of the United States.

Joan is a member of the Town Council. She opposes Hank in every way. Clara's pet name for her is "Joan of Chelsea."

Juanita is a reporter for the local newspaper. As every reporter on every small town paper, she also sells ads, develops and places the ads, does photography and…reports.

Justin is a former bully boy who now works for Boone. Justin is trying to make a break from his former bad partners and has enrolled in community college.

Laila owns Babar Foods. A traditional Pakistani, she is raising her children without the assistance of a husband. Her children are **James**, **Ava** and **Carl**, who lives with Autism.

Marco is a police officer in Chelsea. He is "second in command" because he was the only officer that didn't go off-kilter during a hostage situation. Marco prides himself on being one-hundred-percent-Italian-American.

Martha used to own a bed and breakfast. The cottage was renovated to add an apartment suite, now occupied by Georgia and Little Fred. Martha is retired and enjoys spending time at the Inn.

Mem owns the health food store and cyber café, CyberHealth. Her wisdom is reassuring to everyone, including her daughter, Diana. She teaches the safe use of social media to all ages and has equipment and technology that is helpful to the small-town police department.

Minnie chooses perfect cheeses to accompany the rotating wine selections at Sassy P's Wine & Cheese. She comes from several generations of cheese makers in Wisconsin.

Nancy and Sam are Annie's mother and step-father. They have been married since Annie was a child. They come for extended visits in Chelsea and have learned to call this town their second home.

Pete is a native of Chelsea. He retired from the Marine Corps and is now the Chief of Police. Like Annie, his ancestors arrived in the Civil War era. His, however, came up via the Underground Railroad. He and his wife Janet have three children, the eldest of whom is Ginger. Clarice and Tamara are in high school and junior high.

Ramon is Clara's boyfriend. A Jamaican by ancestry, he plays saxophone with a jazz fusion band called Bergamasco (after the breed of his dog). He and Clara work hard to maintain their mostly long-distance relationship.

Ray owns and operates The Escape, a yacht fashioned into a cruiser for fishing, diving and pleasure. He is married to Cheryl; Chris is his best friend.

Teresa is a newcomer to the area. She came to this community to serve. She pastors a small church, Soul's Harbor, and pastors the community through her outreach.

Terrence & Jerald Timmer-Schmidt have just moved to town. Terrence is a heart surgeon; Jerald is a psychiatrist. They have opened a medical office building in town.

Trudie is the barista at Tiger Lily's Café. She is from Jamaica and ended up in Chelsea when a former boyfriend dumped her at the campground. Felicity saved her, and they have been the best of friends ever since.

WQVX Channel Two. "The Lake Region's good news station" is anchored by **Charles Veritone**. The "ace onsite reporter" is **Dan Tapper**. **Felix** does weather.

Annie's Cats

Annie has seven cats. Most people would call them "rescue kitties." From Annie's perspective, each of them rescued her.

Tiger Lily is a beautiful tabby cat with soft green eyes. She is the titular manager of Tiger Lily's Café, the main gathering place for Chelsea. She is generally calm and logical.

Little Socks is a bright-eyed black cat with white socks. She has a commanding personality and is small and sneaky enough to serve as a cat burglar. She spends time at the yoga studio, L'Socks' Virasana (Veer AHS ana).

Kali, Ko and Mo are litter mates. They shared a secret language as kittens; Kali and Ko now speak "cat," but Mo still speaks "secret." Kali and Ko can be found at the KaliKo Inn, a lakeside bed and breakfast. Mo spends time at Mo's Tap, an upscale blues bar.

Sassy Pants is aptly named; it's difficult to keep this little girl's attention. She is overly sensitive and will react out of emotion instead of reason. She entertains at Sassy P's Wine & Cheese.

Mr. Bean is the baby of the family and is mostly gray with traces of tiger. He has two speeds: fast and love me.

Other Companions

Brown Mousie lives in the long building and roams from the Café to the Wine & Cheese shop. He stays primarily at Sassy P's.

Claire is a blue point Himalayan cat whose human is Frank. She's beautiful and loves people. She is stand-offish with other cats.

Cyril is an English setter whose human is Pete, the Chief of Police. Cyril is friendly and calm. He is an excellent hunter.

Daryll is a multi-colored tabby cat with an air of perpetual confusion. He lives at the state park. His human is the manager.

Fiamma is a Bergamasco. Dreadlocks cover her face. In fact, her entire body is covered with a combination of long dreadlocks and mats of hair. She is an outrageous flirt.

Honey Bear is a large, golden, long-haired mutt of a cat who believes it is his perfect right to be anywhere. Other cats hate him.

Jock is a Portuguese water dog whose human is Ray, the captain of The Escape. Jock is spirited and affectionate; he loves children.

Oscar McMurphy was a stray, named Scaredy Cat by the kids. Despite the name, she is a girl who now lives with Holly and Jolly. She claims Holly as her very own. She is often in and out of the Inn and other places on The Avenue with her brother, Simon Finnegan.

Simon Finnegan was a stray, named Fat Cat by the kids, who now lives with Holly and Jolly. He claims Jolly to be his mom. He is often in and out of the Inn and other places on The Avenue with his sister, Oscar McMurphy.

Speckles is a tortoise shell cat, named for her orange speckles. She belongs to Georgia and is Little Fred's chief nanny.

Tillie came to live on The Avenue with her dreadful family from England. She is a Jack Russell Terrier and now lives with Carlos and Isabel above the Confectionary.

She has free run of The Avenue, including the Inn. She is small enough to squeeze in and out of the cat doors.

Guests at the Inn

Kullen and Barry Knight, brothers, are in town to do some winter surfing.

Robert and Sue have made last-minute reservations. They seem not to have a reason for being in town.

Tom and Helen are from Georgia. They vacation in a different part of the country several times a year to participate in a sport typical to the area. They're in Chelsea to cross-country ski.

Others In Town

Albert docked his boat at The Marina for the winter. He is a newcomer to boats; this is his first winter to be docked anywhere.

Carter docked his boat at The Marina for the winter. He's been living on his boat for several years; this is his first winter in Chelsea.

Randy is a federal marshal, on the look-out for a man in the witness protection program that is on the run.

Kathleen Thompson

1

Someone standing at the bottom of the dune on that Monday morning, had that person looked up, would have seen a tallish man, almost six feet, with the erect bearing of someone with military training. A knit cap covered his hair, but the person looking up would have seen neatly trimmed, possibly prematurely white facial hair, both a mustache and beard.

The man stood half-facing the lake, half-facing something the watcher might not have recognized. The man held something small in his hand.

The watcher, if looking from the proper angle, would have seen a picture taking shape. A watercolor of the lake, whitecaps and drifting snow the only indication of a sharp wind whipping over the lake from the northwest.

By now, most watchers would have moved on, not taking the assault of the wind easily. The man, however, stood his ground on the dune. He was used to the wind, loved it, in fact, and allowed his senses to take it in as he committed thoughts and feelings to canvas.

The wind, harbinger of a wicked storm to come, was cold and sharp with pricks of snow from the last storm. The wind sang in harmony with the song in the man's heart. The watercolor taking shape was building in colors of gray, blue and brown.

Snow clouds filled the sky, lighter gray, turning darker gray and finally slate blue. The gray lake turned darker gray and brown with whitecaps peaking at two feet. Snowdrifts, turning brown with the sand that mixed in, partially covered tall brown grasses.

The man was the Officer in Charge of the Coast Guard Station in Chelsea, a resort town on the sunset side of one of the Great Lakes. The town was insulated from the rest of the world, surrounded on two sides by a wooded state park and on another by the lake. One access road came in from the east.

The town enjoyed a robust tourist trade and was peppered with typical tourist businesses: bed and breakfasts, motels, restaurants, wineries, campgrounds, marinas and a man-made deep water harbor.

To the right and in front of the man were several prominent lake-front houses and a high-end condominium complex hidden from public roadways by the wooded state park.

To the left and behind the man was a lighthouse used as a historic museum. Beyond that, the lakeshore curved around the state park, a rocky, low cliff, and the town park with a white sand beach, currently covered with a mix of sand and snow.

From the middle of the park, a jetty led to another lighthouse. During most of the year, individuals and families fished from the jetty. Today, however, the whitecaps became waves breaking onto the jetty, and access was closed off. Icy tentacles clung to the lighthouse and the jetty, sparkling when some small remnant of sun shone through.

Past the city park beach was a public parking lot, fronted with more beach, which led to another area of white sand. This private beach belonged to the owner of a prominent bed and breakfast, the KaliKo Inn.

Beyond that beach was the local marina, situated on a man-made deep water harbor. Ice was trying to form around the few boats remaining at the piers.

More state park woods were on the other side of the harbor and marina, completing the picture and closing in the town.

The man, his name was Chris, was nearly finished with the watercolor. It needed something. What?

He sat on a canvas chair, sinking into it while he gazed at the painting. It was held fast to an antique easel, a type that came into fashion in the mid-nineteenth century. The easel was self-contained. A box held paints and supplies, telescoping legs fit inside the box, and the easel itself could be easily carried by a leather handle. The easel was made of elm and had been well-cared for over the years. The legs sunk easily into the snow and sand, anchoring the easel against the wind.

The easel had been a gift from a special person, the owner of the KaliKo Inn, Annie. Thoughts of Annie drove his painting into the grays, dark blues and browns today. His paintings usually had at least one element of a brighter color. If his thoughts were not so gray, he would have added a streak of sunshine coming through the clouds, or a splash of coral indicating a sun setting behind the lake.

Perhaps the lack of color left him unsettled. But he couldn't bring himself to add anything.

After several minutes, he packed his supplies into the box, released the canvas from the easel, and prepared to take everything home.

Home. This morning he would go home, not to work, not into town to the Café. Home.

This was a rare Monday.

Annie got to the dining room just as the Inn's two guests were leaving. Annie noticed they had on light but cold-proof outerwear, expensive and appropriate for the weather. They also had backpacks filled with...well, she could hardly tell what was in them, could she.

"Good morning. Headed out already?"

The man, Annie had trouble with names and thought his name was Robert, said, "We want to make the most of this vacation. Today we're doing the trails at the state park."

The woman, Sue, maybe, said, "Your brochures had several places we can try. We'll do a new one every day. Bye!"

Annie waved, and the two left so quickly the door slammed in their wake.

Annie walked through the dining room to the kitchen. "Morning, Henrie. Robert and Sue..."

"Tom and Helen."

"Really? I got it wrong again?"

"Did you call them by name?"

"You know me better than that. I don't call names until I'm absolutely sure."

"An excellent plan for you. Please, continue."

"Oh, yeah, well, Tom and Helen seem committed to their vacation plans, no matter the weather."

"I am somewhat concerned. They plan to go out every day from now through the weekend. I tried to impress upon them the weather situation, but..."

"I don't see the allure of cross country skiing, but at least they are on semi-flat ground."

Annie went into the dining room and poked around until she had filled a plate. There was not much left, but she was able to eke out small portions of several items.

This morning, as well as his typical egg casserole and variety of meats and breads, Henrie served eggnog French toast and a breakfast quinoa that smelled like gingerbread. Ah, December! Annie loved December foods.

Annie set her plate on the dining room table and lifted a corner of the tablecloth covering a table against the wall. She leaned down, looked in and said, "Kids, we'll be leaving for work soon."

One bright green eye opened. The eye was surrounded by a black furry face. It focused on Annie, then closed. Annie caught a whiff of bacon. Henrie was too good to them. Really.

In the kitchen, Annie set her plate next to the cup of coffee Henrie had poured. "We got an early start to the week with..."

"Tom and Helen."

"Yes. Thanks. Tom and Helen. Sunday B&B intakes are rare."

"They are, indeed. Has your committee finished decorating the town?"

"We're done here on The Avenue. We were going to finish the lighthouse today, but Pete called to say we can't get out to it. Something about the Coast Guard calling a gale warning."

"I am afraid you will be hard-pressed to finish it before the weekend. The weather will get worse, not better."

"Maybe Chris can help. He could take us out on a cutter."

Henrie, who had joined Annie at the table, put down his coffee cup and stared at her.

"What?"

"You would not dream of asking him."

"Bad idea, huh?"

"If the Coast Guard has called a gale warning, the Station's Commander cannot be seen to ignore it. Speaking of Chris, I did not see him this weekend. Did he have to work?"

Annie slid her eyes to her plate and didn't reply.

Henrie, more in tune with human nature than most of his fellow human beings, remained silent. After a time, he said, "Hilly let me know that Boone and his boys will remain on duty as often as they can this week, and that they will attempt to stay ahead of the snow."

"We should invite them to stay in the carriage house, free of charge, of course, so they can stay close to all of their in-town customers. And the power where they live can be, well, iffy, on occasion."

"I shall offer the invitation when she arrives this morning. We will count on supplies for all of our guests – I will add Boone, Hilly and the boys to the count – and, frankly, everyone on The Avenue. Our home is the safest by far."

"One of the reasons it's the safest is that you're already working on your lists. Henrie, I often wonder what I would do without you, but most of the time, I wonder what Chelsea would do without you. Thanks."

"You are welcome. Allow me to remind you of our guests this week. Or lack thereof."

"More cancellations?"

"Yes, but we still have the addition, the couple that called last night, the 'Robert and Sue' whose names you have inexplicably entwined with Tom and Helen."

Annie feigned indignation. "I'm working on it. It's a life-long disability. Anyway, what rooms are empty now?"

"The carriage house had been filled and is now empty, with the exception, of course, of Boone, Hilly and company. The brothers arriving tomorrow originally wanted separate rooms. I was going to separate them, now that the room facing the winery cancelled, but...just in case we need it, I shall keep them together. So, we have one floor of the carriage house, the back room on this level, the room facing the winery, and the basement emergency suite. We must name these rooms in January."

"You're right. It gets stilted. Every B&B names their rooms. We're just going to do it later rather than sooner."

Annie finished her breakfast, stood and said, "I've got to go. I'll take the kids with me. By tomorrow, I'm going to have to see if I can borrow Clara's heated wagon to cart them around town. It will be awfully cold on their little paws."

She left, lifting the tablecloth one more time to say, "Come on, kids. Time to go to work."

Annie owned a prime piece of property in Chelsea. On it stood the most prominent bed and breakfast in town, the KaliKo Inn, and a two-story building that started at the Inn and ended at the town circle. In that building were five additional businesses, named, like the Inn, after her cats.

Kali and Ko, big dilute calico girls, walked sedately to the Inn's library to nap on the windowsill. Whatever rays of sun happened to make it through the clouds that day had a good chance of landing there.

As Annie walked toward the town circle, bundled in her warm, durable and less than fashionable winter outerwear, she dropped her kids off at their own places of work. Of course, human counterparts actually managed them, but the cats, to hear them talk, if you could understand them, thought they ran the places.

The first cat to peel off was Sassy Pants, running into Sassy P's Wine & Cheese. Her scattered personality was perfect for chasing after loose wine corks and mingling with a variety of guests. She scooted through the cat door, an accessory on all of Annie's exterior and interior doors.

Mr. Bean, the youngest of the group, a strong gray kitten, ran through the cat door to Mr. Bean's Confectionary, where most of the region came to get their baked goods and truffles.

Mo, who hated to walk, hung onto Annie's shoulder until the last minute, when he finally had to put his paws on the chilly sidewalk. His long gray hair blew in the wind until he was safely inside Mo's Tap, a blues bar that carried the best collection of artisan beers in a multi-county area.

Little Socks, a black tuxedo cat with bright green eyes – and the alpha of the group – walked into Lil' Socks' Virasana, a yoga studio. Before Annie walked past the door, Little Socks was on the windowsill, kneading a black pillow for the next nap.

Alone with her oldest girl, Tiger Lily, Annie looked down as they finished their walk to Tiger Lily's Café. Tiger Lily looked up, expectant.

"Keep an ear out today, honey. Maybe you'll find out what's going on with Chris, and then, maybe, you can figure out how to let me know."

Tiger Lily blinked once, and they entered the Café.

Tiger Lily's Café was a main gathering place for Chelsea. Locals and tourists alike found the food excellent and the atmosphere eclectic and welcoming. Situated on the corner of Sunset Avenue and Main Street, just across Main Street from the Town Circle, it screamed to marketing geniuses, "location, location, location!" Annie and her competent staff made the best of it.

Her competent staff at the Café included chef and manager Felicity. Perky, independent and creative, she kept local and regional customers coming back for more. Her sidekick, Trudie, served as barista and back-up manager.

Today, Annie walked in to the smell of peppermint, white chocolate and gingerbread, the coffees of the month. She stopped at the hostess stand and looked out the window and across and down the street.

Sunset Avenue was one long city block in length, starting at the circle and ending at the lake. Or, rather, at the convergence of the beach, the city park, the municipal parking lot and the entrance to the state park's campground.

Known by everyone as just "The Avenue," the wide street was typically filled with people all day long, from sunup to sundown. Generally, at sundown, one could find walkers and sitters gazing over the lake at the reds, corals, oranges and purples of the sunset.

There were plenty of places to sit. Outside each of Annie's businesses were sets of colorful café tables and chairs, and the median of The Avenue was almost a park in itself. It was wide and outfitted with game tables, benches and landscaping to beckon to everyone wanting to walk or play chess.

On the other side of The Avenue was another two-story building, mirroring Annie's own, but with a few differences. This building had not been as well maintained over the decades. Instead of the original brick façade, it was covered in a variety of pastel paint colors.

Annie loved to look across at it, and today, she had to sigh. A couple of months ago, some vandals had defaced the building. After several weeks of waiting for the insurance company to decide it had not been the fault of the collective owners, they had settled. The building was painted just before the first early snowstorm arrived. The exterior wall was once again a rainbow of pastels, but the logos and business names had not been painted on. Most of the work had been done by one of the vandals, a young man who accepted no pay to make up for his misdeed.

This young man, Justin, now worked for Boone, doing landscaping, snow removal, maintenance and repair of local buildings. Annie thought about that. If Boone trusted him, the young man was on the right track now.

She stopped her daydream and turned to start her day.

Worried about traveling, Sue didn't realize how curt she had become. She put the overnight bag in the back seat, slammed the door and got into the front. She touched her purse again to make sure the pistol was inside.

Robert opened the door and slid into the driver's seat. He checked the atmosphere before asking, "Are you sure about this?"

"Absolutely."

"Why couldn't we have sent that private detective?"

"He doesn't have a personal investment. I do. I'll get the job done."

"I get that you want to do it yourself. Tell me again why we can't just fly?"

"We want to get in, get it done, and get out. We can't be messing around at airports, getting rental cars. And besides, I have this." Sue waggled her purse in the air.

"Oh. Right. Well, let's go. We'll be on the road for two and a half days."

Henrie finished cleaning the dining room. His guests had eaten quite a bit, but then, if they were athletic and planned to work it off on cross country skis, they needed the nourishment. Still…he would have to factor in their appetites as he planned meals for the rest of the week. The two of them were eating enough for six.

Henrie, the manager of the KaliKo Inn, was an enigma. Previously a manager of a five-star hotel, he seemed perfectly content to be the chief cook, bottle washer and toilet bowl cleaner for a B&B in this small town.

His accent was untellable. Some thought French, some thought Rwandan. He read minds, or at least the guests of the Inn thought he did, as he seemed to know what they wanted before they knew themselves.

His tone was always formal, his bearing erect. Due to his manner, female guests prone to swoon did it in private and not in his presence.

As Annie had alluded earlier, Henrie had a way of taking care of all their friends and seemed to do it without a need for thanks. He just did what needed to be done.

Now, what needed to be done was to make another list. Hilly, Boone's wife and responsible for cleaning many businesses in town, all of Annie's among them, had just come from the guest room facing the lake. Tom and Helen's room.

She sat at the table and took the coffee offered by Henrie.

"You should have seen those cats."

"Kali and Ko? What did they do?"

"They went into that room with me. They do that sometimes, and they always sniff the place up. You know, jump on the beds before I change the sheets, get up on the dressers, take a sniff at the shoes that are lying around.

Today, though, they went straight to that armoire. I admit, it had me curious, but I didn't try to open it."

"How long did it hold their interest?"

"The whole time I was in the room. They went at it from just about every angle. Kali even stuffed herself underneath it. I was afraid I was going to have to call you to help get her out, but she made it."

Henrie tucked that bit of information away and turned to the matter at hand. "Hilly, Annie and I discussed the possibility that you and your family may want to stay in town as the weather dictates. No one is staying in the carriage house, and we can make it available to you. In the past, we have had weather refugees. We could hold one floor for that possibility and give you the other."

"That might be a good idea, Henrie. I'll talk to Boone and the boys tonight. Justin, too. He can bunk with the boys if it would help. From current reports, I'd say we might want to move in on Wednesday morning, if we do it."

"I agree. And with that in mind, let us turn to the next task, preparing for the storm. We must assume both the Inn and the carriage house to be full. Overfull, actually. We have bed space in the basement as well."

"Let's get started. What do you have there?"

"This is my winter storm list. We must decide what we have and what we still need. I will take care of the food items. I put an order in with Laila already. Extra food supplies will arrive tomorrow."

"Had you already counted us when you did that?"

Henrie smiled. "Of course. Let us move on to the kinds of things you and Boone can supply."

They discussed ice melt, extra shovels, sand, snow blowers, and fuel for the generators.

Henrie ticked off the number of blankets, pillows, air mattresses, thermal gloves, socks, t-shirts and leggings that were on hand and added a few to the list for purchase.

"Are you sure you have enough blankets on that list, Henrie?"

"You have not been in Annie's apartment since Thanksgiving. You will be surprised at the number of quilts Annie's mother made and left for us."

"Since when does Nancy make quilts?"

"I believe she started in September, and she rarely stopped, even to eat or sleep. Sam, I believe, was beginning to feel like a widower, until he decided to join her."

Hilly laughed and moved on to the next item on the list. "Do we need to take a look at your vehicles, Henrie?"

"Boone took care of that in November. However, we must restock our emergency kits. I have the list here."

Hilly took responsibility for some of the items and Henrie for others as they continued down the list.

Finally, Hilly left, the wind nearly taking her hat as she walked out the door.

2

Ian arrived at the Café just as the lunch rush was ending. He motioned to Annie and sat at a table by the window. Annie motioned to Trudie, who made four coffees. Felicity joined them, and they discussed the most recent Chelsea disaster.

Ian was the king of Chelsea disasters. He had a full-time job at a local bank, and he had another more-than-full-time job, at least for several months of the year, as the volunteer coordinator for Chelsea events. He started as the sporting events coordinator but had the misfortune of being good at it. And the misfortune of being unable to say "no."

Annie took a sip of gingerbread latte and welcomed Tiger Lily to the table. It was Tiger Lily's business, after all. She shared an interest in all the town's disasters.

Ian got right to the point. "At least fifty percent of the vendors have cancelled. They don't think anyone will be able to get into town. I've shut down the spaces at the community building and have everyone that's left coming to your place upstairs."

"How much money are we going to lose?"

"A lot. Our policy states they can get their money back if the event is cancelled due to weather."

"What if we don't cancel? What if we just say it's going on, even if nobody comes?"

Ian's head jerked toward Annie. "Really?"

"It was just a thought."

Significant effort had been put into having crafters, artists, authors, jewelry artisans and antique dealers set up booths for Christmas In Chelsea. There had been enough interest for this first attempt to fill the community building and Annie's second floor catering venue. If there were only enough for her catering venue, clearly, at least seventy percent had cancelled.

As they commiserated over this latest disaster, they were joined by Pete, the local Chief of Police, and his constant sidekick, Cyril. Cyril, a large English setter, white with brown splotches, sprawled under the table with Tiger Lily while Trudie got a coffee for Pete.

"So, you can't decorate the lighthouse, and if you're here, Ian, there must be other problems."

"Vendors are cancelling. We won't be using the community building at all, and, well, I wonder if we'll be doing anything."

"That helps me. I was worried about putting officers in the park in this weather. Maybe I'll just keep them in the office. They can look out the window and patrol this place."

"Be serious, Pete. This is a disaster."

"Not for me, but, you're right. You and most of the folks in town were counting on this weekend. How about the Inn, Annie? What's happening there?"

"Cancellations. At my place and all over town. We got one stray new booking. They must not be watching the weather reports."

"Probably someone coming in to murder someone, with your track record."

"I'm sure, Pete. Well, Ian, there's nothing we can do about it now. Just let us know if it closes up altogether."

"Will do. I have to get back to work."

Before he left, Ian got on his knees to administer his famous two-handed strokes, first to Cyril, then to Tiger Lily. With a wave, he was gone. Pete remained.

"Not going back to work, Pete?"

"It's cold out there. I can see my office from here. I'll stick for a few, if it's not a problem."

"Not a problem. But we have to talk business."

Annie turned to Felicity and Trudie. "We're going to have a Skype meeting Wednesday morning, but that's the day the storm is expected to roll in. We have to be ready before that."

"I've ordered extra food that should hold us for several days, but we're going to have to get creative if we don't use it all. I'd rather freeze things and make casseroles for the rest of the month than be caught short-handed."

Trudie said, "What about the weekend? Do you think Bon Vivant can open?"

The Bon Vivant Grille was Annie's foray into fine dining. Another cook took responsibility for it and opened inside the Café on Friday and Saturday nights.

"I doubt it, but you know, weather reports have been wrong in the past. Talk to Cookie. Maybe his menus for this weekend can be used for your specials next week."

"That should be easy enough. Also, Trudie and I are going to have a big slumber party for as long as it takes. The women will stay in my apartment and the men in hers. I'm ordering enough food for them as well."

"Do you have enough other supplies? Blankets? Pillows? Batteries?"

"I don't even know what to get."

"Call Henrie as soon as I leave here. He'll either know what to tell you to do, or he's already doing it for you. But he needs to know about the extra people. Good idea, Felicity."

"It was Trudie's idea."

Trudie said, "No, really, it was Kate's idea. She needs the money and asked if she could bunk in, to make sure she could get in to work."

"I'll thank her on my way out. Now, hopefully, there will be customers, as long as we'll have the supplies and staff."

"We're the center of everything. We'll feed emergency workers and, well, everyone who has to be in town."

"Good. I wonder if emergency workers will need a place to sleep and clean up. Pete, what do you think?"

"If it gets as bad as it has on occasion, that would be a blessing."

"I think we still have one floor of the carriage house open. I'll say something to Henrie. Pete, count on it, and let the other services know, okay? Utilities, street department, your department, firefighters, the Coast Guard…"

Trudie looked at Annie. "Speaking of the Coast Guard, Chris didn't come in today. Is he out on the lake?"

"Must be," said Annie, and she stood. "I'll thank Kate and see you tomorrow."

She left quickly. Pete, Felicity and Trudie stared as she walked away.

Tiger Lily and Cyril curled into one another on the cold floor. They could have found a more comfortable space, but they wanted to listen to their humans.

"There's a big storm coming," said Cyril.

"I know. Mommy said it will be bad. Henrie's making lists."

"That's both a good sign and a bad one. Bad, because you know he's getting ready for something bad. Good, because you know you'll have plenty of food."

"We'll have enough for you, if you need to come."

"I think we'll be okay, but, it's good to know."

They settled into listening until suddenly Annie was up and moving. Tiger Lily jumped to follow her, but first whispered to Cyril, *"See if you can pick up anything about Chris. Okay?"*

"Sure. See you later."

Tiger Lily trotted after Annie and out the door. "Do you want to go home, Darlin', or do you want to come with me?"

Tiger Lily blinked once and followed Annie to the yoga studio.

The studio was deserted. Apparently, few people were interested in exercise on cold, windy days. Diana lounged behind her counter, feet up, engrossed in a book.

Little Socks curled in her lap, which was probably warmer than the pillow on the windowsill. The sun still had not made an appearance. One green eye opened.

Tiger Lily approached the two and received a caress on the head from Diana. She received a hiss from Little Socks.

Tiger Lily bopped her on the nose, and the two began their own exercise program, chasing one another up and down the room. They ran, turned, skidded on the slick floor, smacked into walls, and missed one another completely.

Annie pulled a chair over and sat next to Diana. They watched the cats, saying nothing to one another for several minutes. Finally, Annie asked, "Is this what the week will be like for you?"

"Probably. I cancelled all of the part-time instructors. They might suffer a little on their holiday cash."

"There are times it can't be helped."

"I know. I hate it, but…."

"Don't worry about it, Diana. Are you ready for the storm?"

"I have a stash of comfort food. I was going to get movies from the library, but I'll rely on Netflix."

"When you think it's time, put the 'closed' sign up and go home."

"I can do that."

At Mo's Tap, Tiger Lily and Little Socks searched for Mo. They found him in the arms of a woman, of course, and they badgered him until he had to leave her embrace and bop noses. There were too many chairs and tables for a good run-around, so they made do with a friendly tiff in one of the private areas.

The cats were always mindful of appearances when customers were present.

Annie said hello to George and Diana but walked to the kitchen.

"Cookie, Felicity will probably talk to you…"

Cookie threw a burger on the grill as he broke into her thought. "She already called. I hope we can open this weekend, but I can alter the menu a bit. Have some things that will freeze well, or that we can make into soups or casseroles."

"Good. I hate to think about not opening, but…if nothing else, maybe we can open on Saturday. Are you staying somewhere on The Avenue this week, or will you try to drive in?"

"I'm staying. Jerry has one of those beds-in-a-sofa. I want to be close, just in case we can open."

Annie leaned against the prep table to talk to Georgia. Georgia worked at several of Annie's businesses, chiefly at the Tap and at Bon Vivant. Today, the Tap had been as busy for lunch as the Café. She remained at the window, triaging orders.

She had a young child, Little Fred, and lived in a recently renovated suite in a former bed and breakfast in town. Martha, her landlord, was getting up in years. Annie assumed she would not have a generator.

"What would you think about moving into the back bedroom at the Inn? The one you stayed in before? It would be a little tight, because we need to get Martha over, also."

"Thanks, Annie. We were talking about that this morning. Martha meant to get a generator this fall, but she ran out of money. Frankly, we talked about the Inn as a possibility if the electricity went out."

"By that time, you'd be snowed in and we wouldn't be able to get you over. I'll call Henrie. Why don't you call Martha and make sure she's comfortable with the arrangement. I think you should move in Wednesday morning."

Annie called Henrie. "So, how about putting Martha, Georgia and Little Fred in the back room downstairs?"

"Excellent idea. I was thinking also about the emergency crews that may need a place to sleep and clean up. We can make one floor of the carriage house available."

"You were reading my mind. I told Pete to let people know it will be open to them."

"I shall stock the larders this afternoon and assure several sets of sheets and towels are available."

"Do we have enough for this?"

"I have added a bit to our inventory. We will get by, if we do laundry daily."

Annie gathered three four-legged children. As they walked to Mr. Bean's Confectionary, she told them, "Your friends Speckles and Daryll will be staying at the Inn, starting on Wednesday. And that sweet baby, Little Fred, will be there, too."

Mo couldn't wait to give Mr. Bean the news. He was generally not the first to hear gossip, and he wanted to rub it in. Unfortunately, all Mr. Bean heard was a series of trills and purrs. None of Mo's usual translators was present.

Mo, chagrined, stomped behind the serving counter to lay close to door behind which the cat treats were displayed.

Tiger Lily told Mr. Bean and Tillie about the upcoming visit. *"Those nanny kitties will be at the Inn this week, and Little Fred, too."*

"Oh, I hope I can come see them!" Tillie, a Jack Russell terrier, lived on the second floor of the bakery with Carlos, the manager and head baker, and his wife, Isabel. Tillie spent her days at the bakery, vying with Mr. Bean for attention from customers. For the most part, they had a workable arrangement, taking turns dancing in the window to lure people in and greeting customers as they arrived. For the most part. Sometimes a little fur flew.

Annie asked Carlos and Jerry about their emergency plans. Jerry was the best candy maker in the region. He was also one of the shyest people Annie knew. She had been surprised to hear Cookie say he would be staying with Jerry.

He handed Annie a cinnamon toffee truffle as he said, "Cookie is staying with me, and I could probably handle others, if anyone else needs to stay over."

"Thanks, Jerry. I appreciate it. Carlos, what about your mom?"

"She's going to stay with us. The girls are staying next door, in Minnie's apartment."

Carlos learned his baking skills from his mother, who used to own a shop in Mexico. 'The girls' were Carlos's sisters, Rosa and Valeria. They moved to Chelsea with their mother some months previously and now had jobs in the community. Valeria worked across the street at Bloomin' Crazy. Rosa worked as the office manager for two doctors.

To say they had moved to Chelsea was putting it mildly. Carlos made a quick trip to Mexico to extricate the family from the clutches of a gang. The three of them, and Isabel, his new wife, were documented and were taking classes to become citizens.

When Annie was ready to leave, she had to go behind the counter and try to pick up the dead weight of Mo. He was in a sulk and was not about to be placated.

"Okay, Mo. It's fine if you stay here. Or walk home."

Mo reached Annie before she got to the door and begged to be held. As they walked out, Annie heard yicks and yowls. Three cats were telling their brother what a big baby he was. Mo pressed his paws to Annie's neck and stuck out his tongue.

At Sassy P's Wine & Cheese, the cats ran to the back dining room. They could count on Sassy Pants being there, most likely in the vicinity of their pet, Brown Mousie.

At least the cats considered Brown Mousie to be their pet. He stayed hidden from humans and was able to help them in their detecting business, usually by being in the right place at the right time. Humans didn't realize their conversations were being overheard, and Brown Mousie could fit into some tight places.

Even Mo came out of his funk and joined the group around a potted hibiscus.

Sassy Pants turned to watch as her siblings ran into the room. *"Hey guys, Brown Mousie has news!"*

"What?" "Huh?" "It's just Monday, and he has news?"

They gathered around, looking expectantly at the little mouse.

Brown Mousie was no longer afraid of this group of cats. He know they could be trusted not to eat him. He kept his family away, however. Cats couldn't be trusted to overlook all the mice. Just him.

"I heard some people from the Coast Guard place talking today. They were getting ready for a storm, and they started talking about the people that work there."

"Did they talk about Chris?"

"Yes. These people, I think one was Trevor and one was Janelle, anyway, they said something about Chris moving away."

"No!" "Trill!" "No way!"

"Yes. They said he was getting a promotion, but he hasn't said anything to anybody."

"Then how do they know?"

"They were talking about someone they called a blockhead named Shorter. He told Trevor someone from some big office somewhere called him and told him he was finally going to get Chris's job, because he'd be leaving."

"Did you hear where?"

"Some big city on some other lake. It sounded really far away."

"Will he take us with him?"

"I don't know anything about that. I only know what they said. They don't want Chris to leave. They like him. They say Shorter is mean, and he can't be trusted."

"Why would he get Chris's job? You have to be good to be in charge."

"*They said he acts different with the bosses. They called it 'sucking up,' and then they laughed about this bottle of mouthwash that he keeps in his desk.*"

"*What's funny about mouthwash? Isn't that what humans use to not smell so bad?*"

"*I don't know. They called it his not-so-secret-secret, and that it's only a matter of time before Chris catches him. Whatever that means.*"

Little Socks finally spoke up. "*Chris wouldn't do that to Mommy. He wouldn't do that to us. They must have been mistaken.*"

Minnie saw them gathered at the hibiscus and said to Annie, "I just know we have a mouse. For months now, the cats tend to gather around one pot or another. They used to run around."

"Have you set a trap?"

"No. Sassy seems happy, and we don't see any evidence. I just know it, though."

"I hear you'll have boarders this week."

Minnie and Jesus, partners in life as well as at the Winery, used to live in separate apartments upstairs. When they made their personal arrangement public, they shared living quarters. Annie offered to renovate, but they preferred having two separate places. Typically living in the larger one, the smaller one was available for quiet time or for guests. Like this week.

"We're happy to have them. If shops on The Avenue are open, Valeria will be able to get to work. I bet Rosa will have some time off, though."

"She can always pick up some hours in one place or another."

"We probably won't need extra help. Even if our staff can't get in, with us living upstairs and Jet just across the street, we'll have plenty of help. During a storm, the winery is the least busy."

"I don't know why. This is exactly where I'd come if I had one street of eateries available to me during a storm."

"My thought exactly." Minnie reached into a cooler. "Here is your to-go order. Having a party tonight?"

"Just Chris, Ray and Cheryl. We haven't spent much time together in the last month or so. Let me get three bottles of wine while I'm here."

By the time Annie got back to the Inn, she had five cats in tow. Henrie, as usual, was ready with snacks.

Chris looked at the cell phone display. It was Ray. Chris sighed and touched the button to answer. "Hi, Ray. Are you and Cheryl ready for the storm?"

Ray and Cheryl owned The Marina, situated on a small deep-water harbor, home to scores of pleasure and sporting craft in season, and The Escape, a yacht repurposed into a cruise and fishing boat for tourists. And locals. Mostly tourists. This time of year, the couple had a lot of free time on their hands.

"Almost. We have a couple of new winter boarders, and I'm worried about them."

"Winter boarders? At The Marina?"

"Yep. You know you can find people all over the lake that dock during the winter and continue to live on their boats, but this is a first for us. We planned for it, sent out flyers and such, but still…we're new to this."

"And you have two? Are they traveling together?"

"Don't appear to be. One arrived just before the last storm. He has a little experience. The other one has been here a few days. Seems he got stuck in a shallow port for the first storm, and they directed him here. Told him to get here 'forthwith.' He's as green as they come."

"Lucky you."

"Yeah. I'll tell you about it this evening. What time are we getting together?"

Chris sighed again, but didn't let Ray hear him. "I think seven."

"Okay. See you then."

"Yeah." Chris hit the button to disconnect and threw his cell phone into a chair. Oh, well. He was going to have to face Annie at some point.

3

Tiger Lily was anxious to talk to her siblings about everything she heard that afternoon, but she had something else to do.

"Let's talk about all of it when Jock gets here. I have something to do before then."

Mr. Bean, always ready for an adventure, asked, *"Can I come?"*

"I suppose. Come on."

Tiger Lily headed for the front door. Mr. Bean, following, asked, *"We're going outside? It's cold."*

"I know. You don't have to come."

The little gray cat followed, vowing not to complain.

They trotted across The Avenue and over to DoubleGood, the combination hardware and technology store. Lucky for the kids, all the businesses on the other side of The Avenue had added cat doors to their front entrances, to allow free access for Annie's cats.

Tiger Lily stopped just inside the door to look, listen and smell. She thought the two she wanted to see were in the back of the building. She moved on, again followed by Mr. Bean. When they reached the back, they were rewarded with a, *"Whatcha doin'?"*

Tiger Lily sat and regarded her two large friends. She knew them best as Fat Cat and Scaredy Cat. They now had a fur-ever home and human-given names, Simon Finnegan and Oscar McMurphey.

Mr. Bean said, *"We came to visit. I'm not sure why."*

Tiger Lily shushed Mr. Bean and said, *"Have you heard about the storm that's coming?"*

"Yeah. It's supposed to be really bad."

"It's going to be real hard on cats. Henrie is going to make sure we have lots of food and stuff, and Mommy has something called generators."

"What's that?"

"It makes sure that the electricity stays on, you know, and heat and stuff."

"We don't have that," said Fat Cat.

Scaredy Cat said, *"Last summer, we had a storm and our electricity went off. We were in the dark all night."*

"Well," said Tiger Lily, *"you might just want to come to our house and stay. Mommy keeps saying something about Wednesday. I think that's the day after tomorrow."*

"What about Holly and Jolly?"

"Mommy will probably call them, but sometimes you guys can't be found when they look for you. And when it starts to snow real bad, you might not be able to walk across."

"But Holly! What about her? If we can't walk across, she can't come in her wheelchair."

"Mommy and Henrie will probably take care of that. But like I said, you guys sometimes hide. Make sure you come, either when they do or before."

"Okay. Thanks for letting us know. Will Henrie have enough food for us?"

"He always plans for extra."

Mission accomplished, they chatted for a while, and Mr. Bean found a rubber doohicky that needed a good swat-around.

Eventually, Tiger Lily said, *"Come on, Mr. Bean. It's almost time for supper."*

Albert sat back, thinking of his situation. No one would find him. The boat was purchased and registered in a name bearing no relationship to his real one. His money was deposited in several banks around the country, easily accessible online, and in several additional names. He used burner phones that could not be traced.

There was just one problem.

He was not going to survive this winter. At least, not alone. And not without some discomfort.

He needed to get the measure of this fellow, Carter. Perhaps Carter could be convinced to take him onboard for the worst of the winter.

The kids had just finished eating when they heard the sound of their friend arriving. Ray and Cheryl knocked on the third floor apartment door and Jock barked for joy. He hadn't seen his cat friends for what seemed like a very long time.

Jock, a Portuguese water dog, didn't get to spend much time with the cats. Usually his friend Cyril got more face time with them. He was going to enjoy having them all to himself. Actually, since he was a tease at heart, he hoped to pick up some gossip on Cyril that he could use the next time they were together.

Sassy Pants lay on the floor in front of a dancing Jock, braving his feet like a rodeo rider tossed off a bronco. She was sure he would see her, stop, and nuzzle her tummy.

He didn't.

When Annie and her friends heard a kitty shriek, they looked over, determined everyone was still alive, and continued with what they were doing.

Jock stood stock still as he watched his humans. They smiled and turned away, and he looked quickly at Sassy Pants, now on top of the refrigerator.

"I'm sorry, Sassy. I didn't see you. Are you alright?"

"Yeah. I thots you wood tickle me."

"I would have if I'd seen you. When you're ready, come back down and I will."

He turned to the rest of the cats, mostly curled up in quiet laughter. *"What's happening around town? Have I missed anything?"*

Jock lived at The Marina and went on the yacht, The Escape, with Ray. Usually, he only came to town – a long city block away – when Ray came. Gossip didn't always travel to The Marina.

Tiger Lily said, *"It was getting so late, we decided to wait until you got here to catch up on our day."*

Kali and Ko said, at the same time, *"We have something!"* *"The new people are hiding food!"*

"What?"

Kali looked at Ko. Ko started. *"We went into the room when Hilly went to clean today. We don't always do that. You know, we sometimes nap when she's here."*

Kali took over. *"But we smelled the food they took upstairs."*

"Yeah. Breakfast. They took a lot of Henrie's breakfast upstairs."

"And locked it in that big thing."

Mo said, *"Trill."* Mo's speaking abilities had not advanced beyond the private kitten language he used with litter mates Kali and Ko. Usually, they had to translate for him. This evening, he worked the plan in the opposite way and tried to translate for them.

"Huh?" asked Tiger Lily.

Sassy Pants, who for some unknown reason could read minds, translated for Mo. *"He saided dat big cupboard dere. He uses a word I still duzn't know. I'ze heard it lots, but I duzn't know it."*

Little Socks, head pressed to the floor, said in a strangled voice, *"Armoire. Armoire."*

"Yeah," said Sassy Pants. *"Dat's it."*

Kali and Ko were embarrassed and didn't acknowledge that they had trouble with this word. This was, in fact, their place of work. They needed to get with it.

Ko tried to pass off the awkward moment. *"Well, we were just saying that these people..."*

Kali offered, *"...Tom and Sue..."*

Ko countered, *"No, Robert and Helen..."*

Slowly, Kali said, *"That's not right..."*

Ko thought for a minute, then she brightened. *"Mommy said..."*

Kali ended the sentence. *"...Robert. Mommy said Robert."*

Ko beamed. *"So his name is really Tom."*

Kali, now that they were on a roll, said, *"Right. And Mommy said Sue."*

Ko responded, *"So her name is Helen. So....Tom?"* Kali nodded. *"And Helen."* Again, Kali nodded.

Kali and Ko, proud of themselves, said together, *"Tom and Helen."* They looked around, smiling and nodding, at the other cats and Jock, who stared back. Confused.

Mr. Bean finally said, slowly, and with emphasis, *"So. Tom. And. Helen. Did. What?"*

"Oh!" said Kali. *"They took a lot of Henrie's breakfast upstairs and locked it up in that case..."* she looked at Little Socks, *"...and I don't have to be able to pronounce it."*

"Why dey do dat? Dere's food everywhere on Da Avenue."

"Trill!"

"That's stupid. That's not a refrigerator, is it?"

"How much did they take?"

Kali and Ko said, together, *"I smelled bacon...."* *"They took sausage...."* *"Egg casserole."* *"That gingerbread stuff."* *"Fruit."* *"Wheat toast."* *"Bagels."* *"French toast."* *"Orange juice."* *"I think cranberry, too."*

"How strange," said Tiger Lily. *"Did they do anything else that was odd?"*

"I think they put lots in their backpack, too."

"Yeah, you're right. It's like they ate a full breakfast and then packed a full breakfast in their pack..." *"and another in the cupboard."*

"Well, that's just great," said Tiger Lily. *"We're going to be locked in with food thieves."*

"What?" *"Huh?"* *"Trill?"* *"What you talkin' bout?"*

Tiger Lily shushed them to get their attention. Mr. Bean was proud to have an inside track on this knowledge. He sat beside her and nodded sagely as she talked.

"Mommy is getting ready for this big storm that's coming in just a couple of days."

"Bigger than the last one?"

"Lots bigger."

"But we already has more snow dan ever before dis early. Mommy said!"

"There's going to be more. A lot more. And that big vendor thing that was supposed to happen this weekend might not happen. And Mommy was saying we might be without electricity."

"No! How Henrie gonna cook bacon?"

"Mommy has generators."

"Oh, yeah. We can still have bacon. And other things."

"Mommy and Henrie are making lots of lists. That's what they do when they have to get ready for parties and things. So maybe it will be like a big party. Mr. Bean and I went over to invite Fat Cat and Scaredy Cat."

"They like to be called by their fur-ever names."

"Okay. Simon Finnegan and Oscar McMurphy."

"Will Holly and Jolly be coming?"

"If the power goes out, they'll have to come, so Mommy will probably get them early, while they can still get Holly across The Avenue."

"Where will they sleep? In the back room downstairs?"

"No, and this is other good news. Martha and Georgia will be in the back room, with Little Fred."

Kali and Ko said together, "Little Fred is coming?" "We get to see Little Fred?"

"Yeah. And Speckles and Daryll."

"Wow. We'ze gonna have a real good time. But it be crowded. We'ze gonna has trouble getting' round."

"Yeah. I guess we don't know everything we need to know yet, though."

"How can we find out what we need to know?"

"Mommy has a Skype meeting Wednesday, and we can listen in, but she said they all had to be ready before that, because it's coming by then."

Jock, who had listened intently to the conversation, said, "That must be why Ray is so concerned about our boarders."

"You have boarders?"

"On The Escape?"

"At The Marina. Not inside. They're at the dock. Two of them. They intend to stay all winter. Ray said people do it every year, but we've never had winter boarders. Ray had to do some special things just for them. He installed this piece of equipment that will keep the water moving, so it doesn't freeze around their boats."

"Wow."

"One of the men got here a while ago. He seems to know what he's doing. The other guy, well, he's kind of an idiot. Ray told Cheryl he hoped the guy would be ready when it hit. He must have been talking about the storm."

Tiger Lily sat up when she heard a knock on the door. She could tell Chris was on the other side and was confused that he had knocked instead of using his key. She watched and listened as Annie greeted him at the door.

When they were alone once again, they talked about The Problem With Chris. Tiger Lily asked Jock, *"Has Ray said anything about Chris moving away?"*

"No. He hasn't said a word. And I've been around them several times. Chris hasn't said anything."

Little Socks said, *"See? That mouse didn't know what he was talking about. Chris isn't moving away."*

"You have to admit, he's acting different."

"Well…"

"We need to keep our eyes and ears open."

Robert and Sue settled into their hotel room. "This was a long day."

"We got a late start today. We don't have to drive so long tomorrow, then we have only a couple of hours the next day. We'll be there by late morning."

"Did you look at that map of Chelsea?"

"Yes. It looks like that B&B we're staying in is close to one of the marinas, the one that gets the most mention on the web."

"Maybe we'll get lucky and get this done right away."

4

Annie greeted Chris at the door, surprised that he had knocked. Stiffly, they leaned in to kiss one another on the cheek.

After an awkward silence, she asked, "Have a good day?"

"Yes, I did. I was out early this morning. Started a new watercolor."

"You didn't finish it?"

"No. It needs something. I don't know what, yet."

"I look forward to seeing it."

They walked as they talked, and by now they were in the dining room where Ray and Cheryl sat, glasses of wine in front of them.

Tonight, Annie served take-out from Sassy P's Wine & Cheese. Since this was "holiday" month, several Christmassy-looking small plates sat around the table. Chris chose crispy eggplant parmesan bites, a couple of beef wellington bites, and churro almonds.

Annie served wine from the Twelve Wines of Christmas list put together by Jesus. Tonight she served Armstrong Family Four Birds Red to represent four calling birds. Annie didn't have to think when she served wine to her friends. They all preferred a dry wine, and this Cabernet Franc fit the bill.

Sitting with their friends, talking about this and that, Annie mused they seemed a contented couple. It appeared neither Ray nor Cheryl picked up on the hint of discord. It wasn't discord, really. Discontent? Fear? Annie tried to put her finger on it but was unable to do so. Fear on her part, certainly, but what was it from Chris? Why would he not discuss it?

Cheryl looked into the living room and said, "Annie, I noticed these quilts as soon as I came in. Where did you get them? They're lovely."

"I didn't tell you about them?"

Cheryl shook her head.

"My mom made them. She started this fall, and, well, she just got carried away. This is the result. They're huge – oversized and large enough to cover a king-sized bed with several extra inches on all sides – so we're going to use them in the guest rooms."

"Why are they still up here?"

"It's time to repaint. Henrie and I decided to do that in January, when we're naturally slow, and we'll pick two wall colors and a trim color to match each quilt. We're going to name the rooms, too. We'll put the quilts out as we finish each room."

"Great idea." Annie and Cheryl moved to the living room where they picked up a quilt to unfold and display. "So this would be for the Hummingbird Room?"

The quilt seemed simple in comparison to the others. On a white background, gray tendrils with sparse coverings of budding green leaves rose from what would be the foot of the bed. Two large blue hummingbirds flew in areas that would take the corners at the foot of the bed. Smaller hummingbirds, in colors of purple, green and orange, flew up to the top and onto the sides.

"Yes, I think so. Henrie and I talked about it and thought using bird names would be good. It would be foolish to get five more cats, just to name rooms for them."

"This is lovely. She's new to quilting?"

"Kind of. She used to do it but got out of the habit. Then she was inspired by – well, who knows by what – and she bought a machine to handle it. She made five for me."

Cheryl looked through the rest of them, each different in style, and each with a different bird theme. The rest of the quilts featured either cardinals, orioles, blue buntings or golden finches.

"I can't wait to see the rooms when you're done."

They moved back into the dining room and caught the end of a conversation about The Marina's new boarders.

Annie asked, "What will they do when this storm comes in?"

Ray answered. "They say they'll stay on their boats. I'm fairly confident the first one to dock – Carter – knows what he's doing. He's actually further south this winter than he's ever been, so the winter, in general, should seem mild to him. Albert, the newcomer, is new to everything. I hope Carter can help keep him safe. It's all new to us."

Cheryl asked, "Who is the couple staying here now?"

"Robert and Sue? No, that's not right…maybe Tom and someone. Helen. That's it. Um…I haven't really talked to them. I know they vacation a lot. They say they go from one region of the country to another doing whatever sport is available. They're here to cross country ski."

"Uh…not so much…"

"What?"

"They came into The Marina a little before noon today, asked if they could use our laundry facilities, and hung out until maybe a little after three. They ate lunch while they were there. It looked to me like carry-out from the Inn."

"From here?"

"Yes. I've had breakfast here a time or two. Looked and smelled like Henrie's cooking to me."

"How did you know they were staying here?"

"They said they'd been on the road for a while, and they hated to ask their inn-keeper to use the laundry. I asked where they were staying, and they just kind of pointed toward town. But I was by the window when they left. They're driving a small camper, right? They parked in your lot and walked in."

"Huh. Curious."

"You know what else is curious?" asked Ray.

Three heads shook as they looked at him. Ray focused on Chris. "We haven't heard how the visit with the parents went over Thanksgiving. It's been a few weeks now."

Chris and Annie looked at one another. Chris said, "Well, Annie's entire family was here as well. Everything kind of got lost in the babble, so to speak."

"Did they have a good time? Get along with everyone?" Ray's emphasis was on the word "everyone," but his eyes pointed to Annie.

Annie answered. "We got along fine, Ray. We had a great visit. Everyone got to know one another, and there was lots of good food…."

"But…"

Cheryl cut him off. "Ray, it's late. We have a big day tomorrow. Annie, thanks for the meal and the wine. Chris, it was great to see you."

Ray, knowing which side of the bread held his butter, took the cue, shut up, and said his good-byes.

Annie and Chris were alone in the apartment. Well, there were seven cats as well, but they politely kept their distance. Chris didn't realize they were watching and listening to everything.

"I should go."

"You can't stay tonight?"

"I have to get in early tomorrow, since I didn't go in today, and I'd hate to wake you up."

"You know I don't mind…"

"I'll see you, Annie. Thanks for dinner."

Chris kissed Annie on the cheek and saw himself to the door. As he closed it, he stood on the other side for a full minute, thinking about Annie, about Chelsea, about his friends. He sighed, feeling every bit as gray as his new watercolor, and finally walked downstairs and outside.

Tiger Lily listened at the door until he walked away. Her eyes were on Annie. She, too, seemed to know he was still there, and she stood, watching the door, as if willing it to open.

When Chris walked away, Tiger Lily didn't know what to do, follow him or stay with Annie. Mo slipped out the cat door with a soft trill. Even though Tiger Lily could not yet understand him, this she knew. He would keep an eye on Chris. She waited until Annie sat in her recliner, tissues in hand, as tears ran down her cheeks. Tiger Lily jumped up and cuddled into her lap, pressing her head against Annie's chest and rubbing to let her know her cats still loved her.

When Mo returned, he sat in conversation with Kali and Ko. Kali came to Annie's lap, snuggled in, and said to Tiger Lily, *"He went straight out the door and to his car. Mo hoped he would talk to Henrie, but...."*

The cats stuck close to Annie for the rest of the evening, sleeping so close – at her side and on top of her – that she wasn't able to toss and turn.

5

Annie was in the kitchen early on Tuesday. The gathering storm clouds kept the rooms dark enough for Henrie to have the lights on. She was happy for that. The lights were low enough in the dining room that the guests would not notice her puffy eyes.

Henrie noticed.

"Is everything alright, Annie? Can I do anything for you?"

"No, Henrie. I'm fine. I'll be fine, at any rate. Sometime."

"Care to share?"

"No, not today. Later. When I know what it is. Are Robert and…"

"Tom and Helen have left for the day. Do you want me to take their photograph? Put their names on it? You are having a particularly hard time with this couple. Your memory of their names is, shall I say, desperately awful."

Annie laughed. It felt good. "I think I've got it now, Henrie."

"As you cannot decorate again today, what are your plans??"

"The walkway is still closed?"

"Yes. I fear the lighthouse cannot be finished until after the storm has passed."

"The merchants are in for a long weekend. All dressed up with nowhere to go, so to speak. We've been advertising the heck out of Christmas In Chelsea in a five-state region. And one of the biggest draws was supposed to be the big 'Christmas tree' in the harbor. Except it won't be there. And neither will most of our vendors."

"Certainly the tourists will understand."

"What tourist has ever understood something that was supposed to happen that didn't? There's nothing we can do about any of it. I should be upset about the vendors, but I'm more upset about the lighthouse. I knew we should have gotten it decorated over Thanksgiving."

"Everyone, including everyone here at the Inn, was busy that weekend."

"I know. Oh, well. Even without the lighthouse being turned into a big tree, maybe the roads will be clear by the weekend and we'll all be able to salvage some sales. At least the area will have the appearance of a white Christmas without having to resort to a snow machine." Annie laughed. "Remember when we had to do that my first winter here? What a hoot."

"A hoot. Yes. And allow me to ask again, what are your plans for the day?"

"Apparently, I have no plans. Can I help you get ready for the storm?"

"Hilly and I have everything under control."

Henrie and Annie looked out the kitchen windows as a blast of cold air came off the lake.

"If it's this bad now, I can't wait until tomorrow."

Annie went to the dining room. As she picked through the left-overs, she called over her shoulder, "I thought you would make more, since they seem to eat so much."

Henrie looked into the dining room. "I made more. They ingested accordingly."

"I thought they must work it off with their sports, but that's not the case. According to Cheryl, they didn't go skiing yesterday."

"I beg your pardon?"

Annie told Henrie the laundry story as she munched on the one remaining helping of egg casserole, some bacon and one sausage link.

"That is curious. They related a story today about the trail at the state park and mentioned they would ski the north shore of Lake Scott today."

"Interesting. Maybe they ski for an hour or two and then do other things."

"Perhaps I should Google them. Just in case."

Annie laughed again. "I love how you've added to your vocabulary, Henrie. Do you need help with the Googling?"

"I believe I can handle it. I will let you know if I learn anything of note."

"Okay. Well, I'm going to run up The Avenue to borrow Clara's wagon. Maybe she'll let me keep it for the week."

"Please do not. I wondered if I should give this to you early, and since you need it now…."

Henrie turned and walked to the back of the kitchen and into his own apartment. He returned, trailing a wagon behind him. It was bright red, made of resin, and sported a bright red raised cover, also made of resin. It was tall enough that her cats would be able to stand or sit without discomfort. A bright blue bow was taped to the top.

"Henrie, it's perfect!"

"Merry Christmas. This is for you and the children. The heater is inside…" Henrie lifted a lid from the top to show her a small heater in the back corner, cordoned off by thick resin bars. "Like Clara's wagon, this heater is battery-operated and will provide significant heat for short periods of time. And, also like Clara's, the heater is, shall I say, modulated so that no harm will come to furry bodies if they must stay in for a time."

Annie didn't have to call the cats to check it out. They already surrounded the wagon, giving it the good old sniff detector test and jumping inside.

Annie and Henrie didn't understand what they said to one another, but a speaker of cat would have heard: *"Iz dis for us? We gots our own wagon?" "This is prettier than Clara's." "Trill!" "Let me in. I want to try it out for size." "This is comfy." "Henrie gets the best presents. I wonder what he'll get for Mommy." "This is for Mommy." "No, this is for us." "Get in, it's time to go to work." "Make room." "Get out of the way!" "Fat butt!" "Stupid head!" "Ko, Kali, stop fighting. You don't need to get in. You work here!" "Fat butt!" "Sigh."*

By this time, Annie and Henrie had reached in to pull Kali and Ko from the middle of the wagon. Annie said, "You'll get your chance, girls. You'll probably ride to the New Year's Eve party in this, if it's still cold and snowy."

The girls would not be mollified. They jumped out of human grips and ran to the library to hide under the television table.

Henrie shook his head. "I will make a special treat for them later this morning."

Ray walked to the boats docked for winter, Jock at his side. Carter was on deck, tying down equipment.

"Mornin'. Do you need anything today?"

Carter looked around and waved. "I was going to come in and ask if I could borrow a car or truck. I'm going up to town today to get some things I forgot to stock."

"Sure. We have something you can use. Come up when you're ready and we'll give you a key."

Carter turned away to finish a knot. He turned back. "Say, have you seen the other guy? Albert?"

"Not today. Were you looking for him?"

"Yeah. I heard some loud talking before I came up this morning. Sounded like arguing. I couldn't tell if it was one voice or two, you know, like he could have been shouting into a phone. When I came up, no one was around. I yelled, but he didn't answer."

"Haven't seen him, or anyone else, but I was out back for a while."

"I've been worried about him, wanted to invite him to go up to town with me. Thought maybe if I talked about what I had and what I was still getting, he might get an idea of the kinds of things he needs to do."

"You think he could be, um, unprepared?"

"That would be one word. Another word would be kick-butt-stupid for doing this."

"That's a word, alright."

Ray looked at Albert's boat. Jock, upon hearing about the loud voices, had jumped on to take a look. Ray watched as Jock sniffed around and poked his nose flat against all the windows. Jock jumped down and made no attempt to take Ray up.

Ray looked back up at Carter. "I don't think there's a problem today, but let me know if I need to get him on land."

Ray turned to go, glad to get his face out of the wind. As he walked to the office, he saw Albert coming from the parking lot. A silver pick-up truck was driving away.

Jock saw a dog; it stared at him from the passenger window.

Chris sat in his office, considering his options. He could do this himself or send someone else.

Channels and harbors were icing up. Someone needed to get around with the boat they used in the winter to shave and break up ice. Chris liked to get out in the winter, but he knew his bosses would prefer he delegate this task.

So much for his bosses. Chris grabbed his winter gear, headed for the door, and acknowledged his second in command, generally called by his last name, Shorter.

"Shorter, I'm going out. I'll head north first, open up the harbors and rivers in that direction, then wait to hear from you if I should keep going or turn back."

"Chris, you know the big guys aren't gonna be happy. Send me."

"I'll do it. Is the boat stocked? In case we get stuck out there?"

"Sure is. And it has emergency rations in case you have to pick up any stragglers." While Shorter continued to talk, Chris turned to go. He stopped when he heard, "But really, send me. This could put a kink in your plans."

Chris turned around slowly. "What plans?"

Shorter didn't even blink. "Oh, you know. Just a rumor. I was told to polish my resume, so to speak."

Chris turned again to leave and said, over his shoulder, "Please make sure the crew's ready to go."

On any other day, he would have been concerned about Shorter's desire to move up, would have said something encouraging. Today, he was too concerned with his own train wreck of a life to care.

He shrugged into his outer gear and left the building, welcoming the cold rush of wind in his face.

Randy pounded the dashboard hard. Three times.

The dog jumped and leaned against the passenger door.

Randy didn't notice. Finally! His payday was here! Now he had to decide how to move forward. He would get the money, then tell his boss the story.

He could say Gerald, well, his name was Albert now, had gotten away. He found the boat, but the witness was gone. He had cleared out his cabin.

His boss would demand photographs, witness testimony…he could get the photos when he got the money. Albert would cooperate. He could probably get witness statements from the people at this marina and doctor them.

What was next? Back to work. That had to be the plan. Then he would put in for a vacation, maybe in a couple of weeks, and disappear.

Randy turned to his dog. Sis. His faithful companion. "I'm sorry, girl. I've been pretty angry recently, haven't I. Things are gonna get better. We'll head home tomorrow. Everything will be fine."

The dog, a dark gray giant schnauzer, got as small as she could in the passenger seat.

Randy reached into his pocket and pulled out a pill bottle. Just one. He'd take just one.

Albert had the appearance of a man without a care in the world. Inside, he was seething. The feds found him. He had been so careful. So careful.

Oh, well. If it was money his handler wanted, he had enough on the boat to throw his way. He would throw him a bone. Satisfy his need for now, then disappear forever.

Where had he slipped up? How many identities had been discovered? If it was only the name he currently used, he could fix it. Hidden in his cabin were five more, ready to go. If they had found some or all of the accounts' names, well, then, he had a problem.

Before telling the handler anything, he would have to learn what they knew. He had been in tougher situations before. He could talk his way out. And then he would move on.

There was one upside. When he moved on, he could leave this lake and the boat behind. His next life would be on land, and somewhere warm.

6

It seemed that all of Chelsea wanted to eat out today, probably because they knew they would be snowed in later in the week.

Annie helped behind the coffee bar until she noticed the servers getting behind on bussing tables. There seemed to be no end to the stream of people bustling through the door, eager to get out of the wind.

Friends from across The Avenue, Mem and Clara, stopped in for lunch. Annie had time to acknowledge them, then she was back to work.

As they left, Mem said, "Come over to my place when you're done here. We need to talk about this weekend."

Annie gave a quick nod. As she bussed a table, she noticed two men at the hostess stand. She left the bus cart at her table and walked to the stand.

"Please, come with me. I'm just finishing this table, and I'll get a server right over."

As the men sat, Annie finished wiping the table and asked, "Can I get you something to drink? Coffee?"

"Sure, ma'am. I'll have a cup of black coffee."

"It looks like you have some special coffees? I'll have a mocha latte, please."

As Annie turned away, from the corner of her eye she caught the look the first man gave the second. It appeared to be a look of incredulity. Piqued, she motioned to the table's server that she would take care of the men.

She approached with menus. "I guess I'll be your server. I'm Annie. Do you want to hear about our specials?"

Black Coffee said, "Just give me a burger and fries. Put everything on it. Extra onion."

Mocha Latte said, "I'd like to hear about your specials."

"We're getting ready for this storm with some comfort food. We have a combo pork and beef meatloaf, served with sliced and broiled garlic new potatoes, beef and noodles over mashed potatoes, and chicken stew made with Indian spices, served with chapati."

"Do you make the chapati here?"

"Our bakery makes the bread."

"I would like that stew, please, with a little extra curry on the side."

"Certainly." Turning her head, she asked, "How would you like that burger?"

"Well done."

Annie handed the tickets to a server on her way to the kitchen, standing for a while longer. "Are you from the area? I haven't seen either of you before."

"We're docked here for the winter. I expect you'll see us every now and then."

"I heard we had a couple of winter folks in the harbor. Are you ready for this storm? It's supposed to be bad."

"I am. Don't know about Albert, here."

"I'm fine. I have everything I need. At least for bare bones living. Doubt I'll be able to make a meal like we'll have here."

Mocha Latte's name is Albert, thought Annie. He thanked Trudie as she handed him a steaming cup. He smelled deeply and smiled. "Or this. I won't be able to make this. But we're not that far away. I can just trot up here."

"I don't think 'trotting' will be possible after that storm gets going. Unless you have insulated hip waders, or maybe snowshoes. I'm glad you came in. I own the KaliKo Inn, you may have noticed it? In between here and The Marina?"

"Yeah. We noticed it on our way into town."

"Well, just to let you know, we have a generator, so we'll have heat, and we're planning on enough food to feed an army, just in case the power goes off around town. You're both welcome, if things get bad."

Black Coffee said, "Well, thank you kindly. I think I'll be fine, but Albert, you might want to…"

"Quit worrying, Carter." He looked up at Annie and shook his head. "He's all worried that I won't be able to handle a little snow. Dragged me shopping today. He filled up on all kinds of things and tried to get me to do the same, but really? We're right here, close to downtown, lots of people, and I can't believe we'll be in trouble."

Annie said, "I've never been on a boat all winter, so I don't know…"

"He doesn't, either. When he wakes up in the middle of the night, frozen to the bone, and his generator is out of fuel, or broken down, then he'll know what it's like. It's not easy, Albert, to get yourself warm, off the boat and somewhere safe in the dark, wind and snow. Especially if anywhere else is on the other side of water."

"But you have extra fuel, and you said you have a couple extra generators. If that happens, I'll just hop over to your place."

Black Coffee just shook his head. Annie heard her order come up, excused herself and returned with a tray. Placing dishes in front of the men, she repeated her invitation. "Really. If you feel the need or just want to get warm or get a hot meal, come over. I doubt you'll be able to get there once the storm is really going. It's supposed to lay in for a couple of days. But..."

"Thanks," said Black Coffee.

"Yeah. Thanks."

Annie turned to go and saw Shorter, Chris's second in command. Try as she might, she couldn't get a good feeling for the man. He was apparently very good at his job, but there was just something about him. She put on her customer-friendly smile. "Hi, Shorter. Here by yourself today?"

"Yep. Picking up a to-go order."

"Oh. I saw that one going together. Let me check on it."

"Thanks. I'll get the coffee."

Annie glanced back. Tiger Lily had followed Shorter to the coffee bar. She seemed to be listening to everything he said. Maybe she's trying to pick up gossip, thought Annie. Then she laughed and shook her head. She had such an imagination!

Annie picked up the to-go bags and took them to the coffee bar. "Trudie will finish this up for you. What's happening at the Station today?"

"Oh, same old stuff. Chris is out on the lake, busting up ice, looking for folks in trouble. Should be me."

"He enjoys the lake."

"He does, but the bosses don't want him out there. They can't understand why he's dragging his feet on that promotion. Sweet for him. Big city, big pay increase, and it would move me up the ladder. But...thanks, Annie. I'm sure it will be great, as usual."

Shorter picked up the tray of coffees and the bags, turned and walked out the door.

Annie and Trudie stared at his back, shocked into silence.

Tiger Lily, not so much. A low growl sounded in her throat.

Chris and his crew were three hours north of Chelsea. They had opened several river harbors, knocking ice into chunks that rolled in the wake, grinding and splintering off the hull. One of his best crew members kept an eye on the prop, watching as ice got sucked in and exploded out, assuring each time the prop continued to turn.

Chris himself stayed on the wheel, whipping it back and forth, right and left. The boat rolled violently, sending waves toward shore, shaking up the ice in its wake.

The goal was not to open up a channel; instead, they loosened jams and allowed the rivers to do the hard work. On occasion, they would stop to assure other boats were loose and running.

Chris loved the exhilaration of the work. It kept his mind off his other troubles. Somehow, picking ice from his beard was comforting.

As he turned to check on the crew one more time, he noticed – with both satisfaction and pride – they seemed to stay upright without having to hang onto railings or ropes. Feet planted firmly and apart, they stayed at their stations. Only rarely did one or another reach out to grab a rail or a rope.

Chris turned to face the front, rolled the wheel to the right, and wondered if he could be as steady if he were positioned on the deck. Maybe a few years ago. Not today. Maybe he should take that promotion. Get himself off a boat and into an office.

The wind hit him in the face and he breathed in deeply. An office wouldn't be his first choice.

Annie had a hollow feeling in the pit of her stomach. She had not recovered from Shorter's revelation, and she had not responded to Trudie's pointed look, then her words of sympathy.

She put on her coat and walked out the door. When the cold air hit her, she had the presence of mind to step back inside. At the hostess stand she asked, "Do you want to come with me, Darlin', or do you want me to pick you up on the way back?"

In answer, Tiger Lily jumped into the wagon behind the hostess stand. She settled on one of the cushions that Henrie had placed, always thinking of their comfort, and sighed. It had been a busy day, and she would prefer a nap. But she was not about to let Annie spend a minute alone.

Annie sent a quick text to Mem, pulled the wagon through the door and started across The Avenue. Somehow, Little Socks caught Annie's mind's eye. She looked back to see a chagrined black cat staring through the window of the yoga studio. She pounded on the glass, unable to make any noise.

Annie pulled the wagon to the door and out came the cat. She barely hit the cold sidewalk and made a neat jump into the wagon. Annie closed the lid and started across again.

Inside Mem's teashop, she took a deep breath, smelling the fragrance of several kinds of hot tea, blended with the aroma of essential oils in diffusers around the room. Today it was a citrus smell, orange or tangerine.

Mem was the most mature business owner on The Avenue. Her combination health food store, tea shop and cyber café, CyberHealth, was warm and welcoming. Everyone on The Avenue came to her for advice, even her daughter, Diana.

Diana was the head trainer and manager of Annie's yoga studio, Lil' Socks Virasana. She and Mem had been estranged for at least a decade. Now they made up for lost time, sharing Mem's apartment above the shop.

Tiger Lily and Little Socks jumped out and followed Annie, listening to her conversation with Mem.

Mem had already pulled three square tables together and set them with mismatched china cups and saucers, lemon, milk and honey. She walked from the kitchenette with a tray of teapots, each covered in a colorful, funky cosy.

"Everyone else will be here in a few minutes."

"Everyone?"

"As many that can come. All of us stand to lose income. I expect someone from every business on The Avenue, some from Main Street, even a couple from the big box stores. We need a Plan B."

Christmas In Chelsea was supposed to be a major event. Hotels and B&Bs in the area were booked with people planning to eat, shop and gaze at holiday decorations in a lakeside setting. But, like Annie's KaliKo Inn, the local hostelries were suffering cancellations.

Merchants who had stocked special items, advertising them for sale at discounts worthy of an overnight trip, were over-stocked and over-expended. Artisans and vendors who would have drawn buyers into local businesses were cancelling. If they did open up, it would be at one location and would not pull foot traffic from one end of The Avenue to the other.

Annie answered Mem. "We do need a Plan B. The Café and, well, all my places that serve food, are doing the same."

Annie sat, poured a cup of tea and stared out the window. Mem sat beside her.

"What is it, Annie? Where are you?"

Annie shook her head and brushed a tear from her cheek. "I don't know if I can talk about it, Mem. I've been so…worried…about Chris. Well, about Chris and me. And I didn't know why he was so…distant. And now…"

The door blew open, partly from the force of the woman coming in – Clara – and partly from the wind. Annie was thankful to be saved from the conversation.

She hard Mem say, "You won't get out of it this easily, Annie. I'll expect you to stay when we're finished here."

Mem turned to the vivacious Clara, a Haitian beauty who owned the flower and gift shop, Bloomin' Crazy, and who was never without a signature red tropical flower in her hair. This time of year, the flower was silk.

Clara was not in a good mood. "Ramon can't make it this weekend. His band is in Minnesota, and they're already snowed in. By the time they get out, we'll be snowed in. I'll be all by myself, sittin' in that apartment with nowhere to go."

"Come to the Inn if you get stir-crazy."

"If I understand the projections, I'll have to tunnel across The Avenue."

Despite her bad humor, Annie laughed. "Boone will keep at least one path clear, two if they can stay ahead of the snow. And anyway, you don't have a generator. If we lose power, you have to come."

Mem added, "I'm sorry Ramon won't be here. Don't worry. This winter you'll have plenty of opportunity to get snowed in with him."

Clara poured a cup of tea, pouted, and went behind the counter to escape the wind when the door opened again.

Tiger Lily and Little Socks jumped to the windowsill, out of the way of feet and into the meager sunlight of the afternoon. They were joined by Fat Cat and Scaredy Cat, blowing through the door as one of their humans came in, followed by several more people.

Annie lost herself in a flurry of activity, setting cups, plates and silver around the tables. Jerry came from Mr.

Bean's Confectionary with a deep dish fruit and berry pie, hot from the oven. Almost hot. Cooled considerably from the cold wind on the short walk across The Avenue.

Jerry counted heads and cut the pie into ten pieces. Annie laughed to herself when she heard Clara say, "That's not nearly enough for me!"

"You can have mine," said Jerry. "I had a piece earlier."

As Annie poured tea, she smelled the mixture of tartness and sweetness of the pie, still hot in the center. Mem brought vanilla bean ice cream and added scoops to the pie.

Soon, the meet and greet chatter turned to the reason for the gathering. What-will-be-our-Plan-B-if-the-weather... no one wanted to say the words.

Annie was uncharacteristically silent during the exchange.

Someone said, "We were thinking about a new years' sale if this one falls through. Maybe the first weekend of the new year."

"We can't count on the weather cooperating."

"Certainly the bad weather won't go on that long."

"We'll get a break, but it could start up again. I don't know about the rest of you, but my advertising budget is shot for the year."

"If we advertise everything together..."

"We did that this time, but I spent all I could afford for my portion of that."

"We could include some dynamite food offerings."

Jerry added, "We have the raw supplies already. We could enhance them and come up with some great New Year's baked goods and candies. The Café and Bon Vivant, well, all of us, could do something and keep morning, noon and night-time specials going."

"Our Christmas decorations could, for the most part, stay up. And we can add something different for the weekend."

Clara offered, "My decorator friend probably has lighted things. I'll call her. We could keep up the winter things – you know, like the snowmen – and replace the Santas."

"And the Nativities."

Pastor Teresa, from the nondenominational church on the corner, said, "Not the Nativities. Those days won't have ended until Epiphany, and that's the first weekend of January."

"You're right. Sorry."

The room went silent. Eventually, all eyes were on Annie.

"What?"

Mem finally spoke. "You've been awfully quiet. What do you think?"

"About?"

"Let's start with New Year. What do you think about a New Year sale the first weekend of January?"

"I think it would work. Unless the weather doesn't cooperate."

"Okay. And what do you think about advertising?"

"Well, we could advertise together again…"

"And taking down those Nativities. We should do that, right?"

"Oh, yes. I'll make sure mine come down."

"Annie."

"What?"

"Have you listened to a single word?"

"Um…no?"

Eyes rolled, heads swiveled, and hands went to foreheads, cheeks and chins. All eyes were on Annie.

"What? You can't do this without me?"

"We can, and evidently, we will. Why don't you take a break, Annie? Go home. You're tired."

"I'm not. I'll just sit here and soak it in. I promise to listen."

Mem sighed, turned to the group and continued the discussion. Every now and then, she reined in the people having private conversations on the side.

Ian rushed through the door, coatless and windblown.

Mem said, "Where is your coat? You'll catch your death!"

"You sound like my mother! I just ran over from the bank. Two blocks. Piece of cake. And I have bad news."

Several voices sounded at once. "No!" "What now?" "What else could go wrong?"

"We're down to ten vendors. Ten. And frankly, they're idiots. They think the snow will pass us by."

"Do you think they would come if we tried it the first weekend of the year?"

"No. I thought about that myself. Thought I would come here with good news as well as the bad. I sent out a text blast, and only a few can do it. Less than a dozen."

After a prolonged silence, Mem said, "Well…maybe we need to downscale our ideas."

Teresa said the last thing that could be said. "Let's see what happens this weekend. It may not be a bust, after all. We could be surprised."

A couple of minutes after the group left, two men rushed in, looked quickly at Annie and Mem, then to the back of the room. They went straight to the computers at the back, checking in with Mem's assistant.

Annie watched as they rushed through. Strangers. Men certainly on a mission.

7

At the windowsill, Tiger Lily greeted Fat Cat and Scaredy Cat, then turned to Little Socks. *"Brown Mousie was right. Shorter came in to pick up lunch. He said something about Chris getting a promotion and moving to a big city."*

Little Socks sat still, crestfallen, staring at Tiger Lily. *"He's really leaving us? I didn't believe it. I still don't!"*

"Maybe he really is. Maybe Mommy knew, but she just hasn't said anything. We need to find out what everybody in here knows."

Fat Cat said, *"We'll help. We're getting the hang of this detecting stuff. We walk around, make nice to people, listen, and pretend we're looking for food."*

"We don't even have to pretend," said Scaredy Cat. *"We can really look for food!"*

The four cats roamed the room, picking up stray crumbs that had fallen, leaning up to receive a stroke here and there. They kept their ears open.

As the humans wound down their discussion, they met at the windowsill.

"What did you hear?"

Fat Cat, licking her lips after eating a piece of pie crust, said, *"Jerry and Teresa said Annie's been unhappy, and they haven't seen Chris for several days."*

Scaredy Cat wanted to contribute. *"I heard Clara and Jolly, and then Gema and Laila say the same thing. Gema told Laila that if she was Mommy's best friend, she should ask her about it."*

"What did Laila say?"

"She said she would wait until Mommy was ready to talk."

Little Socks stomped a foot. *"I wish we could go over to the Coast Guard station. We could hear what Chris is saying, or what that Shorter guy is saying."*

"We'll need to work on that. Maybe we can get him a cat."

"Or a dog. His friends have dogs. We could find a stray one."

"And how do we get it to him?"

"I don't know! You're the oldest cat! Figure it out!"

Tiger Lily and Little Socks hissed at one another, earning a reproving glance from Annie.

Henrie's day was busy. Not rushed, as he was never rushed, but busy. He and Hilly completed their storm preparations, he spent time on Google, and he prepared for the arrival of two new guests.

When he made the reservation, he had, well, reservations. The men, brothers, relayed their intentions to surf the lake. In the winter. While Henrie had heard of people crazy enough to surf the Great Lakes in the winter, he had yet to meet anyone so inclined. Perhaps, he thought, Chelsea would have yet one more winter sport to advertise.

Now, as he checked the rooms to assure they were ready, he thought about his Google search of Tom and Helen. He found more than he wanted.

As reported, and as stated on their driver licenses, they were from Georgia. At least, Henrie found a former address that matched the address on their identification.

Acting on some type of instinct that his newly-found interest in Google seemed to inspire, a further search of real estate in that region let him know the home at that address was now for sale. It was a home in the upper middle income range and in a pleasant sub-division. Three bedrooms, two and a half baths, two levels, a good-sized piece of property, and outside amenities that included an in-ground pool and bath house. The home was listed as vacant and move-in ready, including furniture, appliances and decorative items.

The virtual tour of the home showed tasteful art, paintings, prints and sculptures, a cabinet filled with china and crystal, and expensive, yet homey, touches in the bedrooms. The advertisement listed one price as-is, and one price with furniture and personal items removed, the inference being that an auction would probably take place.

It was as if the occupants had died suddenly, leaving no heirs.

A further search found Tom on Linked-In and Helen on Facebook. Tom's personal information boasted a management positon at a prestigious national accounting firm. Helen's social media account included photographs of the couple in a variety of locations, doing, apparently, what they told him they did. Pictures were posted from Vail, Colorado (downhill skiing), the Bahamas (hang-gliding), Florida (deep-sea fishing), Appalachia (biking the Appalachia Trail), Minnesota (fishing from a small boat), and other places, participating in other sports he could not recall.

Helen did not list children or extended family in her account. Nor did her account say anything about her personal situation, if she worked, if she volunteered, if she had a life outside their vacation habits. Her account listed only ten friends, and Henrie learned nothing about Tom and Helen from a quick look at their accounts. All of the friends were from the same town in Georgia.

Something had apparently happened to change their personal situation. Henrie was concerned for the couple's personal well-being, but he did not yet know if he should be concerned about the Inn.

Now, he heard a commotion in the foyer. He walked to the railing on the second floor and looked down. Two men, both on the young side of middle-aged – Henrie guessed in their thirties – had blown in through the front door with a gust of wind. As the men laughed at the wind and the weather, dropping bags and looking around, Henrie thought to himself that they would be pleasant guests, after all.

He called from the second floor, "Good afternoon, gentlemen. Welcome to the KaliKo Inn. You will notice your hostesses on the bottom step. May I present Kali and Ko?"

The cats slid noiselessly into position on the bottom step. Ko looked up at Henrie with reproach. He should have been ready. At his post. Down here. Before the men arrived. How gauche.

Kali had eyes only for the men. She purred, smiled and simpered, giving each one a coquettish wiggle of her right shoulder. Before they could succumb to her charms, however, there was Henrie, walking past them on his way to greet and shake the hands of the new guests.

"How do you do. I am Henric. And you are?"

"Kullen Knight," said the taller of the two. And this is Barry. My bro. My real bro. Says he won't surf with me. Says he's gonna watch as I drown my fool self."

"Charmed. Allow me to take your coats."

"Oh, we'll keep them. We're going to leave our bags, check in, you know, and then we're gonna hit the cyber café."

"You will enjoy the cyber café. I will point it out to you. I thought, pardon me for asking the question, you were here to surf?"

"Oh, yeah. We'll do that in the morning. We'll check out the beach this afternoon, maybe, and the walk to the lighthouse, too, but this afternoon, who was it, Barry?"

"Oh. Some guy. Some guy from my group, you know, he's expecting us to be online by…" Barry checked his watch. "Gosh! We're already late!"

Kullen put his coat back on. "Hey, dude, okay if we leave our bags here? We'll be back to check in later."

"Certainly. But I must tell you about the lighthouse…"

"Yeah. Later, dude. In a couple of hours."

"The cyber café does not have a sign. It is…"

But they were gone. Out the door, buttoning coats and putting on hats and gloves as they hit the porch at a run.

Henrie looked at the bags and sighed. Better to cut his losses. He would put the bags on the cart but would not take the cart upstairs until the gentlemen returned with credit cards. He wondered briefly if he should have barred the door while he told them about the lighthouse.

Kali was crushed. Ko rubbed it in as she pushed her sister back to the library. *"They didn't even notice you."*

Annie thought about bolting for the door, but she knew Mem would come hunting. So she stayed, cleaning up the tables and helping with the dishes, saying nothing until everyone else was gone. Eventually, they were alone, with the exception of the two computer gamers in the back of the room. Evidently, they conversed with someone online, because the banter between the two left some things out.

She looked at Mem. "Do they talk to other people while they're online?"

"Yes. There are earpieces with microphones."

Annie made a face. "Gross!"

"Don't look at me like that. They get rubbed down with alcohol in between uses. But yes, to answer your original question, they can, and sometimes do, talk to other people online."

Annie ran water into the first sink, preparing to wash the cups and saucers. Mem's china may have been mismatched, chipped and scratched, but the pieces were still too delicate to put into the dishwasher.

As Mem readied the second sink with a bleach rinse, she asked Annie, "Are you ready to tell me about it?"

"I don't know what to say."

"Just start talking. We'll figure it out."

Annie sighed, and was once again grateful for Mem's calm reassurance. "It's Chris."

Annie went silent. Mem didn't say a word.

"Well, ever since his folks were here, you know, at Thanksgiving, he's been this way."

Annie went silent again. This time Mem asked a question. "What do you mean, 'this way'?"

"Distant. Both emotionally and physically. I really didn't know what was happening. I didn't know what questions to ask. I didn't know if it was something I had done, something that was changing in his feelings, or…I hated to think it…but something that was related to his family."

"You still haven't talked about it? That's been weeks, Annie."

"I know. And today, Shorter came in to pick up a take-out order, and he said something about Chris's promotion. That he'll be moving to another location."

Annie wasn't looking at Mem, but she could tell Mem stopped rinsing cups and saucers. Finally, Mem dried her hands, put them on Annie's shoulders and turned her in for a hug.

Annie couldn't help it. The tears came, and they wouldn't stop.

Chris got home and thought about calling Annie. He decided instead to call his mother. Finding his mother more and more difficult, he now dreaded calling her.

She answered with a cheery voice. "Chris. It's so good to hear from you. Have you taken the position yet?"

"No. I haven't made a decision to do that."

"Why not? It's everything you want!"

"It is not everything I want. I have been clear, Mother, that everything I want is here. Right here. In Chelsea."

Chris heard a dramatic sigh. "After you see reason, you'll be happy. You'll be close to home. You can live in the guest house. The decorator is almost finished."

"Decorator?"

"I'm just thinking ahead. I know you want to stay with the Coast Guard. This is how you'll do it."

"So you know I was given an ultimatum. Promotion or resign."

"Of course I know. We talk to the Senator every week, sometimes every day."

"I am old enough to manage my own life, Mother. I've told you this."

"I just know you'll make the right choice, Chris. Oh, your father just came in. Do you want to talk to him?"

"No. I have to go."

Chris could hear his mother say something, but he clicked off before she could go further. He wished he was not a dutiful son.

8

Annie built a fire in the library and sat in one of the comfortable chairs in front of it as Henrie brought in a tray. It smelled of food from Mo's Tap.

"This shall be the last peaceful evening. Tomorrow, about the time the storm hits, our last guests will arrive. As will our local guests."

"I take it the brothers arrived?"

"Yes. They went to the cyber café, and they planned to look at the lake."

"I saw them at the café. They seemed to be on a mission."

"They were late for some type of online appointment."

"Ah. That explains it. They were talking to someone on the internet."

"I believe they may turn out to be quite interesting."

"Are they surfing in the morning?"

"So they say. I have not seen them. I do not know if they were able to investigate the lake, but I am sure they were not able to get to the lighthouse walkway."

Just then, the front door opened. They heard a few people walk in, and then Pete's voice. "Henrie? Annie?"

Henrie stood and walked to the foyer. Annie followed. Kali followed as well. They found Pete and Cyril, accompanied by the two men Annie had seen at Mem's cyber café.

"These two staying here?"

Henrie answered. "Yes, Chief."

Annie chuckled to herself. Sometimes Henrie was so formal with Pete. Probably when he thought the situation demanded. She watched as Cyril left, in search of cats. Except that Kali was here, rubbing the ankles of one of the men, then the other, then back again.

"Is there a problem?"

"I'll say. This one, says his name is Kullen, says he's here to surf?"

"Yes. That is what I understand."

"And his brother...Barry?"

Barry nodded. "Yes, sir."

"Said he's here to make sure Kullen doesn't kill his fool self?"

"Also, that is what I understand."

"And did you tell them the lighthouse was closed?"

"I did make an attempt. The gentlemen were in a hurry."

"Well, I can hardly blame you, Henrie. You would think that the barriers and signs, bright yellow tape and flashing red lights would have stopped them. But, no. Apparently, Kullen here is looking forward to killing his fool self and taking Barry with him."

"I do apologize, Chief. I will have a stern discussion with them about the dangers during a winter gale."

"I would appreciate it." Pete turned to the two men. "First and last warning. Stay off that jetty. And if you've half a brain between you, stay off that lake."

Both answered at once. "Yes, sir." "Yes, Chief."

"Cyril! Let's go!"

As Pete left, Henrie asked the brothers, "Have you had the opportunity to eat?"

"No, sir."

"We shall see to the details, get you checked in, and I will direct you to the establishment closest to the Inn. Just a few steps away, as a matter of fact."

"Does it have a sign?"

"Pardon me?"

"A sign? You know, something that says it's a restaurant."

"Certainly."

"Well, you oughta tell those folks across the street that a sign or two would be helpful."

As they walked toward the check-in area, Annie heard Henrie say, "I did attempt to tell you…."

Kali dropped her head and walked to the library. Neither of the brothers had noticed her.

Cyril gave a short bark and cats came running from the library. Tiger Lily said, *"Come in here, Mommy has a fire."*

Settled in front of the fire, Cyril told them about their guests. *"These guys have half a brain between them."*

"Their bags are still downstairs here. They ran out to go somewhere as soon as they came."

"Are these the ones that are going to surf?" asked Little Socks.

"Wot's surf?"

Cyril, wise in the ways of the world, said, *"Normally, people do it in warm weather and in warm water. And in the ocean, not on a lake. Not even on a Great Lake. You get a big board, and you take it out into the waves and glide – they call it surf – back to shore.*"

"*So you let the waves carry you?*"

"*Yes. That's it, exactly.*"

"*But do they know how cold it is?*"

"*Dat water gotsa be really really cold. Ice cold.*"

"*That's why they have half a brain between them.*"

"*Golly. I guess we'll have to keep an eye on them.*"

"*Our work never ends.*"

As Cyril left, Kali rejoined them, dejected.

Annie had already turned to go back to the fire and did not hear the rest of Henrie's conversation. Best not to interrupt his process of checking in. She could have taken the bags to their room, but this, too, was part of the process for Henrie.

When Henrie led them upstairs, Annie went to the kitchen to retrieve a bottle of wine. By the time Henrie returned, a glass of dark red sat beside his chair, along with the burger and sweet potato fries from Mo's Tap.

Henrie struggled to keep his chuckle quiet. "I do believe they will be interesting."

Annie laughed, but turned serious. "So, we have brothers bent on drowning or succumbing to hypothermia, and a couple that is.. what? What did you find out?"

Henrie told her what he learned.

Each took a bite, chewed, swallowed and repeated, for several minutes. Annie then asked, "Did you run their credit card?"

"I did, for the number of days they plan to stay. Today, I locked that amount in. They may be saving their card for other expenses, taking food from breakfast to last throughout the day. Hilly informed me Kali and Ko are very interested in the armoire. I assume they are storing food there for supper, and possibly taking food with them as they leave for mid-day."

"That squares with Cheryl's information. Should we say anything?"

"What do you propose we say?"

"Um...I don't know. They must have clothes and sporting equipment in that camper. I wonder what else?"

"Perhaps we would find an automatic weapon."

"Henrie!"

"Joking."

"You don't do it often enough to do it well."

"So sorry. And now, are you of a mind to tell me about yourself?"

"I suppose. It's easier now. Mem forced me to talk earlier. I didn't know what's been going on with Chris, and I've been afraid to ask him. Today, though, Shorter said he was offered a promotion. One that would take him to a larger port, a larger town. Probably more pay. Shorter is looking forward to getting the Chelsea post."

"Oh. I had no idea. Frankly, I thought he was receiving pressure from his mother about me."

"You? What haven't you told me?"

"Well, you know, it was nothing. She offered me a position as her house manager. At a magnificent salary, by the way."

"You. Are. Kidding. Me."

"I kid you not. She was quite brazen, but not in your presence. And, if I think about it, not in front of Chris, either."

"But you thought that somehow…."

"Not understanding the issue of what had come between you…"

"That would never create a strain for Chris or for me, Henrie. Never. No matter what your decision."

"I thought as much. I do wonder if his mother had something to do with the promotion. As they left, she said they would not see me again. I thought, perhaps, that they decided not to return because of my decision. Now, apparently, she was certain Chris would no longer live in Chelsea."

They stared at the fire for several minutes, until Henrie said, "Call him."

Henrie picked up the to-go containers and his glass, returning to the kitchen and leaving Annie alone for the evening.

Tiger Lily, on a pillow in front of the fire, told her siblings, *"Leave her alone."*

Sue took the pistol out of her purse and held it in her hands. "Do you think I should have gotten training?"

"How often do you plan on using it?"

"I hope I never have to."

"Then I'm glad you didn't waste money on the training. I set the alarm for six o'clock. We'll be there before noon tomorrow."

Carter was fixing dinner when Albert called to him from the deck. "Okay if I come down?"

"Sure. Come on."

Albert ducked his head as he came down the steps. "They don't make these very big, do they?"

"Actually, mine has more head room than most."

"Well. Huh. What are you having?"

"Just finished. Bacon and eggs. Toast."

"Smells good."

Carter argued with himself but finally said, "Did you have anything?"

"I got a burger from the bar up the street. Nearly froze my toes off coming back. Straight into the wind. Worked up an appetite, I guess."

"Huh." Carter figured he didn't have to offer anything, if he had just had a burger. "What's goin' on?"

"Just visiting. It's pretty darned lonely out here. I didn't realize…"

"Why are you here, Albert?"

"No reason. Just saying hello."

"I mean on the lake. In the winter. Why are you doing this?"

"Well…I need to…you know…make a new life for myself. Needed to…leave a bad situation."

"Hiding from an ex-wife?"

"Yeah. That's it. Hiding from an ex. And hiding some assets. Have to stay under the radar."

"Huh. Was that her on the telephone this morning?"

"What? Oh. You heard that?"

"Two things you need to learn. One. Sound carries over water. Two. When it's windy, and the wind is coming from your boat to mine, sound carries. Yeah. I heard ya. Didn't hear the words. Just the sentiment."

"Oh. Well, yeah, it was…my ex."

"She can find you using your cell phone."

"I called her. I have a couple of burners. She won't be able to figure it out."

"Well…I wish you luck. But what you said about it being lonely out here, it is. Most of us that live on the water do it because we want to be alone. If that isn't comfortable, you need to change your plan. You might want to do that before tomorrow afternoon."

"I'll be fine. Really. Just need to get in the groove, you know. I've got books, cards for solitaire, stuff like that. Well, I'll get out of your hair. How about we have breakfast tomorrow, before this big, bad storm comes in?"

"Sure. Sounds good."

Chris looked at the watercolor. He still didn't know how to finish it. He opened the closet. The closet with watercolors, sketches and photographs of Annie. The ones he would not show her until she was ready to see them.

Now, he didn't know if he could ever show her. He would be gone; she would be here; she would never know how much he cared.

He chose a photograph, a close-up of her hand with the ring he had given her. That hand. The hand that never touched a cat in anger. The hand that touched him with such tenderness.

Would he ever feel that tender touch again?

His phone rang. He looked at the display. He could not talk to her. Not now.

He walked out to his deck and felt the cold wind on his face.

Annie picked up her phone and called his number. He didn't answer. He could be on the lake. Or....

9

Wednesday morning, the brief calm before the storm, saw Henrie up long before the light of day. Kullen and Barry requested an early breakfast. Henrie would hold his comments. He had said what needed to be said the night before.

Kali and Ko sat at their places on top of the buffet. When Kullen and Barry arrived, Ko huffed and jumped to the floor. She stalked out. Kali jumped to the floor as well, to rub against their ankles, one after the other.

Henrie noticed thick, dark, wetsuits under their street clothes and asked about them. Barry answered.

"These are made for winter surfing. I could give you some technical terms, but what it all means is that they can protect an idiot like my brother from getting hypothermia. We have caps, too. And glasses."

"And while they would keep your brother from harm, what is the purpose for you to wear one?"

"Oh. If I see him go down, I'll start out. If he comes back up, I go back to shore. If not, then I get my sweet behind out there and save him."

"I see."

Henrie did not see. He could not imagine a lone man on a surfboard would reach a man in trouble in time. But he held his tongue.

Kullen said, "He's just being a namby."

"A namby?"

"Namby-pamby. He thinks he has to keep me safe, so I let him think that. I'll be fine. I'm pretty good on a board."

"In the winter."

"Well, this will be a first for me, but yeah, I'm good. Anyway, it will probably be warmer when we get out there. We're going to the cyber café first."

"I can assure you it will be no warmer. Not later this morning. Not this afternoon. But I am happy to hear you are starting with an indoor sport."

"It's not really a sport. Well, it is a sport, but for us, it's a living."

"I beg your pardon?"

Barry answered. "We got tired of the nine to five, the corporate rules, dressing for work. We quit, and now this is how we make our living. We're professional gamers."

"I have never heard of this."

"We'll tell you about it before we go. But to give you a hint, in China, some people rake in over four million a year."

"Yeah. You could get rich. And you might like it better than putting in your time here. I mean, I'm sure it's great and all, but if you game, you call your own shots. Every day."

Henrie nodded, he hoped sagely, did not say, 'we are not in China,' and returned to the kitchen. He motioned to Kali to follow him. Kali had been trying to catch the attention of either of the brothers, to no avail. They would not look at her.

The brothers ate well, putting away helpings of egg and sausage casserole, bacon, sausage links, gingerbread-flavored French toast, coffee and juice. They shied away from the oatmeal, grits and ham.

After having seconds of most things, when Henrie offered more, Kullen said, "No, thanks. I have to keep my girlish figure."

Henrie laughed softly as he turned to go. When he returned to the dining room, they were gone. He looked down. "It's okay, Kali. I still think you're beautiful."

Kali dropped her head and hid under the detective table.

Tom and Helen appeared.

Tom looked at the breakfast, already severely depleted, and asked, "Is this all you've got?"

"I am sorry, yes. I prepared breakfast for six adults, and two of the four in residence ate enough for four."

"Instead of serving breakfast, you're going to make me do math?"

"I do apologize. However, I must inform you that we can no longer afford to provide enough at breakfast to sustain you throughout the day."

Tom started to sputter. Henrie held out a hand to silence him.

"We have remained silent. However, we now have additional guests, and tomorrow there will be many more. Two scheduled guests will arrive this morning, and we will have several people from town who need a place to stay during the storm. As the week progresses, I must be able to plan meals – not only breakfast – for several people, and I will need your cooperation."

Helen, who had remained silent, now said, "Come on, Tom. Let's eat. Remember, we wanted to eat light today, anyway."

Henrie went into the kitchen, mulled over the situation, and returned to the dining room.

"Pardon me for the intrusion. Is there something we – I – can do to assist? I happen to know you are not skiing as you say. I shall not say how I know, and believe me, it is not my place to meddle. However, we are preparing for a significant weather event, and we will be, shall I say, locked up together for a period of time."

Helen and Tom looked at one another, then down at the table. A tear escaped from Helen's right eye. Henrie said nothing, but he dialed down his gaze.

"Well. If you desire a conversation, you know where to find me."

Carter and Albert sat at a table next to a window. They watched the clouds over the lake move at a menacing pace.

Carter said, "It won't be long. Did you check your generator?"

"Nah. I know it works. Say, Carter, did you ever wonder what you would do if you came into a lot of money?"

"I will, one day."

"Really? How?"

"Eventually, my old lady will kick off. She's got a lot."

"What will you do then?"

"Buy a bigger boat."

"Seriously?"

"Yeah. Have it picked out already. Hope she goes soon."

Albert thought this guy might turn out to be helpful when he worked his plan. He could be bought.

After breakfast, they walked briskly from the Café to The Marina. It was too cold and windy to talk. Just before they passed the winery, Albert noticed a car slowing down, turning into the parking lot of the Inn. He looked at the driver and passenger, a man and woman, who seemed to look intently back.

Carter was oblivious. Albert didn't give it a second thought as they continued to The Marina.

Henrie had barely cleaned the dining room when the next set of guests arrived. Robert and Sue. A lean-looking couple with rather stern faces.

"Welcome to the KaliKo Inn. May I introduce…" Kali and Ko were in place on either side of Henrie.

"Can you tell us which room we'll be in?"

"You will be on the second floor," Henrie pointed, "in the room that faces The Avenue."

"Perfect. Why don't you give Sue the key and I'll check us in."

"If you would…"

"We're in kind of a hurry. There are things we want to do."

"Certainly."

Henrie gave the key to Sue, and Robert moved Henrie to the check-in computer. He took care of check-in details with efficiency while Sue took their bags to the room.

Kali said, *"I'll stay with him. You go with her."*

Ko responded, *"I don't need the exercise. You do."*

Sue ran down the stairs. She said, "Come on, Robert. We're just in time."

Kali and Ko had not yet decided who should follow whom, and they were out the door. They looked at one another, confused. Henrie looked confused, too.

Annie was out of the house early, earlier than most days. She dropped the kids at their places of business for probably the last time they would see them for the rest of the week.

She helped the Café through breakfast rush, probably the last rush of the week, and sat at the laptop to set up the Skype session. Snow was headed in and would make landfall within two hours.

Today, everyone on The Avenue was included in the Skype session. While businesses remained open, staff appeared on the call, left, returned, always leaving someone at the monitor.

At the Inn, Henrie, Kali and Ko were at the monitor most of the time, with Hilly filling in. "We've moved into the carriage house, Annie. We took the upstairs. Having the boys and Justin, the sleeping arrangement is just better. And we can keep the steps cleared as we go up and down."

At Sassy P's Wine & Cheese, Annie talked to Jesus. "We have everything we need, probably until the middle of next week. It's hard to plan. We figure we'll have fewer customers, but as soon as we order accordingly, we get slammed."

Sassy Pants seemed to nod in agreement.

Carlos called out. His face wasn't at the monitor, but they could hear his voice, probably from the ovens. The monitor was filled with Mr. Bean and Tillie.

"We're going to keep lots of sweet breads – donuts and the like – on hand for street crews, but we won't make much ahead of time. We'll have enough for sandwiches. By the way, Mother and the girls moved over this morning. We're packed in like sardines."

Across The Avenue, Jolly said, "I think I should get Holly and our things over before the snow hits. I'm really happy the cats are sticking close today. I'm not sure why, but maybe they'll come over with Holly."

"We gave that downstairs accessible room to Martha and Georgia. With Little Fred, they needed the extra room. We have the generator, so the elevator will always work. Take the room that faces the winery."

"Okay. As soon as we're off this session, we'll head over, then I'll come back to the store."

Jennifer asked, "Hilly, is Boone going to keep the ambulance plowed out?"

"That's the plan. He's working with the street department. They'll keep at least one lane open, probably on the north side, and Boone will do the walks. When it gets heavier, Boone's crew will help with the road. They'll do their hot spots first, the ambulance and the police department. They'll keep at least one point open from one side to the other."

Teresa said, "Where are they going to put all that snow? Did anyone live through the blizzard of seventy-eight? I've seen pictures from Indiana. The roads were one lane wide, and the snow was at least twenty feet high!"

Hilly said, "The snow has to go somewhere, so the plows and blowers shoot it up. That's what made those walls of snow so high."

Teresa sounded hopeful. "Maybe it will be that way this week. That would be awesome. Hey, don't forget. I have the efficiency apartment if anyone needs it."

"Only until the electricity goes out."

"Everyone expects the electricity to go out. Why is that?"

"This will be heavy snow. It will weigh down the power lines. Keep your bag packed so you can come to the Inn."

George stuck his face in front of the monitor, moving Mo to one side. "If there's an emergency on the lake, I might be called out."

George, bartender and manager of Mo's Tap, was a volunteer with the Coast Guard. He was one of the more experienced of the rescue crew.

"I know, George. We'll have to hope that no one is stupid enough to go out there."

"It could be someone that is stranded both by land and water, and the easiest way to get to them is water."

"Oh. I didn't realize that could happen."

"In a bad one, it can. Surprised Chris hasn't said anything to you."

"Well, he's been busy."

"Hey, Annie," this from Clara, "do you have a couple of youngish men staying at your place?"

"Yeah. Two brothers."

"They are some sort of crazy. I was takin' my time getting' back to work yesterday, and they were runnin' into every place from the corner all the way up. They were in a hurry. They saw me and yelled, 'cyber café?' and I pointed them to you, Mem."

Annie said, "They are serious about their gaming. And they surf, too."

"Surf the web?"

"The other kind."

"The other kind? Are they from California?"

"No, here in the Midwest. They want to surf the lake."

"The lake? In the winter?"

"Yep. And I imagine they ran into every place because you don't have names on the building yet."

Marie, one of the sister set of nurse practitioners, said, "We were going to put temporary banners up for the weekend, so everyone would know who was who, but…I guess we don't have to do that now. Maybe we'll do it for the weekend after New Year."

Annie noticed Mem had her head in her hands. "What, Mem? What's wrong?"

"Those young men were in this morning. When they left, they were doing the high five and chanting 'surf's up.' I thought it was something to do with their game. I bet they were headed to the lake."

Annie groaned. "I'll have to make sure they made it back to the Inn…."

Annie asked for time with her staff alone. The others logged off. Annie and her staff made plans for use of food items, including the best case scenario, the worst case, and any contingency in between. "Diana, close up. Go home. Come to the Inn and visit. Do anything. Just put a sign up and close."

"It's already up. Everyone should feel free to call me if you need help, and in the meantime, I'll check in with each place every day."

Just as they were logging off, Henrie came on. "Martha is settled, Kali and Ko are reacquainting themselves with Little Fred, and the little cats, Speckles and Daryll, are running through the house like wild ponies. I imagine we will find things...well...everywhere."

Annie laughed and logged off. While she puttered with the computer, Tiger Lily tapped her leg and ran to the hostess stand. A couple had come in.

Annie followed. "Hello. Welcome to Tiger Lily's Café."

The woman said, "You must be Annie. I saw your picture on the website."

"Yes. And you are?"

"I'm Sue. This is Robert. We were going to stay at the Inn."

"Oh, yes. Have you checked in already?"

Annie walked the couple to a table. Tiger Lily followed and jumped to her ledge.

"Yes, but we've finished our business. We're probably going to go ahead and go home."

"We're getting ready for a storm. I doubt you'll get very far."

"We hear people up here are good with snow. We'll be fine."

"The only reason we could give you a room was that almost everyone else cancelled. Because of the snow."

"Cancelled? You were full, and they cancelled?"

"Well, yes. We were supposed to have a huge shopping weekend. The local motels and B&Bs were completely booked, but now we're going to be empty, for the most part."

"A shopping weekend?"

"Yes. Christmas In Chelsea? Isn't that why you're here?"

Robert and Sue looked at one another. Sue said, "Well, no. We hadn't heard about it."

Robert added, "We knew it was supposed to snow, but it hasn't even started. And people cancelled?"

"It will hit soon. In the next couple of hours. And then no one will be going much of anywhere for a few days."

Robert and Sue looked at one another again, concern on their faces. Robert looked up at Annie again. "Well, you know, we decided to eat lunch, then check out. We only came to town to do one thing, thinking it might take us a while, but, well, we got finished early. Do you think we should get on the road now?"

"Um…no. Definitely not."

"We're headed south…"

"The storm is a big system. It already hit north of us, it's bearing down on Chelsea, and shortly after that, south of us will be covered. Just a minute. I'll show you."

Annie went to the hostess stand and picked up her cell phone. She found her weather app and walked back to the table.

"Look."

Robert and Sue looked at the massive block of blue covering the lake. Worry creased their foreheads and their mouths drew into tense lines.

"The room is available to you for several days. We were planning on having you. Don't get me wrong. If you want to cancel, you can. We won't charge you even for a day if you leave this afternoon. But I strongly, very, very strongly, recommend against it."

"Thanks. We'll think about it."

Annie left the table, signaling to a server to take over. This couple blew in from somewhere, knew nothing about the weekend event, knew nothing about the weather, and were here to do…what?

Unable to stop herself, she returned to the table. "Do I detect a southern accent?"

Sue answered. "We're from Texas. South Texas."

"You're not used to snow, are you?"

"We were looking forward to seeing it, actually."

"In Texas, roads are closed when you get a half inch or so, right?"

"On those rare occasions, yes."

"We're going to get a few feet of snow."

"What?"

"A few feet."

"Oh. Well, Robert, let's get back to the Inn. Maybe we can get right on the road."

Annie shook her head and walked to the kitchen to cancel their order.

10

Chris was on the lake again, this time moving south, breaking up ice in river harbors and getting boats to safety.

It was warmer today. The ice didn't form as quickly as earlier in the week. He could tell the snow was upon them, however, and he called in to check out the situation at the Station.

Shorter answered. "I've got a boat by the lighthouse, pulling a couple of guys out of the water."

"Did they capsize?"

"No. They weren't in a boat. They were on boards."

"What? Say again?"

"Boards. Surfboards. One guy is pretty cold. Well, they're both cold, but one guy is in trouble. I've called for an ambulance to get to the Station. Guys are doing what they can to warm him up."

"Who is it?"

"Don't know for sure. One of my guys said they're staying at the Inn."

"The KaliKo Inn?"

"Yep. Say, I hope I didn't cause you a problem. Keep forgetting to tell you I may have let slip to Annie about that promotion…"

"What?!"

"Hey, sorry. Didn't mean to."

"When was this?"

"Yesterday. When I picked up lunch."

Chris took several deep breaths, told himself that it wasn't Shorter's fault, and got back on the radio. "No problem. Do you need me? I think we've done all we can here."

"No, but…wait a sec."

Chris fumed while Shorter went offline. Soon, he came back. "I hate to do this to you, keeping you out with the snow coming in, but you need to head down to Bayless. They have to get a barge out of the ice before it gets socked in."

"That will put me…well…another half hour down there, an hour or two to break it out…it will be pretty late in the afternoon before I can head back."

"You may have to sit there."

"I'll keep in touch."

Chris thought about calling Annie. Instead, he told his crew where they were headed, and he pushed south.

The snow was coming down. It was wet, heavy snow. It came fast, at least two inches, maybe three, per hour.

Annie got Tiger Lily into the wagon and they rushed up the street, picking up cats at the rate of one every minute. By the time she got to the Inn, it was difficult to get the wagon up the ramp to the house.

She burst into the house to be greeted by some extra cats. Kali and Ko were not to be seen. They were probably with Little Fred, wherever she was. But the others – Simon Finnegan, Oscar McMurphy, Speckles and Daryll – crowded around her for attention. Annie was startled to see Ben.

"Hi. Are you on break from school?"

"They cancelled all of our classes until Monday, so I called Henrie and asked if he could use some extra help."

"And he said yes."

"Of course. JoJo is here, too. We're staying in the basement. Again."

"What will he have you do?"

"Everything. I'm on my way outside to get ahead of the snow on the sidewalks and steps. Kind of helping Boone, too, but I'll concentrate on this side of The Avenue. Up and down the street, keeping the sidewalks and doors cleared."

"Good deal for us. Thanks for coming."

"You're welcome. Thanks for always having a job for me!"

"We have to keep those places open for workers."

"Yes, ma'am. Like a postman, my job will never end."

Annie went through to the kitchen, dragging the wagon behind. Henrie was making a pot of fresh coffee. Of course.

"Where should we keep this wagon? I left in on the porch last night, but that won't do."

"Let us put it on the all-season porch. It will fit behind the sofa and will be out of the way."

"Good idea. I'll take it in a minute. Have all of our guests made it in for the day?"

"I have not yet seen the brothers. However, in regard to the other guests, we need to talk."

"I figured. Who first? Tom and Helen? See? I got their names right!"

"You did. Yes. Let us start there. I conversed with them today. While it had not been my intention to embarrass them, I realized that we must have some accounting of our food items for the next several days. I pointed out that I need to manage our meals. While I did not use the term 'hoarding,' I believe I conveyed the essentials."

"Did you ask them about their house? Their jobs?"

"I did not. I left the door open, so to speak, for conversation. However, since I have embarrassed them, they may not be forthcoming with me."

"Noted. I'll be available and…kind. Did they go out, um, skiing again today?"

"They were appropriate enough not to mention skiing, but they did leave. They returned a short time ago."

"I'll knock on their door and tell them of our snowed-in plans for meals, and make sure they are comfortable mingling with others. Tell me about this other couple, Robert and Sue. They came to the Café after our Skype session. Did they say why they were coming to town? They know nothing about dealing with this much snow, and they didn't know about Christmas In Chelsea."

"Do tell." Henrie's voice was pointed.

Annie turned from pouring a cup of coffee and looked Henrie in the eyes. "What?"

"It was a, shall I say, unusual check in. The gentleman kept my attention to check in while the lady took their bags to the room. She was down almost immediately, taking the gentleman with her. Somewhere."

"You say 'gentleman' and 'lady' rather than husband and wife, man and woman, Robert and Sue."

"Yes. I have a feeling about them. I cannot put a finger on it, but the feeling is not what you would call warm and furry."

"Fuzzy."

"I beg your pardon?"

"Warm and fuzzy. That's the phrase."

Henrie shook his head, rolling his eyes up, then closed.

"Yes, that. They returned, probably from the Café, with the apparent new information about a storm coming in, and did they have time to, they used this phrase, 'get out of town.' Of course, I assured them they would be welcome to go or stay, but highly recommended they stay. It was about that time that the heavens opened, and the rest is history. She looked at the snow with something akin to horror, and they went directly to their room."

"Are we going to have to spend the week with crazy people?"

"I hope not, but it is beginning to appear that could be the case."

"Wonderful. What about the brothers? Mem said they were at her place, then left, talking about the surf being up."

Henrie sat at the kitchen table with his head in his hands. "Do you know the time they left her establishment?"

"I don't. Let me call her." Annie hit speed dial as she said it. Mem picked up on the second ring. "Mem, what time did the surfers leave?"

"Oh. Hmmm. They were online for a couple of hours at least. Let me look at their ticket."

Mem's end of the line went silent while she looked up the charge. "They left here about eleven o'clock."

Annie hung up. "Eleven."

She looked at the clock. "It's two thirty. I'll call Pete."

Before she could make the call, the Inn's landline rang.

Henrie answered. "This is the KaliKo Inn. How may I help you?"

Annie could hear only Henrie's end of the conversation, which went something like this. "Yes, I … Yes, they … How … Which hospital … Certainly … I am not their father … Of course … Good…"

Henrie put the phone in the cradle and shook his head. "Well. That was Mr. Shorter. Officer Shorter. Whatever. And may I say I hope not to have to deal with him on a regular basis. Our young men are on their way to the hospital with varying degrees of hypothermia. Apparently, Barry is not as severely affected. We should, well, one of us should get to the hospital."

"How?"

Henrie looked out the kitchen window. "That is a very good question. How do you suppose the ambulance will get there?"

"I don't know."

They heard a commotion at the front door. As Annie and Henrie moved to the foyer, they heard Jennifer, the other sister in the nurse practitioner set, shout, "Special delivery! Two nuts in blankets!"

Annie couldn't help it. She laughed. Until she saw the two nuts. Barry was dressed in hospital scrubs and slippers with a blanket wrapped around his shoulders. Annie ran to him and took him to the library, seating him in the chair in front of the fireplace. She turned immediately to get the fire going, then grabbed two throws. One went over his lap; the other, she wrapped around his feet.

Henrie helped Jennifer with Kullen. They put him in the other chair, wrapped in three blankets. One was tight around his trunk, a second over his shoulders, and a third around his legs. Annie grabbed more throws and covered his head and shoulders, his mid-section and his feet.

"What are we supposed to do with them?"

Jennifer smiled. "They'll be okay. They had these expensive wetsuits designed for cold water surfing. I say 'had,' because we had to cut them off."

"Ooof."

"Yeah. Ooof. Anyway, I'll bring that stuff in. I figured we'd all be better off not making that trip to Marsh Haven in this snow, and they will be fine. I'll run over in a little bit to check on them. You need to keep them here. Their trunk sections were warm before we left the Station, so I want them to keep their upper bodies warm, and work on their hands and feet."

"Should I run a hot bath?"

"No. No. No. If they warm up too quickly, it could affect their hearts. Oh, and if you get out a hot water bottle, it has to be wrapped in cloth. Frankly, I would just do what you're doing now. Maybe get one large blanket to cover everything, and every now and then, get in there and check their fingers and toes. Once everything gets back up to normal body temperature, get them some warm tea. Warm, not hot. I don't want them drinking anything hot, or anything alcoholic. And don't let them get into a warm or hot bath until they are no longer shivering and their temperature is normal. Do you have a thermometer?"

Annie looked to Henrie, who nodded. "Guess so. How long will this take?"

"Don't know. It could take a while. If you have the time, I would suggest keeping them awake for a couple of hours with some light reading. If one of you can do the reading."

"Henrie, is JoJo busy?"

"No. I am certain she would be most pleased."

"Any suggestions on reading material?"

"Yep. Winter Water Sports For Dummies." Jennifer laughed. "I wouldn't be so snarky, except that in their more lucid moments, these guys are pretty funny."

Barry gave a brief smile and Kullen, from under his blanket, gave a thumbs up.

Barry asked, "How soon can I go to the cyber café?"

Jennifer howled. "See what I mean? Tomorrow, rock star. Tomorrow! If you can get across the street!"

11

Tiger Lily wanted to take advantage of the fire, but those goofy guys were in front of it, and JoJo sat between them, back to the fire, reading some nonsense magazine.

Magazines came to the Inn regularly, but neither Mommy nor Henrie read them. They went to the library, the foyer, on the second floor landing…places where guests would sit and want something to keep them occupied.

She wasn't sure she could carry on a conversation with the rest of the cats with JoJo and the men in the room. So she rested on cushions underneath the window.

Little Socks settled in beside her. *"What's the matter? Cat got your tongue?"* She rolled onto her back, feet in the air, laughing out loud. It was unusual for Little Socks to be amused with anything, much less herself. She must have snow sickness already.

Soon, all of the household cats joined them. The cushions were full, with seven of Annie's cats, two from Holly and Jolly, and two from Martha and Georgia.

Kali told the group about the wetsuits, how the men would use them to keep from being frozen. She remembered to say, *"And then they talked about something called gaming. They make money on it, somehow, and they can do it at Mem's."*

Ko added, *"Those new folks are really strange. They wouldn't let Henrie take them on the tour, and they stayed just a minute and ran out the door."*

As the cats grew quiet, they gazed out the window. It was only mid-afternoon, and there was no sun, just layers upon layers of snow, coming down in a straight line like hard rain.

Other cats seemed to be affected by the snow. Fat Cat and Scaredy Cat seemed to embrace one another as they lay in the cushions. She wondered what they were thinking. Probably thanking whatever gods they believed in for saving them before this winter.

Sassy Pants seemed to have a similar thought. She scooted close to Kali and Ko, snuggling into their sides. They seemed to sense she needed comfort and allowed her to stay there. Sassy Pants was an older kitten when she was found. It was possible she either remembered snow like this – having to live outside and against the elements – or she knew enough about fear of the elements to think, "what if…."

Mr. Bean sat in the window with his nose pressed against the pane. He wanted to go outside to play, but Mommy had wisely locked all of the exterior cat doors. They wouldn't be going anywhere for a while. Tiger Lily wondered briefly if she had remembered the cat door in the basement. No matter. The way the snow was coming down, they wouldn't be able to get out, anyway. It would be buried.

Tiger Lily watched Speckles and Daryll for a while. They acted like they were on vacation. They were, in a sense. There were plenty of humans on hand to keep an eye on Little Fred. Even Kali and Ko had given her over to the care of humans.

Maybe Little Fred didn't need nanny kitties anymore. Maybe Speckles and Daryll could become real cats. For now, they quietly batted a funny piece of metal back and forth. She wasn't sure where they had found it.

Tiger Lily kept an eye on the men. They seemed to doze, off and on. When that happened, JoJo would rouse them and start to read again.

Now, it sounded like she was reading a recipe. It actually sounded pretty good. Turkey breasts stuffed with butternut squash, figs and spinach. They were browned in a black skillet, then baked, still in the skillet. Tiger Lily stared at JoJo, willing her to give the recipe to Henrie. Or Felicity. That would be better.

JoJo responded to the stare. Somewhat startled, she turned her head and looked at Tiger Lily. Their gazes melded for a moment, and JoJo said, "How about I get this recipe to Felicity? She'd like it."

Then JoJo turned back to the magazine, checking on the men before turning her eyes back to the recipe.

Tiger Lily broke her stare and licked her lips. Mission accomplished.

Henrie came in on occasion, checking on JoJo and the men, bringing warm tea and occasionally small snacks.

Once, he came in with eleven little dishes. Tiger Lily knew it was coming. She smelled it the second Henrie opened the refrigerator and reached in to get the Tupperware dish that had bacon. He opened the door, and Tiger Lily knew. She sat up straight, and just like that, so did ten other cats.

They had gotten down from their cushions and were milling around the floor long before he arrived.

Henrie was always impressed when they did something like that. Today, he said, "You knew I would not forget you."

They ate, they cleaned up, they went back to the cushions. They were affected with lethargy. The lethargy that occurs at the beginning of a storm. The lethargy that occurs when you know you won't be leaving the house for any reason, and you'll be stuck, stuck, stuck with these people and these cats, and there was nothing to be done.

She breathed deeply. The thing she was most happy about was that the detective agency could take a break. There would be no crimes committed in Chelsea on this day or in the days to come.

One of Justin's jobs was to keep the sidewalks of the Inn clear, in case people from town needed to get in.

Justin took his job seriously. He wanted to prove himself. Stay out of trouble. Make as much money as he could. Continue with his classes at the community college.

He was living at home again, having forged a tentative truce with his parents. He knew it was all on him. He would have to work – maybe for years – for them to believe in him again.

For now, he was on his own. They didn't charge him rent, but he was more or less a renter in his own home. When they joined extended family for holidays, he was not included. When they visited their other children, both successful in the beginning of their careers, he was not included. When they sat down to dinner, he was not included.

He could tell his mother wanted to fully welcome him back to the fold, but his father would not. Not now. Maybe when he had that degree and he started a career of his own. He paid for school on his own. He paid for everything – his clothes, meals, anything extra – on his own. They allowed him a bedroom that was heated in the winter and cooled in the summer. That was all.

Thoughts of the coming holiday filled his mind as he used a combination of snow-blower and shovel to stay ahead of the snow. He wondered where he would spend Christmas Eve, Christmas Day.

In years past, he spent all his free time with his rotten friends, even the holidays. They didn't have families that cared. They only had one another. Every now and then, Justin had wished he was with his family rather than with the delinquents.

Now, when he thought about them, he realized they didn't have a chance in the world. Not the kind of chance he had. They were living up to the expectations of their parents. Justin was the opposite. He had drug his parents' expectations down.

No more. No more. He would get through this Christmas, and maybe next Christmas….

Justin realized he had worked his way around the house. He was at the basement steps. Oh, well. May as well keep that clear, too. They might need an emergency exit. Justin cleared the steps all the way to the door, making sure the door could open all the way. Hey, there was a cat door here, too. That Annie didn't miss a trick.

By the time Justin had gotten around the house, clearing off the steps and ramp to the porch and a good section of the porch as well, over to the carriage house, the steps to the second level, from the carriage house to the back of the house and back to the basement, several inches had fallen. He cleared it again.

This was his job today, and he was going to do it well.

12

By Wednesday evening, nothing moved outside. Annie walked through the Inn, inviting everyone who was there to a buffet supper. She knocked first on the door of Tom and Helen.

"Hello. It's Annie."

She heard movement, and soon, Helen opened the door. Annie could tell she had been crying.

"Hi. We're putting together a buffet supper for everyone. We've got lots of people here now, including some people from town. I wanted to invite you down. And I want you to feel free to mingle."

"I don't know…"

"Please join us. We're all going to be here for a few days, and we may as well get used to one another."

"I suppose…well…we'll come down for supper."

"Great. I'll see you down there."

Annie told Holly and Jolly the meal was ready and knocked on Robert and Sue's door.

"Hello. It's Annie."

Robert answered.

"Hi. We have a buffet supper ready downstairs. Please come join us, and feel free to mingle. We'll all be here for a few days."

Annie thought he seemed ill at ease, but he said, "Sure. We'll be down in a minute."

Annie started for the kitchen, but she could stand it no longer. She stopped at the second floor landing and tried again to reach Chris by cell phone. There was no answer.

She called his house. She finally called the Station. Shorter answered. Annie felt an inward groan coming on, but she pushed forward.

"Shorter, this is Annie Mack. Is Chris still there?"

"No. He's not in yet. Still on the lake."

"On the lake?" Annie took a deep breath to calm herself. "When do you expect him?"

"Frankly…about an hour ago. But it's snowing pretty hard. Wind is up on the lake. They're coming in against it."

"Have you been in touch recently?"

"Are you telling me how to do my job?"

"No, Shorter, no. I'm sorry. I'm just worried. Will you please tell him I called when he gets in?"

"We're pretty busy, but if I remember, I will. You know this line shouldn't be used for personal calls."

Annie took a deep breath and continued to the kitchen. Henrie and Martha had deli meats, breads, deli salads, lemonade and coffee for what looked like a hundred people. Before she could say anything, however, Donnie and Daryl, Boone's sons, stomped in, brushed off snow, and dropped their coats. They made up plates and went to the small table in the dining room.

On his way by, Daryl said, "Thanks, ma'am. This will be real fillin' whilst we warm up."

Annie smiled. Sometimes, the boys backed into their Appalachian slang at work. She supposed they didn't backslide at community college, nor with their girlfriends or at family meals. But at times….

"Where's your mother?"

"She tole all her folks to stay home, so she's takin' care a the places that's closed up fer the day, the Café and the bakery, now, I suppose. She got that yoga place early."

"How kind of her. Well, we will be opening at least the Café and bakery tomorrow for crews, so it's good to know we'll be ready."

"Yes'm."

Annie walked past Henrie and sat at the end of the counter. "Should we keep food out all day, so they can eat when they get a chance?"

"I will make sure we have supplies in the Keurig corner, and let them know. They can manage on their own."

"That's a very relaxed approach, Henrie."

"Desperate times call for desperate measures."

JoJo came in. "The guys are hungry. I'll make a couple of sandwiches."

"Are they okay?"

"Barry is. Kullen doesn't look so good. He just started coughing."

"I'll check on him. We might need to call Jennifer and Marie."

"Thanks, Annie."

Annie went to the library, surprised to see all of the cats still there. Part of her surprise was that she had forgotten their supper. "Golly, kids. Let me check on Kullen, then we'll go upstairs to eat."

Tiger Lily stared at her.

"Maybe I'll bring it down."

Tiger Lily licked her front paw. Two for two. She was on a roll. Maybe this snow was helping her powers of persuasion.

Chris ordered his crew into their rescue wetsuits. They wore outer gear as well, but the suits would be the best protection in the event of a tragedy. He was beginning to think more favorably about an office job.

They were a third of the way back to Chelsea when the snow hit. The wind had been against them for longer than that, however, and their progress was slow.

Halfway back, the radio stopped working. Chris had to wonder about that. This was an expensive piece of equipment. There was no reason for it to be out.

Just as he turned around to shout to his crew, one of them shouted to him.

"Boat! Boat to starboard!"

Chris saw it. Between them and shore, a fishing craft that had seen better days struggled in the wake of their much larger craft. Steering into the snow, Chris had not seen it. They were all lucky they didn't have a collision.

The boat, Chris could not see a name, struggled in a sea of ice chunks, icy waves breaking over its bow.

As Chris wondered about his navigation gear, why the boat had been invisible to him, he and the crew rushed to the task of rescue. There was no way this boat would make it to safety.

Chris saw three men on deck. They had clearly given up on making it to shore and waved their arms to indicate that yes, please, they would very much desire a bigger boat!

Navigating the rescue would be tricky. Between dangerous ice chunks, wind, snow, limited visibility, waves and currents, they ran the risk of crashing into it and sending all its inhabitants into the water and probably to their deaths.

His crew had already dropped buffers over the side, to mitigate damage if they did hit the craft, but still…they could be sent up and over, mitigating nothing.

One of his senior staff, Janelle, shot a tow line across. It missed. After retrieving the line, she shot again. Again, it missed. By now, the smaller boat had started to upend, waves pushing it against ice that was now packed against the shore.

Janelle shot the line and they caught it. The crew of the battered boat worked to secure the line to the bow, but a wave, larger than all that came before, hurled two of the men into the water.

Using hand signals, the remaining man understood he was to tie the tow line around himself, and while that rescue went on, Chris grabbed another line and jumped. The men in the water had minutes to live. No time to think.

He knew he could be crushed by the ice. He knew he could be crushed by his own boat, or by the smaller one breaking loose and barreling down the icepack. But he had no other choice.

Annie put a hand to Kullen's forehead. He was warm, alright. Burning up. She put the thermometer under his tongue and waited a few seconds. One hundred two. Annie called the sisters.

Kali jumped to the arm of Kullen's chair, to see if her mere presence would ward off any illness.

Marie stomped through the door. As cheerful as her sister, even in dire circumstances, she had nothing but praise for Boone and his crew.

"It's blippin' cold out there!" she said. "And the snow is already over my boots."

Henrie appeared. "Coffee or cocoa?"

"Cocoa. Heavy on the chocolate, no whipped cream or marshmallows."

Henrie left to do her bidding and Marie approached Annie. "Which one? Oh, I didn't even need to ask. Nurse Kali is on duty. You must be Kullen."

Kullen nodded his head briefly, but his eyes remained closed. His breathing was labored.

Marie did a quick check of his body temperature, skillfully finding fingers, toes, arms and legs. "He's warm enough." She looked at Barry. "You the brother?"

Nod.

"Why don't we take Kullen up to your room, get him in some comfortable clothes, sweats, if you have them, and we'll take it from there."

Barry and Marie helped Kullen from his chair, out and into the elevator. Annie followed as far as the doorway, then she turned. "JoJo, could you please wait on the landing upstairs? If they need anything, you can just call down and I'll bring whatever they need, right away."

JoJo nodded and trotted up the stairs.

No one noticed when Kali slipped upstairs, into their room and under the bed.

Henrie appeared with a tray and two steaming cups of cocoa. Annie said, "I'll take one. We'll have to keep one warm for Marie. I think I'll add a little something to mine."

From behind the second cup, Henrie produced a shot glass filled with dark liquid. "I thought you might need this."

"Ah, Henrie. Thank you!"

"Have you heard from Chris?"

"No. He's overdue. Out in that storm."

"Come. Sit in the dining room. There are many people. Many conversations to keep your mind from going to dark places."

And that's when the power went out.

Randy jumped into the truck. The snow was coming down now. He couldn't see out the front window. He pounded the dashboard. Once. Twice. Three times.

The dog huddled against the passenger door and whined. "I've had enough!" Randy turned and hit the dog with his fist. Once in the face, and once in the ribs.

She yelped and cowered, then melted into the foot well in front of the seat.

Randy finally realized what he had done. "Sis! Sis! I'm sorry, girl. I didn't mean it. Really, I...I'm sorry, girl."

He leaned into the steering wheel, head down, trying to think. He had come away with nothing. The guy tried to give him five thousand. As if that would be enough. He'd disappear again, and that would be it. And what would he say to the bosses? The guy's dead now.

That gave Randy pause. Need to get rid of that gun. He reached into his coat pocket. The gun came out, but....where was the silencer? Gosh darn it! Where was it? Was it the agency's silencer? Or was it his own? The agency silencer could be traced to him, couldn't it?

He got the bottle out of a pocket and took one more pill. Just one. You aren't in trouble if you only take one at a time.

Gotta hit the road and think. Just gotta think. He finally thought about Sis. "You need to go out, girl? Here, let's go out."

Randy got out of the truck and held the door for Sis. She crept toward it, keeping her eyes on his face, then his hand, then his face. Finally, she was out and in the snow.

"Be quick, girl. We gotta hit the road."

He leaned against the truck, letting the snow hit him in the face. He waited. Waited some more. Stood up, called out, "Sis! Come on!" Waited some more. His heart fell. What had he done? What had he become?

Carter always went to bed earlier than most. He woke up in what, for him, was the middle of the night. He had been getting power from The Marina, but apparently, the grid went down. He wasn't sure when, but it was awfully cold. Had to have been a couple of hours.

He reached over to turn on a battery-powered light, then put on a coat, hat and gloves while he got the generator started. Once it kicked on, he checked his heater. Yes, it was on. It would take a while.

Carter didn't mind situations like this. In fact, he got a secret enjoyment of having to rely on the barest of threads to survive in the winter. He began the process of making coffee, then thought about Albert.

Darn it. Why did a newcomer have to pick his dock? Well, there was nothing to be done.

Carter put on heavy pants and added a sweater to his layers of clothing. He struggled on deck, putting his hand against his eyes to shield them from the driving snow.

Sure enough, there was not a single light on Albert's boat.

Carter reached inside for a flashlight. He waded through snow past his knees, tripping on occasion over items that were in place, but invisible in the dark and under the snow. Eventually, he made his way to the dock and waded over to Albert's ladder.

Up he went, cursing under his breath, for the most part, and only yelling a few bad words per minute. Much slower than the snowfall.

On deck, he bumped into many things that were under the snow. He stepped on something small, rod-like and unsecured, losing his balance and landing on his back. His head went all the way back to the deck. The snow was too soft to shield it from the hard deck. He was going to have a knot. And maybe worse.

He cursed again. This time he cursed Albert directly for not keeping a proper deck.

Carter knocked on the door. No answer. He put his weight into it, and the force of his upper arm. No answer.

The guy could be in hypothermia already.

He took hold of the handle, expecting it to be locked, but it was not. He opened it and blew down the stairs, partly on his own volition and partly with the help of the wind. He got to the bottom of the steps and turned to push the door shut. Snow had already coated the top inner step.

When Carter turned and aimed the flashlight into the room, he realized he had no need to wake Albert. He was sprawled on the floor, torso upright against the bed. He sprouted a new eye in the center of his forehead.

Annie and Henrie found places to sleep, pillows and blankets for almost everyone on the other side of The Avenue. Annie's buildings were powered by generators, and Jennifer and Marie kept The Clinic, The Drug Store and their apartments powered as well.

Everyone else, though, needed a warm place to stay.

Laila packed some bags and bundled her three children across The Avenue to the Inn. James, a freshman in college, carried the largest bag, while Ava, in high school, and Carl, in junior high and living with autism, carried pet carriers and pulled a wagon with other pets in cages. The menagerie – ferret, turtle, parrot, hamster and lizard – traveled in high style.

Laila worried as they walked across. "I hope the power comes on soon, or our refrigerated items are toast."

James, her oldest, said, "If the freezer things are still cool, we can cook lots of deli food. And freeze it. And hope…"

Annie gave Laila a hug and said, "It will be alright. Tomorrow, if the power is still out, we'll get what we can and put it in our freezers."

Henrie shook his head. Annie had not seen the state of their freezers. He carried bags as he led the children and Laila to the all-season porch.

Holly and Jolly had a room. They would be joined by Holly's friend Jet as soon as he finished at the Winery.

Annie placed two mattresses on the floor on the far south side of the library for Mem and Diana. She asked Mem, "Where is Frank staying?"

Frank was Mem's special friend. He owned a three-story building around the corner on Main Street. His apartment was on the third floor. His store, Antiques On Main, was on the first.

"He added a generator. He asked me to come over and stay, but I wanted to stay home, so I could keep the store open. If the power comes on tomorrow, I can still open up. Even though he's as close as you, just in another direction, I stand a better chance of doing that if I stay here."

"Where's Gema?"

"She's in Frank's guest room. She packed for a few days, just in case. She's being very positive that customers will be here to buy her jewelry."

Annie had to laugh. But it was a quiet laugh. She was dead on her feet.

The last people to settle in were Pastor Teresa and Clara. They had called dibs on two long sofas at the front of the library and were in the process of making beds out of them.

All of Annie's new quilts were in use; every pillow, blanket, towel and washcloth had been given to a guest; everyone knew where to find food, water and coffee.

Annie and Henrie stumbled to their beds, exhausted.

13

In what Annie's mother called "the wee hours of the morning," Annie heard someone pounding on her apartment door. Groggy, she struggled out of bed, into a robe and out to the kitchen.

She hoped it was Chris. Then she growled under her breath. He had a key. He had no need to...

Annie swung the door open and saw a very wet, very cold police chief and his dog.

"Thank you for keeping the front door unlocked."

"We always do in an emergency. Get in here. Let me get a towel and...well...I have a robe and some sweats that belong to Chris."

"Will he mind?"

"We won't tell him."

Cyril, thankfully, had shaken most of the snow from his body somewhere else in the house. Someone would find it later. Annie still took a kitchen towel to his fur, getting most of the water out.

He gave her a grateful lick and padded into the dining room, where the cats waited.

Annie watched as two big cats, looking at her as if they would be scolded, then two smaller ones, pushed through the cat door. Without a sound, they joined the group in the dining room.

Annie looked at Pete. "Detecting."

"I wish they spoke human."

"Come with me, Pete. I'll get you those clothes."

Pete came from the bedroom, cell phone in hand, and dressed in warm, dry sweats and slippers. Annie had a cup of coffee and a shot of whisky ready at her favorite reclining chair. Being extremely generous, she gestured him into it and covered him with a throw.

"Thanks, Annie. There was no way I could make it home in this mess. I need to call Janet."

Pete made his call while Annie stared out the window at the snow. When he hung up, Annie asked, "You told Janet you were at The Marina. Did you hear anything about Chris? Had Ray talked to him?"

"He heard radio chatter. He knew Chris was south somewhere, getting a barge out, and then he didn't hear much of anything."

"I haven't been able to reach him, and Shorter is so…so nasty. He pretty much told me not to call again."

"Annie, everything is probably fine."

Annie looked at her hands. For no particular reason. She didn't know where else to look. Until she remembered.

"What were you doing at The Marina?"

"Murder."

"Are they alright?"

"Ray and Cheryl are fine. And Jock. It's one of those boaters."

"Which one?"

"Uh… the inexperienced one."

"Oh. Mocha Latte."

"What?"

"I remember him more as Mocha Latte than by his name, but anyway, what happened? He didn't slip and fall. You said murder."

"Shot. In the head. Dead."

Annie heard a knock on her door. She went to the kitchen and opened it. Henrie, with his hands behind his back, asked, "Is everything alright?"

Annie smiled. "Yes, Henrie. It's Pete and Cyril. Come in, and put that bat down."

Henrie stepped in, dressed in his snappy tuxedo-style pajamas and wearing black leather slippers that looked like dress shoes. He put the bat on the floor, leaning it against the door jamb.

"How about coffee and a shot?"

"I do not mind if I do."

"He's in the living room. I'll bring it in."

Pete was telling Henrie about the boater. He had just reached the good part. "So anyway, the other guy blew into The Marina and collapsed on the floor. When Ray got to him, he was saying 'murder, he's dead,' and then he passed out."

"Was he shot, too?"

"No. Jennifer thinks it was a mild case of hypothermia."

"Jennifer was there?"

"Yeah. Ray felt a knot on his head."

"Pete, you're talking in circles. Slow down and make it a straight line. What happened?"

Pete looked at Annie, shivered, pulled the throw around him and said, "I wonder if I've got a little hypothermia?"

Annie brought another throw, tucked the first one tightly around his midsection, and covered his legs and feet with the second. She brought a third and tucked it under his neck, making sure to cover everything but the arm holding the coffee. She took the shot, not yet touched, back to the kitchen.

"Wait…"

"No. Not until you're warm. I bet talking will warm you up. Talk. Tell us what happened."

"Okay. Actually, this will help. Take notes, will you, Annie? This might clear my confusion."

Pete took a deep breath and started at the beginning. "So Carter, the alive guy, thinks this guy Albert, the dead guy, didn't know much about living on a boat in winter. He didn't want to, but he kind of took him under his wing. He woke up cold, realized the power was off, and bundled up to get his generator going. The heat was on and was going to start working, and he realized, hey, this is exactly what I told that idiot could happen. I'd better check on him."

"So the other guy, Mocha Latte…"

"Albert. He was on the other boat. Again, what Carter told Albert could happen. Getting from one boat to another is not a straight line anymore. They were close enough that when the weather was good, they could jump from one boat to the other. But now, with several inches of snow, he had to wade through snow and wind to get to the front of his boat, get down to the dock, find the ladder to Albert's boat, and do it all backwards. When he made it into the cabin, he saw Albert. He was shot. In the head."

"Dead," said Annie. "And then he had to do all of that in reverse, this time getting to The Marina. Where Ray and Cheryl decided to stay, thank goodness, rather than go home. Any idea who did it?"

"Not one."

"And what was the knot on his head?"

"Oh. He said Carter didn't keep a shipshape deck. His foot went out from underneath him when he stepped on something, and he hit his head on the way down."

"Lucky man. If he had passed out…"

"I know. Jennifer thinks he's okay. More hypothermic than concussed. They're keeping him in the office overnight."

"So did you have to go onto the boat?"

"I did. I could kind of tell where Carter fell down. The snow was covering it up, but there was still an indentation. I felt around, and look what I found."

Pete reached under the throw for his pocket. Then he realized he wasn't wearing his uniform.

"Just tell me."

"It was a silencer."

"No!"

Pete yawned. "Yes. And then I went into the cabin, saw the dead man. Snapped some photos. Got his fingerprints. Backed out."

This time, when Pete yawned, Annie had to join him. "I shut that door and wrapped crime scene tape through the latch and around anything I could find. It's cold in there."

Pete yawned again. "At least until the power comes back on. Guess I'll have to get out there by then with techs."

There was one final yawn as Pete rolled onto his side in the reclining chair.

Annie said, "You could ask Ray to cut the power to the boat, keep it frozen until you can get back out."

"Good idea....gotta call...." Pete nodded off.

Before leaving, Henrie wrote a note and left in on the table for Pete. "Call Ray. Put crime scene in deep freeze."

Randy had a work-horse of a truck, but it wouldn't make it in this weather. This weather was too extreme. He needed to think. How could he blend in while he looked for Sis? This was a small town. People would know he was a stranger.

Maybe in a couple of days, maybe even by tomorrow, emergency crews would arrive. He could figure out something, insert himself into a crew.

He had some time. No one would be missing Albert. Not for several days. He'd kept his radio on, and there was no chatter about a murder, about a body.

He just hoped Sis was safe, wherever she was. She could handle cold weather, but how long could she stay out in this?

He pulled out the bottle and took two. It was night. Two at night. Got him through the tough hours.

He would hang around this street. It looked like people were working around the clock to keep it cleared.

Certainly he would meet emergency crews here, and certainly, this is where Sis will find shelter.

The cats piled on top of Cyril to help him warm up. *"It's cold. I don't remember ever being this cold. I think Pete's a little confused."*

"Why do you think that?"

"He was going to go home. I figured that out and started barking while we were still in the parking lot. Then I acted like I was going to break the window once we got to the Inn. He kind of realized maybe I was right."

"That's a good thing. It looks like Mommy's wrapping him in a million blankets."

"Is you warm enuff to tell us wot happened?"

"I guess." Cyril told them what he knew, and added that Jock had seen people on the dock in the middle of the day.

"Who'd he see?"

"He didn't go outside. Just saw them from inside. Two people, a man and a woman. But Cheryl called him for lunch, so he didn't see if they went on one of the boats."

"Did he see anything else?"

"A little later, he saw a man get out of a silver pick-up truck, one he had seen before. Ray was in a hurry to get to town, so Jock didn't see what boat he was going to, but he saw a dog in the truck. There was something else. Something about an argument, maybe on a telephone, that the Albert guy had yesterday morning."

Tiger Lily made her list. *"There was a man and a woman, and then a man. And an argument the day before. We'll probably have to think about this."*

She looked at Speckles and Daryll. *"I thought we would be crime-free for a while, but we're not. We have to be on our toes. The two of you were playing with a funny thing today in the library. What was it and where did you get it?"*

Speckles and Daryll looked at one another, then back at Tiger Lily. They answered in turns. *"I don't know what it was." "It was in one of the rooms." "We smelled food in one of the rooms that the people stay in." "The food smelled real good, but it was locked up." "We tried to get it." "But we weren't going to make a mess, honest." "We found it under a big chest where the food was."*

The little cats ran out of steam. They looked at one another, then at Tiger Lily, expecting to be scolded.

"It's okay that you were in the room. We go in all the time."

"Really?"

"Yes. But that thing looked really interesting. What is it?"

The little cats looked at one another, then back at Tiger Lily. Speckles finally said, *"You don't know?"*

"No, but Cyril knows lots of things. He might know what it is. Is it still in the library?"

"No. We took it to our bedroom. It was fun."

"Can one of you go get it?"

Speckles exhibited her ninja abilities. She jumped straight up, turned in mid-air, and landed on running feet.

Daryll laughed. *"She does that all the time. She's so cool!"*

Kali cleared her throat. Everyone looked at her. *"I've been trying to get those goofy guys to notice me, but all they do is ignore me. It's like they can't see cats."*

"That's pretty goofy, all right."

"Yeah, but they were talking tonight, right after Marie left. It sounded a little funny."

"What were they saying?"

"That one guy, Barry, said he would go to work tomorrow and take care of it. And Kullen, he said, 'love ya, bro, but you got us into a real mess.'"

Several cats asked at once, *"What did he mean?" "What kind of mess?" "Trill!"*

"I don't know. I guess it's one more thing we'll have to watch out for."

Then Little Socks did something totally out of character. She went to the kitchen, picked up a mouthful of cat food, and dropped it on the floor in front of Cyril.

"Thanks. I'm really hungry."

"We'll gets you more!" Sassy Pants ran to the kitchen, Mr. Bean on her tail. Between them, they pushed the dish almost to the end of the kitchen floor, where it ran into two feet. Mommy's feet.

Mommy picked the bowl up and went to the cupboard. "Here, kids. Let's take this to him instead."

Annie set a bowl of food and another bowl of water within Cyril's reach at the same time Speckles returned with her prize.

"What's this?"

Annie took the metal thing from Speckles, looked at it, then looked at Tiger Lily. "We'll talk about this in the morning."

Annie tucked the metal object into her pocket and returned to bed. Tiger Lily asked Cyril, *"Did you see it? What was it?"*

"It was a bullet."

14

Annie fed the cats and Cyril, then made coffee. She poked Pete until he woke up.

"I left out a towel and everything you need in the bathroom. Don't tell Chris."

"Thanks. Where's my uniform?"

"Hanging in the bathroom. I hope steam from the shower will fix it."

"Pretty wrinkled, huh?"

"You treated it badly."

Annie opened the door to let Cyril out. "Go downstairs and ask Henrie to let you outside, then stay down there. I'm going to keep this door closed today."

She filled the cat dishes. Tiger Lily, cleaning herself from breakfast, stopped long enough to look up.

"I'm putting your supper out now, kids. Things have a tendency to get confused with everyone here. Don't sneak up here all day long, Ko. Ko?"

Ko looked at her from around the corner of the kitchen island.

"I mean it. This is all you are going to get today. No more until tomorrow morning."

There was no need for anyone to get going early on Thursday morning. Snow continued to come down. Boone and his crew, in cooperation with the Street Department, kept the walks, steps and roads clear from the municipal parking lot to the police department, and life went on for businesses on The Avenue. Somewhat.

Power was restored to The Avenue early in the morning. Most of Annie's guests – the ones that lived on The Avenue – left their bags at the Inn, but after breakfast they bundled up and left for work.

Holly, Diana and Teresa stayed in to enjoy a rare day without work. They found movies that involved winter storms and went to Holly's room to enjoy a marathon.

Henrie waved Laila and her children out the door.

"I've left the menagerie here, Henrie, but the kids are better off being bored in their own home. If the power is still on this evening, we'll come get the pets."

"Must I do anything with them in the meantime?"

"No. They have all they need. It would be best if they're left alone. If they get out of their cages, we won't find them."

Henrie checked in with Annie's staff via Skype. Cooks and servers made buffet breakfast for emergency workers at the Café. Donuts and breads were in plentiful supply at Mr. Bean's. George made sure the bar was open for burgers and beer during lunch, and, for the most part, Jesus, Minnie and Jet relaxed at the winery.

Jennifer and Marie were up and on duty, and the other businesses were open. They didn't expect a lot – if any – business, but if someone should wander in, they were ready.

Barry was the first guest – guest that was also a tourist – to arrive in the dining room. Henrie stood, leaving his coffee on the side table. "Good morning, Barry. How is Kullen today?"

"He's feeling better but moving slow. That woman said he needed to be careful he didn't get pneumonia, so she gave him something and told him to stay in for the next couple of days. He's taking a shower now, and he should be down in a bit."

"That is good to hear."

"It would be really good if I could work today. Is it possible the cyber café is open?"

"It is. I spoke with Mem briefly. She does not have a tech assistant today, but as you are proficient and have been there before, you should have no difficulty."

"Great. I should really get going…would it be a problem if I took breakfast to go?"

"Not at all."

"Will she mind?"

"Typically, we do not cross our meals with her establishment, as she does serve food. Today, however, I believe everyone will make an exception."

Henrie gave Barry a carry-out box, thought again, and gave him an additional box with a bag and a thermos for coffee.

Barry had been gone for a few minutes when Tom and Helen arrived. They greeted Henrie and served themselves, being careful to take small portions.

Tom said, "I think we'll spend some time in the library today, if that's alright. Maybe we can find something on TV that would be good for everyone…"

He was interrupted by the entrance of two people. "That sounds good. It's what we planned to do. I'm

Robert. This is my wife, Sue. I guess we're stuck here together for a while."

"Yes, I guess so. I'm Tom. This is Helen."

Henrie retreated to make another pot of coffee and to replenish the breakfast items. He heard the four chatting, friendly enough, if a bit distant. Typical for guests whose plans had been changed.

He heard voices, now female, talking about their reason for being in town. He recognized Helen first.

"We came to cross country ski. The winter weather was quite beautiful until…well, until yesterday."

"How nice. We, well, we heard there was to be a winter extravaganza of some sort. Shopping, decorations, vendors of all sorts. We hoped to relax and do some Christmas shopping."

Henrie caught the lie, even though he was not in the same room. The other female voice continued the conversation.

"I heard about that. It wasn't our reason for coming, but we understand it was to be quite the affair. I would imagine it is off the table now."

"You never know. The snow could be gone by the weekend."

"That would be tomorrow."

"Oh. Yes. Silly me. Time does fly."

"Some of the stores may be happy to let go of their merchandise, even if the entire affair doesn't happen. Will you shop, as long as you're here?"

"Well, probably. Tell me, how long do you plan on staying?"

"We should have left today. Perhaps we'll leave as soon as the highways are clear."

"Oh. Well. We might do that as well. Silly to shop during a winter emergency, really."

Voices stopped suddenly. Henrie stopped working, listening carefully. He turned back to his work when he heard Pete's voice, followed shortly by Annie's.

"Good morning. Sorry to join you wearing a wrinkled uniform. Got caught in the snow last night."

Annie's voice added, "This is Pete, our Chief of Police. He's not really a guest, just a casualty of the snow."

Henrie heard low murmurs of greeting. Then, a subdued, somewhat stuffy male voice. Kullen.

"Morning, everyone. Oh, hi."

Silence.

"Me and my brother, we're the ones that bumped into you in that parking lot yesterday. Remember? I'm the one that smacked you with my surfboard. Again, I'm sorry for that. I wasn't looking."

Henrie heard a mumbled response. He wasn't sure of the voice. Perhaps he should fashion an excuse to go back in. He then heard the sound of chairs pushing back.

One of the men said, "Excuse us. We've got things to tend to in the room."

After a pause, a man's voice, probably Tom's, said, "I thought they were going to join us in the library."

The next voice Henrie heard was that of Little Fred. She was angry and punctuated her cries with shouts of "Mamamama!"

By the time Georgia and Little Fred were in the dining room, Henrie was there, warm baby oatmeal in hand. Pete stood to take the crying little dear.

"Hewo dare, wittle girl. It's your Uncle Pete."

Little eyes went wide, and the cries became a smile and a laugh.

"Thanks, Pete. We've had a rough morning. We're without nanny kitties, and she will not be placated."

"You left the cats at home?"

"No. They're here. Seems they've taken a little vacation."

Thunderous footsteps on the stairway announced the arrival of Kali and Ko, the original nanny kitties. They took care of Little Fred when she first arrived in Chelsea and only grudgingly trained Speckles when the baby moved away.

They surrounded Pete, reaching up as far as they could to get to Little Fred. Pete went to the corner to sit at a small table, the better to get the child close to the cats.

Henrie glanced at Tom and Helen. They were entranced. Either by the baby or the cats trying to get to the baby. He could not be sure. But after a nod of welcome to Kullen, he left to return to the kitchen. Today would be a busy food preparation day.

Randy filled his plate at the buffet. The people in this Café were friendly, and they didn't seem to care that they didn't know him.

A dark-skinned woman handed him a cup of coffee and asked what crew he was with.

"I just came on my own. They told me to hook up with the first crew I found. Do you know where they get their assignments?"

"Over at the Street Department. But someone will be here soon, surely, and you can just go with them."

Randy sighed when she left. He could do this.

Should he ask people about Sis? Or just keep his eyes open? He couldn't take the chance of someone putting two and two together: stranger, dog, murder. Well, that was one and one and one.

He shivered. He was cold. It might be affecting his thinking. He pulled out the bottle and took two.

It didn't take much to catch Pete's attention, and he had far too many years of experience to let it show.

He surrendered the child to Georgia and turned to Kullen. In a stern voice, he said, "Surfboard, huh? You went against all of my instructions and went out on that lake."

Kullen sunk into his chair as he stared at Pete.

"I think we're overdue for a serious conversation. Finish your breakfast. Make it a good one. Might be a while before you see food as good as this. When you're done, we'll find a private place to talk."

Kullen swallowed the bite he had been holding. "I think I've had enough, sir. Don't think I can eat any more."

Pete kept the stern look on his face. Without turning away from Kullen, he asked, "Where could Kullen and I go have a talk, Annie?"

"Um, I think maybe the best place would be the library. No, it will be in use. Maybe on the back porch? I think all the kids went back with Laila. You'll have to work around their luggage and things, though."

"Good enough. Tell you what. Kullen and I are going to head that way. Could you please ask Henrie if he can put a carafe of coffee together? Kullen and I are going to discuss the error of his ways. It may take a while."

Pete stood. Kullen stood, not as quickly, and certainly not with as much confidence. He followed Pete to the porch, eyes downcast.

Tom and Helen beat a quick retreat to the library while Georgia made a plate for herself. Annie went into the kitchen.

"What do you think, Henrie? Do you think Pete is really going to go after Kullen?"

Henrie kept his voice low. "No. I believe that Pete may have heard something suspicious. It is certain he wants you or me to join him on the porch. Which do you prefer?"

Henrie had filled a carafe and was making a tray with cups and condiments.

Annie thought quickly. "I'll take it. Could you do me a favor and call the Station? See if Chris made it in, or see if you can find out anything? Shorter won't take my call. He's…well, he won't take my call."

"Certainly. That will give me an excuse to join you on the porch."

Annie took the tray and walked down the hall to the porch, wondering if the corner heater had been turned on. Kullen didn't need to get cold.

She put the tray on the table in front of Pete and went to the corner, switching the heater on. On her way back, she picked up a large throw and put it around Kullen's neck and shoulders.

Kullen stared at the cages on the table. A parrot. A ferret. A turtle. A lizard. A hamster. And Kali. What was she doing in here? She sat on top of the ferret cage, staring at Kullen.

"No matter what happens, you have to stay warm."

"Yes, ma'am."

"Don't ma'am me."

"Yes, ma'am. Um, ma'am, do you always eat with the animals?"

Annie shook her head. "Bad weather makes for strange bedfellows. Pete, put this boy out of his misery. Why are we here?"

Pete let his face soften and looked straight at Kullen.

"Tell me about that couple you saw on their way to The Marina. What are their names, and what time did you see them?"

Kullen looked at the cages. Annie realized he was the kind of person that had to keep moving when he was nervous. His fingers played with the latches.

"I don't know their names…"

Annie said, "That was Robert and Sue. I think. Yes. Definitely Robert and Sue. Henrie will have intake cards."

"What time?"

"Um…I don't know? We'd been at the cyber café, and we left, um…I'm not sure of the time…"

"Eleven. I called when we got worried about you."

"Okay. You left there at eleven. What did you do then?"

"Um, this is important? I mean, I'm real sorry I went to the lighthouse. Really. I didn't mean to make all those people come rescue me. I didn't mean…"

"Hold on, now. Let's do one thing at a time. And now I'm going to start over." Pete's face was stern again, and his voice was inordinately low and strangled. "You really went back out to the lighthouse? You went into the water? You had to be rescued?"

Kullen fingers flipped open the lid to the lizard cage.

Annie said, "Um, Kullen, could you close that, please?"

"Oh, yeah. Sorry." Kullen was able to keep his eyes off Pete's face while he closed the cage door. "Um. This isn't about that?"

"No! This was about something else, but now, I guess yes! What were you thinking? What happened?"

Kullen's nervous fingers found the door to the rabbit cage. He flipped the latch open and closed, open and closed, until he finally had to say, "I couldn't help it?"

Annie couldn't help herself. She started to laugh, and she curled into her chair, tears running down her cheeks.

Henrie stepped into the porch. "Pardon me. Annie. Pardon me."

By the second 'pardon me,' her laughter was gone and she stared at Henrie's face.

"First of all, I understand that Chris is fine. Well, he is in a hospital south of here, but he will recover. There are no serious injuries. He had a concussion, and he was hypothermic."

Henrie looked at Kullen and Pete. "There is quite an epidemic going around."

Annie saw things in slow motion. She watched as Kullen fumbled the latch, and the rabbit leapt for freedom. He caught it just in time and shoved it back into the cage. He latched the door.

She turned to look at Pete, whose face was filled with concern. He was saying, "Annie? Are you alright?"

She looked back at Henrie. He was weaving back and forth. No, he wasn't. Her eyes were doing the weaving.

Kullen was now playing with the parrot's cage door.

She felt herself going into shock. Mouth open, body going slack, she nearly melted out of her chair except that Pete caught her. He moved her to the sofa, closer to the heater, and put a throw around her.

From a distance, she heard, "Come on, Henrie. Keep talking. I've got her."

Henrie had moved closer. He wasn't weaving so much now. He was nearly still. He was saying something. "...not bore you with details...some kind of hero...managed to get into a harbor..."

Annie cleared her throat. "Can I talk to him?"

"I have the number. All I have to do is press 'send.'"

"Please press it, but don't leave me."

Annie took a deep breath as she took the receiver from Henrie. She felt stronger now. The phone rang on the other end and was answered by a woman.

"Hello, this is Annie Mack. May I please speak to…"

"Annie, this is Janelle. I'm so glad you called. He's awake, and he's being a real S.O.B. But he wouldn't call you."

"Why not?"

"Some fool reason. He keeps saying, 'she hates me,' or 'why would she talk to me.' Anyway, he's makin' faces at me, so I'd better give him the phone before he fires me."

Annie waited until she heard his voice. She knew they couldn't talk. He had people on his end, and she had people on hers. After he said, 'hello,' she took a deep breath. "Hey, sailor. I hear you were trying to be a hero."

"Don't believe it."

"I won't. Tell me how long I have to wait for you to tell me yourself."

"They say I'll be released tomorrow."

"Tomorrow, huh? Well, there ought to be a road or two clear by then. Think you remember how to get here?"

"I do."

"Then I'll see you soon?"

"Soon."

"Okay. …. Okay. I can't wait."

"Neither can I. … Annie?"

"Yes?"

"Nothing. I'll see you as soon as I get out of here. They owe me a few days off."

"Good. See you soon."

Annie gave the phone to Henrie and wiped her eyes. "He'll be here tomorrow. I don't know what time."

"We will be ready." Henrie turned to Pete. "Do you require my assistance?"

"Yes. Please have a seat. I noticed you put four cups on that tray."

"I would have made an excellent Boy Scout."

"I'll bet. Hey, it's nice and warm over here. Kullen, make yourself useful. Bring that tray and your little self over here."

Kullen coughed. He had been twirling the latch of the ferret cage. He flipped it and picked up the tray. Annie motioned him to the chair on the other side of the heater.

Pete stayed where he was, leaning back, looking at the ceiling. He sat forward and looked at Kullen. "I believe you were going to tell me about your little adventure."

"Yes, sir. I'm pretty confused right now, but I'll just start at the beginning. Kind of. The part when we told you we'd stay away, but we knew we wouldn't."

"I think you already told me that. Let's just start where you were not in the water, then you were."

"I can do that. Let's see. We went to the pier. We'd passed a few folks on our way out, people who like to walk in all kinds of weather, you know. But no one that went past the closing barriers, like we did. It was probably one of those folks that called the Coast Guard."

"Called the Coast Guard."

"Yes, sir. I was out there, on my board. I'd just caught a wave." Kullen sat up straight. "It was really exciting. I was in the zone, man." His arms were out in imitation of a surfer riding a wave. "I hit that wave just perfect, and I was headed back to shore, and, well…," he slumped again. "You know how you're in the middle of something great, something you've always wanted to do, but then you remember what you should have seen?"

"Uh huh. What should you have seen?"

"Well, in all that excitement, I thought the clouds had gotten grayer or foggy or something, and I was riding that wave and got hit with the first wall of snow. It was intense. Really intense. Knocked me off. I couldn't see anything, and I guess Barry couldn't see me, because he got into the water on his board, and, well, the next thing I know, some frogman is lifting me out of the water."

"A frogman."

"Yeah. Like I said, I think someone that saw us going out called the Coast Guard, because they were right there, man. I woulda died in that water. I think I passed out."

"And then what happened?"

"Well, they started trying to get us warm, and they took us to their base. What do they call it? A station? Yeah. And then…well…this paramedic brought us here. Busted us a little bit."

"Jennifer."

"Yeah."

"Marie would bust you, too, but Jennifer would do it better."

"She did it pretty good."

"And you're okay?"

"Gotta stay warm. If I don't, could get bad."

"And your brother?"

"Oh, he's good. He's back at the cyber café, I think."

"And will you ever do this in my town again?"

"No, sir. I've done it once. That's enough. Plus I can't afford to buy another suit."

"Right. Now let's get back to my original agenda. Tell me everything about meeting that couple in the parking lot."

"Well, okay. We left, like she said, at eleven, and we walked, I don't know, pretty fast, it was cold. We left the car in the public lot, over by the pier, or walkway, or whatever you call it, that goes to the lighthouse. So I have my board, and I'm holding it between my upper arm and my body, and I'm trying to pull my glove tight, so I'm not paying attention, and I must have turned, because my board whacked this guy on his butt. Just whacked him."

"Did you speak?"

"Well, yeah. He yelled, and I dropped my board and turned around, and I said, 'hey, man, I'm really sorry,' and he was like, 'you'd better be,' and I was like, 'I didn't mean it, sorry, I was puttin' on my glove,' and he was like, 'just forget it.' And they left. They were walking toward The Marina, and we watched them for about half a minute. Then Barry said, well, he said something that wasn't very nice about them, and I agreed, and we went to our rendezvous with destiny."

Kullen sat back and looked expectantly at Pete. Pete nodded his head as if in thought. He turned to Henrie. "What time did the guests arrive?"

"I will have the arrival time on the card, but if memory serves, it was in that general vicinity of time. And they did leave quite suddenly shortly after their arrival."

"Kullen, I'd like you to leave us now. Can I count on you to say nothing to anyone? Not even your brother? You never know when someone will overhear you."

"Sure. You can count on me, but hey, what's this about, anyway?"

"Dead body."

Kullen laughed out loud, then noticed no one else was laughing. He shut his mouth, looked at all three, then said, "Seriously?"

"Seriously. Not a word."

"No, sir. … I think I'm gonna go back to bed now…."

When Kullen was safely out of the door, Henrie told Pete about the lie.

"They professed ignorance of the winter festival to Annie but claimed to the other guests that was the reason for their visit."

"Have they done anything else suspicious?"

"They planned to spend the day with the other guests, but went to their room after seeing a police officer. The two acts may or may not be related."

Annie leaned in. "Pete, I forgot. The kids gave me a bullet last night."

"Where did they get a bullet?"

"I don't know. Hey, where are they, anyway? Did they come down for bacon, Henrie?"

"They did, early. I let Cyril out, and then they went upstairs."

"All of them?"

"Yes. Come to think of it, with the exception of Kali and Ko just now, they have been exceptionally quiet this morning."

"Where's the bullet?"

"In the pocket of my robe."

Pete looked at her. She looked back.

"And you're going to get it, when?"

"Oh! Now. I'll be right back."

Annie walked quickly to the stairs and up. As she rounded the steps to go to the third floor, she stopped. And looked. All of the cats were on the second floor landing. They stared down the hall. Annie looked in that direction, but could see nothing. Tiger Lily joined her at the landing.

"Are you guarding something?"

Tiger Lily blinked once.

"Is it the door where the bullet was found?"

Tiger Lily blinked once.

"Can you show me the door?"

Tiger Lily looked at Speckles and nodded. Speckles walked slowly, looking back the entire time, until she reached the door of the room facing the lake. The room of Tom and Helen. She crouched in front of the door, looking back at Annie.

Annie reached down to stroke Tiger Lily's head. "Thank you, big girl."

Annie continued to the third floor, retrieved the bullet and returned to Pete.

"Your dog and my cats…and the guest cats…have staked out the door where the bullet was found. Tom and Helen's room."

"You know this how?"

"Tiger Lily and Speckles told me."

Pete and Henrie closed their eyes, shook their heads and declined to comment.

Henrie finally said, "They were away from the Inn during the period in question. They left following breakfast and returned in the early afternoon. Before two thirty."

Annie finally said what they all were thinking.

"We're stranded with murderers, and no good reason to trust either couple."

For some reason, her eyes turned to the table with the menagerie. The ferret was no longer in his cage.

Randy was told to hook up with the crew from Indiana when they got in. In the meantime, he could go to the carriage house of the KaliKo Inn. They would have food and beds.

He took the slip of paper with directions, nodded his thanks and left, taking a pill before he started the truck.

Kali rejoined the companions on the second floor landing. *"Guess what? Mommy and Pete don't know which of these couples killed that guy on the boat."*

"It has to be the ones with the bullet."

"Not necessarily. Those other people were out there at the right time. The goofy guys saw them."

"We're snowed in with all kinds of murderers?"

"Not everybody is a murderer. We just don't know who is. And guess what else?"

"What?"

"Kullen let Freddie lose. He was jiggling the latch, and he didn't get it closed. Freddie got out."

"Oh, no!" "He's a pest!" "He stinks!"

Ko asked, softly and even kindly, *"Did he notice you?"*

"No." A tear trickled down Kali's nose.

15

Chris asked everyone to leave the room with the exception of Janelle. She pulled a chair close. "Want to talk?"

"Why do you say that?"

"Why did you make everyone else leave?"

"Good point."

"Professional or personal?"

"Professional. When's the last time you piloted?"

"Few weeks ago."

"What did you think of the equipment? Communications, navigation?"

"I thought it was sluggish."

"Why didn't you say anything?"

"I did. I talked to Shorter. That's his command."

"What did he say?"

"Said it was due for service and he'd look into it."

"Did he?"

Janelle didn't answer.

"Janelle, did he?"

"Don't know that he did. Haven't had an opportunity to check."

"Which boat?"

"The one we were just using."

"Ya don't say."

"Yep."

"Still, woulda been nice to have a heads up."

"Probably shoulda said something."

"Yep."

"Yep."

"Did you check on our rescues?"

"Yep. All doing well. The last guy you pulled out, the one that nearly drowned you, he's got lots of company."

"Big family? Girlfriends?"

"Big daddy. Lots of media."

"Who is he?"

"Apparently, he's the son of the Governor."

"You're kidding. Did he say why they were out there?"

"They had permission from the electric company to fish in their warm water discharge. Of course, the permission was for on-shore angling, and for January and February."

"They were in a boat."

"Yep."

"This is December."

"Yep."

"Was there a breakdown in communication?"

"I don't believe so, sir. While you were out of it, I looked around."

"I knew I could count on you."

"Yep. I got a look at the letter. Specifically said they were not to be out when the lake is treacherous."

"Like when the Coast Guard calls a gale warning."

"Yeah, like that. And the letter is specific to shore fishing."

"Huh."

"And the boat they were in, the one that had seen some better days?"

"Yeah?"

"The owner of that boat, the first one you pulled out, he was operating without a license."

"You don't say."

"Yep."

"Have you said anything to anyone?"

"Nope. But I do have a good deal of a paper trail started in my handy, dandy, all-purpose laptop computer."

"You do understand that a computer file is not made of paper, right?"

"Right."

"In that paper trail, do you notate the kind of fish they were going after?"

"They were happy to get about anything. Brown trout, steelhead, Coho, even Chinook."

"You don't say."

"I do say."

"Any word on how much they had? I'm assuming the catch was lost."

"The catch – not much, but let's say it was above the daily limit for three men – was lost. The boat was lost. Their lives, however were not.

"Have you and the rest of the crew steered clear of the media?"

"For the most part."

"Most part?"

"You might want to watch the noon news. Catch the replay of Shorter's interview about the rescue of the Governor's son. The high seas adventure. The great work of the U.S. Coast Guard, no names mentioned, in the..."

"I get it."

"And, sir?"

"Yes?"

"On a personal level, I think you need to make this decision using your heart."

"What decision is that?"

"The one you haven't talked about to any of us."

"Right."

"Off the record, I like her. I think she should be part of the equation."

"Dismissed."

Tiger Lily was in the library, on the windowsill, staring at the snow, when she saw movement. She sat up straight. There it was again.

It was a dog! A big dog! A big, cold dog! On the sidewalk, which was barely visible in front of the wall of snow growing ever higher on the median.

She jumped off the sill and yelled, *"Come help me! We have to rescue a dog!"*

She ran to the front door and was stopped. They were locked in, and Tilly wasn't here to unlock the cat door. Darn! Then she thought of the basement. She ran downstairs, several of the cats following, while others stayed in the windowsill to keep an eye on the dog.

She was relieved to find the door open and the stairs and walkway nearly clear. How did that happen?

No time to think about it. She and two others – Fat Cat and Scaredy Cat, both used to cold weather – ran out and around the house. It was a good thing the walk was shoveled. Tiger Lily would have had to jump to get on top of the snow, and she was smart enough to know she could fall in and be smothered.

They stopped at the shoveled junction of front sidewalk and front porch steps. The dog stood there, looking up at the porch.

"Hello."

The dog turned. She was shivering, and her paws looked raw.

"I'm Tiger Lily. Are you cold?"

The dog nodded.

"We need to find a way to get you inside."

The dog stared at Tiger Lily, who turned to give instructions. *"You guys go in, and have Cyril bark real loud at the front door. Someone will come let him out, and we'll go in."*

As the cats scooted back to the basement door, Tiger Lily walked up the steps. She turned. *"Come on. We have to wait by the door. When it opens, we'll run in. They won't send you out. Trust me. You'll get warm, and they'll give you food and water, too."*

The dog followed, still saying nothing, but trusting that the cat had her best interests at heart.

As they waited, Tiger Lily said, *"This is my house. My name is Tiger Lily. Oh, I said that already. What's your name?"*

"S-S-S-S-S-Sis."

"Sis? Do you always stutter, or are you just cold?"

"C-C-C-C-C-Cold."

"Okay. Well, it's almost time."

Sure enough, they heard Cyril on the other side of the door. Loud barks and a bay or two brought Henrie to the door. Soon, the door opened, Cyril scooted out, and Tiger Lily rushed in, Sis right behind.

Henrie let out a shout, Cyril jumped back in, and Tiger Lily led Sis to the basement.

Henrie was held captive by ten cats and a big dog.

Pete was at The Marina, having left a pouting Cyril at the Inn. He had already interviewed Ray and Cheryl, learning nothing more than Albert's supposed argument on a telephone and someone in a silver pick-up truck.

Ray was outside now, keeping a snow blower going, trying to keep ahead of the snow. He did a path to the municipal parking lot, meeting up with a city truck's plow line, and a path to Carter's boat.

Pete was with Carter in the office, whose information was more complete, although…Pete doubted he could put a case together.

Carter was saying, "I didn't hear any words. Just a tone, you know. I asked him about it later. He said he had a couple of burner phones, and he'd called his ex."

"He said that?"

"Well, kind of. Actually, now that I think about it, I might have suggested it was an ex, and he might have agreed. He offered something about hiding assets, so it fit with having an ex-wife."

Pete nodded, thinking. "Did he say where those assets were? What they were?"

"No, he didn't."

"Did you see him with anyone?"

"No, can't say as I did."

"Did he seem to be afraid of anyone? Seem to be hiding?"

"Remember, now, I only met him a few days ago, but no. Not when we were together. Which wasn't often. Shopping once and lunch after. Breakfast once. A couple of times visiting on one boat or the other."

"So you were on his boat?"

"Once."

"Did you notice anything out of place?"

"No, well, I wasn't inside. Only on deck, and it's been cold, so that wasn't for long."

"You slipped on something going over in the snow. Did it look to you like he had things out of place, messy?"

"No. Actually, I thought about that. When I slipped, that's exactly what I thought. This morning, though, I was thinking about it. He was really pretty neat. It's possible the wind blew something out of kilter."

"Did you have any visitors since docking here?"

"No."

Pete thought he said that pretty quickly. He would circle back.

"It's possible a couple – a man and a woman – came over here. Neither Ray nor Cheryl saw them. They didn't come into The Marina. It's possible they went to one boat or the other. They didn't come to yours?"

"Come to think of it," Carter's eyes stayed planted on the floor, "A couple did come over yesterday. They asked for him and I pointed them in his direction. I went down, didn't watch them, didn't see if they went on or when they left."

"What time was that?"

"Don't remember exactly. Mid-day or somewhere around there. After we got back from breakfast and before that storm hit."

"You didn't hear anything, a shot or anything, when they were in the area?"

"Nope. Never heard anything like a shot."

"Well, actually, you probably wouldn't have. You slipped on a silencer."

Carter finally looked up and met Pete's stone face.

The snow had let up some. Pete glanced out the windows. The snow had slowed, allowing him to see, but there was no way he was getting out to that boat. At least he didn't have to worry about anyone messing with the crime scene.

Ray came in, stomping snow off his boots and brushing it off his face and hat. "Sleet is mixed with snow now. I hate to say it, but Carter, you have to make a decision. You're staying here or on your boat. I can't keep this up in both directions."

Carter looked out the window, thinking. Finally, he turned to Ray. "I'm crying uncle. I'll go out right now, get some things together and be back, if that's okay with you."

"Do it. Do it quick. That path is getting pretty deep and narrow."

Carter looked back at The Marina. Ray hadn't come back out. He was either resting or visiting with that cop.

He didn't have to worry about protecting her anymore. Not that he particularly worried about her. But at least he was sure that wild shot didn't kill Albert. He had been sure it had…but now…a silencer?

There was a lot more to that guy Albert than he figured.

As he packed a duffel, moving quickly through the small cabin, he thought, "I've gotta get on that boat before the cop comes back. There may be something there worth having."

The cats and Cyril gathered around Sis, who still shivered, as much from fright as from cold.

Tiger Lily said, *"Mommy and Henrie will be down pretty soon. They'll feed you. And probably take care of your feet."*

"Why would they do that?"

"They're nice people. Anyway, I'll introduce you to everyone later. Right now I have to take care of something. Cyril here will keep you company until Mommy gets here."

Tiger Lily moved to the side room, where her paper and paints were kept. She had to look around for them. She sniffed. JoJo had been in here doing laundry. She must have moved them. While she looked for the paint pot, Cyril talked to Sis.

"My name is Cyril. I'm the town's police dog. How did you end up here?"

"I had a problem with my human. I had to run away."

"Do you need a new human?"

"Maybe. I don't want to go back to him. I ran away yesterday, and...well...I don't know anyone here, and the snow's so high...and it's so cold..."

"We'll take care of you. If you need to find a fur-ever home, you happened upon the right place."

"Are you sure?"

"Yes. Do you see those big cats?" Cyril nodded his head toward Oscar McMurphy and Simon Finnegan. *"And those little ones?"* He nodded toward Speckles and Daryll.

"Yes..."

"Annie rescued and found fur-ever homes for them. Well, I guess Annie didn't rescue Speckles..."

"She didn't rescue any of them," said Mr. Bean. *"We found them. They were ours."*

"Yes, but she had to agree to help."

"I guess so." The young cat looked down at the floor.

"I didn't intend to be mean, Mr. Bean. I just wanted this dog to know..."

"My name is Sis..."

"I wanted Sis to know she was safe here."

"Well, that's true. But we found them. They were ours."

Randy was sure of it. He was getting ready to call her name, but she went into that big house – the KaliKo Inn – with another dog. She was safe. And right here! How lucky was that? He couldn't go in and ask for her. The people here would ask questions. He took a pill. Just one. He had to think.

Henrie and Annie walked to the basement with dog food, a water bowl, a handheld phone and Annie's picture book of dog breeds.

Annie knelt in front of the dog while Henrie placed the food and water close by. Annie leafed through the book until she found the right page. "I think you're a Giant Schnauzer. I wish I could ask what your name is."

Few humans knew that Tiger Lily, during a game of Candyland, had mastered the art of reading. During an emergency, she pushed herself to learn how to write.

She could write simple words. Annie and Henrie helped. They taped pictures of things Tiger Lily knew – cats, dogs, humans, simple things – and one syllable words to describe them.

Henrie kept paper and edible colored inks in the basement so she could practice. The inks had to be edible, because Ko could not help herself. If something was in a bowl, she had to have it.

Now, Tiger Lily pushed a dirty piece of paper toward Annie. She picked it up. In dark blue, she saw what could be three letters. S-I-S. She looked at the dog. "Is your name Sis?"

The dog looked back. Cyril walked to Annie and tapped her right foot once. "Yes."

"Well, then, Sis, we'll have to see to those paws. But first, have some food and water."

Henrie and Annie backed away. Tiger Lily gently put her shoulder on the right leg of the big, cold, wet, scared dog. She eventually walked to the dishes and ate. First tentatively, then with vigor.

While she ate, Annie dialed the emergency room of the veterinary clinic. Dr. Ralph answered. Annie described the state of the schnauzer's paws, and he prescribed petroleum jelly in copious amounts, and a trip to the clinic as soon as possible.

"You'll need to get him checked for everything. Worms, viruses. It would be best if you kept him separated from the other animals until we have time to check him out."

"I'm not sure how we can make that happen, but I'll work on it. Right now, they're all together. The cats and our local police dog found her – I think it's a her – and decided to save her."

"How does she look otherwise?"

"Healthy, but scared. I can't tell if she has problems with her teeth, but she doesn't seem to have a problem eating."

"She may not have eaten for a while, so let her go out pretty soon. Put a collar and leash on her, so she doesn't think you're throwing her out of the house."

"Good idea. Thanks, Doctor Ralph. Is there anything else I should know?"

"Yes. Find her a good home. If you have a book there, read up on her. When she's healthy, she'll be active. And I believe she's a high-maintenance dog."

"I'll read up on it. Certainly, in all of my circle of friends, there's a man or woman who will want her."

Sis had cleaned the bowls. Annie poked around in a drawer until she found an old scarf and a piece of rope. She approached Sis slowly. When Sis started to back away, Cyril blocked her way. Sis stopped and allowed Annie to tie the scarf around her neck and the rope around the scarf. Annie opened the basement door. Sure enough, it was clean, and since the snow had slowed, she could see remnants of cat paws.

"Come on, Cyril. Come outside with us so she doesn't think I'm kicking her out. She needs to do what all dogs do when they go outside."

Cyril led the way, then Annie, then, tentatively, Sis. Outside, Cyril demonstrated what she was to do by peeing gleefully into a wall of packed snow. Sis got the hint and led Annie to another area of packed snow. She walked around a little more, did a little more business. When she finished, she turned to look at Annie.

"You bet. It's time to go in. Let's take a look at those feet."

Janelle camped in front of the hospital door and refused to let the media or the Governor's aides into the room. She kept the media at bay because the Coast Guard – Chris – did not care to make a statement. She kept the Governor and his aides at bay because Chris did not want to be pressured to go easy on his son.

She would not leave the hospital until Chris was ready to go. They would have to go over land, and the roads wouldn't be passable until tomorrow. If they were lucky. She had time for more research.

She had gathered as much information as she could about the boaters, their illicit fishing, and the unlicensed boat. What she wanted to do now was get a look at the Coast Guard's maintenance logs. She couldn't do that from a hospital in Bayless. And she couldn't call her friends at the Station.

She called George.

"You know what you're asking me to do, Janelle?"

"I do. Can you do it?"

"I can get to the Station. I think the roads are clear, to there, at least. And I can ask if they need volunteers. They'll wonder why I didn't call."

"Shorter isn't that bright, and they're having an all-hands-on-deck day."

"How do I go about getting my hands on those logs?"

"Well…first of all, just get there. Send me a text. Let me know who else is there, and we'll figure it out."

"Okay. If they grab me and send me out in this weather, just because I'm there, you're gonna owe me big time."

"Copy that."

While Henrie rubbed petroleum jelly into an unusually compliant large dog's paw, Annie read from the book.

"The Giant Schnauzer was created to be a working dog, so he has intelligence and drive."

She paused. "This book is written for boys. I'm going to say girl words. She can be a loyal and courageous companion, she needs training, exercise, and attention. Huh. Intelligent. Loyal. Courageous. Sounds like two other dogs we know."

"Three, actually. One is just smaller."

"Forgive me. Sometimes I think Tillie is another cat. Hey, Doctor Ralph was right. The book says she is high maintenance. She has to be groomed often. Do we have dog brushes?"

"I am certain we can find something to work."

"And she needs to be professionally trimmed. Hmm. Looks like she's had some trimming recently. She must be loved by someone."

"Perhaps Doctor Ralph can find an embedded chip."

"Good idea. Let's see, she doesn't shed much. That's good news. And she's easily trained. So far, she's done pretty well with plain-spoken English."

"She does have the assistance of eleven cats and a dog."

"You got me there. She's active. She'll need regular exercise, and she's good with kids. She seems to be good with cats, too."

"We must introduce her to Little Fred, with caution, to assure the truth of this statement."

"Oh, well, reading further, she's good with older kids. We should probably not leave her alone with Little Fred. Here's the last thing. She won't be good with new owners. People who have never owned a dog. We'll need to find someone who already has or had a dog."

Tiger Lily looked at her siblings and shook her head sadly. She had hoped Chris would take this dog.

Little Socks knew what she was thinking. *"He's not inexperienced. He kept Cyril for a while, and he's always around Cyril and Jock. Maybe it rubs off."*

Annie continued to read. "One reason she lasted so well in this storm is that she's adaptable to cold weather. More to cold than hot. Oh, and she has a tendency to wander. Maybe that's why she's lost."

"So many of our community dogs work with water. How will she be in that area?"

"Let's see…it looks like she can be conditioned to like the water. It's not a natural thing, but she can be trained."

Little Socks nodded to Tiger Lily. A good point for a Coast Guard man.

16

Annie hated to leave the beautiful dog locked up, but she knew the health of her cats and Cyril could be at stake. It didn't seem possible. Sis looked perfectly healthy. But just in case, she had a stern talk with the cats. And Cyril.

"I'm going to let Sis stay with us, but you have to leave her alone. She can stay with me, wherever I am, on this…well, let's call it a leash. She has to eat from a separate bowl, drink from a separate bowl, and you are not to cuddle. Do you understand?"

Eleven cats and two dogs looked at Annie as if they understood. They were not happy.

Tiger Lily said, *"We found her. She's ours."*

Annie heard "Meow, hiss!"

Henrie had already gone to the kitchen to replace breakfast dishes with lunch items. Many people to feed. Not enough chairs in the dining room. He didn't ask, but Annie figured she should try to be helpful.

Annie led Sis upstairs and pointed to a dog pillow. Henrie was always prepared.

Sis lay down without hesitation. Annie looked at her pads. She added more petroleum jelly. Sis seemed to help her by moving her paws this way and that. When Annie finished, Sis heaved a large sigh and fell asleep.

Annie shooed Cyril and the cats out of the kitchen.

Henrie turned on the news. WQVX had already begun its noon showing. Anchor Charles Veritone was giving an update on regional power outages.

"Thousands of residents were without power for ten to twelve hours overnight. Great Lakes Electric Company is working to get hundreds more back in working order. They issued a statement that residents should be prepared for further outages."

Charles turned to face another camera. "Well, the snowfall has slowed somewhat, but we expect it to continue throughout the day. By this afternoon, I understand sleet will be added to the mix. With twenty-six inches already on the ground, this remains our top news story of the day. Let's turn to Felix for an up-to-date weather report."

Henrie hit the mute button, unwilling or unable to listen to the message of doom. The electricity in the kitchen flickered. Annie checked the monitor. The generator did not turn on. It was just a flicker.

Annie set stacks of plates and silver on the dining room table and came back into the kitchen. She saw Shorter on the TV. "Henrie, where's the remote?"

Henrie turned, saw Shorter, and reached into his pocket for the remote and the sound. Shorter was saying, "...we mounted a rescue effort, priority one. The fishing boat was in serious trouble, breaking apart at the seams. My crew handled the emergency in the way you would expect. We extracted the men from the boat just in time and transported them to the hospital. Hammond Junior and his friends have been effusive in their compliments."

The screen cut to Dan Tapper, ace on-scene reporter. Annie felt the corners of her mouth go down. Dan was onsite at the Station.

"Charles, that was Officer In Charge Shorter at the Chelsea Coast Guard Station. In our interview this morning, he related the heroic actions taken by his crew. Our sister station in Bayless submitted this report."

Video of a scene inside a hospital rolled. In it, a female reporter interviewed the Governor, Hammond Senior. "I just can't say enough about our proud men of the Coast Guard." Annie noticed one of those "proud men," Janelle, standing to the left of and slightly behind the Governor. Janelle's expression didn't change.

"These men risked their lives to save my son. Risked their lives. I've been unable to talk to most of them personally, only the gentleman here…" the Governor turned to indicate Janelle, did a bit of a double-take, and continued. Ever the politician. "He assures me they were only doing their duty. Again, I can't thank them enough."

The reporter didn't miss a step. She aimed the microphone at Janelle. "And can we have your name?"

"Janelle Charles."

"Can you make a statement?"

"I'll have to decline to comment at this time, but I would like to thank the Governor for his kind words."

Janelle and the reporter shared a smile and a nod, and once again, Dan Tapper was on screen, standing at the desk with Charles Veritone.

"There you have it, Charles. And thanks go to our sister station in Bayless. For once, I was unable to be onsite for that interview."

Charles turned to Dan with a question. "Do you know, Dan, how Officer Shorter was able to make it back to

Chelsea? I understand the remainder of the rescue crew is still stranded in Bayless."

Annie laughed out loud. Charles Veritone had long since stopped covering for his ace onsite reporter. Dan must be related to someone a bit higher up, to have retained his position.

"I understand, Charles, that he airlifted back."

"By helicopter?"

"Yes, that is usually how they travel."

Charles turned to face the camera; the zoom squeezed Dan out of the picture. "There you have it, folks. Our Coast Guard is not only brave, they defy all logic and reason when traveling in this weather! We'll be back after this message from our sponsors."

Annie and Henrie looked at one another, then burst into laughter. Annie finally got herself under control. "I don't care what job they offered him. He can't leave if Shorter is going to be his replacement."

Randy stayed at the carriage house. When the crew from Indiana dropped their gear, he told them he was waiting on the crew from Kentucky.

He had time to think, and his thoughts veered one way, then another.

He could just leave. He heard things about the woman that owned the Inn. She would find Sis a good home.

But he couldn't leave. If she was that good, she'd find the chip. They would have his name. They would put the pieces together.

So, what was the best way to go? Leave her in good hands and disappear? He couldn't do that. He didn't have enough money.

Get her? Come up with some story to get inside the house, grab her and go? That way, he might have a chance to go back to work. Make up a story.

No. They would find the body. And he hadn't checked in with his boss yet with a cover story. That ship had sailed.

He just needed to think. He needed another pill. Or two.

There were too many cats to fit under the detective table. The library was in use by humans. They finally found a place to talk and nap on the second floor landing.

Cyril said, *"It's too bad Sis can't join us. It would be nice to be with a girl dog and not have Jock interfere."*

Mr. Bean asked, *"What did Mommy mean? Why can't we cuddle with her?"*

Cyril was the person they looked to for answers, whenever he was in the room. *"She may have a disease or something that we can't tell. Whenever you get a new kitty, doesn't it have to stay separate?"*

"I think that's supposed to happen, but it doesn't. Not always, anyway. I don't think we kept Speckles or Daryll separate. Or Fat…Simon Finnegan and Oscar McMurphy."

Speckles sat up. *"That would have been mean."*

"It seems mean, but it's for everybody's good. You could have had worms or something. And Sis might, too."

"Worms? She hadded worms? Where?"

Little Socks bopped Sassy Pants on the nose.

Soon, they fell asleep, waking when Henrie brought little plates of bacon for their lunch. For Cyril, he had a dish of dog food sprinkled with bacon.

Cyril fell asleep again, thinking that if he had to leave Pete, this is where he would want to be.

Henrie went in search of his guests. Kullen was in bed, but he was hungry and said he would be right down.

Robert and Sue were in their room. They had to be convinced to come down, but agreed, after some urging.

Tom and Helen watched a movie in the library with Martha and Little Fred. Well, Little Fred slept or played with her toes.

Martha looked up at Henrie. "Is lunch ready, Henrie? I should be helping you."

"Lunch has been prepared, and no, you are not required to help. You are a guest, and frankly, it is probably best you stay with our girl."

"Thank you, Henrie. It feels good to be off my feet. But I'll get a tray for the three of us and bring it in here, if that's okay with you."

"Certainly. We lack for dining room chairs as it is."

Henrie watched Helen as Martha rose to get the tray. Her eyes went to Little Fred and stayed there, a combination of wistfulness and peacefulness.

As people gathered, moving in and out of the dining room, Henrie caught whiffs of unbathed bodies. He wondered if this was a Midwest anomaly. Have snow day, don't bathe. If that were the case, he would have to pray for a break in the weather.

Holly and Clara came out of the elevator, followed by Diana, who wore a coat and boots. She made a sandwich to go. She wiggled her fingers as she walked out. "George got called in. I'm going to work the floor for Candice. An electric crew from Indiana just got in, and they're hungry."

Henrie had not known George was on the lake.

George sent a text to Janelle. It was a few minutes before she got back to him. In short bursts, he told her who was on station that might be able to get to the logs. He ended with, "Barge stuck in Haverport. Guess who gets to go out?"

He was shucking into winter gear when Janelle texted back. "Ask Trevor."

George stuck the phone in his pocket, grabbed a hat and gloves and walked over to Trevor.

"Hey, man, got a minute?" George motioned with his head toward the coffee pot. Trevor looked around, saw he was currently unsupervised, and nodded.

While they pretended to pour coffee, George filled him in. "Janelle wants the maintenance logs for the communication and navigation equipment. She thinks Shorter might try to lose them or change them as soon as he gets a chance."

"I wondered why he got them. They're on his desk. I saw him take them, but we've been busy. He hasn't had time to do anything."

"Any chance you can get them? Put them somewhere for me? I'll get them to Janelle."

Trevor sighed. "Man. You know how much trouble…. Man. I'll work on it."

"Thanks. I gotta go. This is the classic example of no good deed goes unpunished. Janelle owes me."

"She'll owe me, too."

Tiger Lily woke to find Freddie the ferret staring at her. She knew Freddie had gotten loose, and she had met him before, in his cage. To see him here, uncaged, was unnerving. She screamed, waking the others.

Freddie ran.

A drowsy Mr. Bean said, *"What happened?"*

"Freddie was here. He just scared me, is all."

"Where'd he go?"

"I don't know. He ran downstairs. He's either somewhere on the first floor, or maybe he went on down to the basement."

Tiger Lily yawned and went back to sleep.

Annie couldn't help herself. Normally the last person to put on layers of clothing in the house – she would turn the thermostat to sixty three if Henrie would let her – she pulled a fleece sweater over her head. She supposed it was mind over matter.

The Inn was warm, too warm, for her liking. But the snow continued to come down. It had begun to drift over the bottoms of the windows on the ground level. Since the Inn's ground level was raised to allow for the porch, the snow had to be every bit of the twenty-six inches WQVX reported, if not more. Just looking at it made Annie cold. She was glad she was not assigned duty outside for any reason. She sent up a silent prayer for the men of the Coast Guard Station.

She dug through her dresser drawers until she found a linen and cotton blend scarf in rainbow colors. It was perfect.

Annie went to the library. Tom and Helen had fallen asleep in front of the television. Martha was asleep on a recliner in the corner, covered with a blanket. Little Fred was asleep in her chair on a side table.

Annie picked up lunch dishes and left as quietly as she had entered.

In the kitchen, she checked on Sis, who was still asleep. The dog roused a bit as Annie untied the old scarf that served as a collar and replaced it with the rainbow-colored one. The dog was so tired, she went right back to sleep.

Annie thought about knocking on Henrie's apartment door. No. If he were not asleep, he should be.

She got a gallon of apple cider out of the refrigerator, poured it into the crockpot, and added the spices Henrie had already measured out. While the pot simmered, she went to the basement to find a bean bag chair. She ran into JoJo in the laundry room.

"JoJo, have you been down here all day?"

"Not all day. I've spent a large part of it in and out of rooms, here and at the carriage house. Do you know how many towels and things have to be kept clean?"

"Do you want a break?"

"No, thanks. Really, I kind of like working alone. I've been online all day, off and on, in between washing, drying and folding. This is the last load. I'll finish it and take them around."

"And you'll just drop them in the rooms, right? You won't try to put everything away, will you?"

"No. I'll just drop them. I know how many people are in each room, and frankly, I'm not even concerned that every room gets a matching set."

"Next time we have a storm, make sure you get here. You're more valuable than Henrie."

"Not more. But close."

Annie found the bean bag chair and took it upstairs. She placed it on the floor beside Sis, got a blanket and pillow from the back porch, and snuggled up for a nap.

Sis stirred as Annie got comfortable. She readjusted her position to keep her nose and a front foreleg on Annie's thigh.

This is how Mem found her. Mem and Barry – her sole customer for the day – returned to the Inn before darkness took over the street. It came early. The sun was still blotted by heavy snow, now mixed with sleet.

Mem went to the computer banks and sat down beside Barry. He was on one of the sofas set up for gamers, engrossed in something she didn't understand. He seemed nervous. He had broken into a sweat, but she knew the building was on the cool side. When she spoke, he jumped."

"Are you…I'm sorry. I didn't mean to give you a scare."

"Oh. Sorry. I was concentrating."

"Yes. Well, I was thinking we should get back to the Inn before it got dark."

Barry looked behind him, out the windows. It looked dark already.

"Okay. Um. I can finish in just a few minutes."

"Thank you. I'll close up and wait for you."

"Um, ma'am? Could you tell me the name of this place again? My, um, friends, might want to come down this weekend."

"Really? They would rather play from here than where they are?"

"Um, well, sometimes everyone needs a change of pace."

"I'm sure. The name is CyberHealth. Tell them we're on the north side of Sunset Avenue."

Barry logged off and put his coat on. At the door, Mem gave him an umbrella. "What's this for?"

"You'll see."

They stepped into the street. Mem's umbrella was up, and it took Barry only seconds to realize he needed it. Sleet, invisible in the snow, drove down at a relentless pace. It was still afternoon, but the street lights were already on.

Boone and his boys could shovel some, but most of the snow had to be thrown up by blowers. The wall of snow was at least fifteen feet high.

Each business had a slender walkway from their door to the cleared sidewalk. The sidewalk was one pedestrian

lane wide. It abutted the one-truck-width lane on the
north side of The Avenue.

They kept one walkway clear from the north to the
south. In front of The Clinic, one pedestrian-width lane
was carved through the road, the median, and the road on
the north side, ending at the pedestrian-width sidewalk in
front of the Inn.

Justin was working on the porch steps – his lane was
two pedestrians wide – when Mem and Barry arrived. She
stopped to give Justin a hug. She whispered, "Bless you."
From Justin's smile, she knew she had done something
right.

Mem opened the door and smelled the mulled cider
right away. What a wonderful way to enter a home from a
blizzard. She looked back across the narrow walkway to
the north side of The Avenue. One street light was visible.
It flickered once, then went out.

Mem stepped into the Inn. The lights were out here, as
well. In a few seconds, they powered back on. Mem opened
the door and looked across the street. Still dark.

Thank goodness she was able to stay right here. They
would be warm and dry.

Mem found Annie in the kitchen, asleep on a bean bag
chair, next to…who was this? How did Annie get a new
dog in the middle of a blizzard?

The dog, a beautiful dark gray giant schnauzer, looked
at Mem drowsily, closed her eyes and went back to sleep.
Mem could see Annie had ministered to her raw paw pads.
Or Henrie. Probably Henrie.

She took off her outwear and padded through to the library in her stocking feet. Martha, Little Fred and two of the guests were asleep. A quick look told her no other humans were on the main level. The cats and Cyril were on the landing.

Mem did not want to drink alone. She found a carafe, filled it with mulled cider, put that and several cups on a tray. She opened Henrie's cookie jar and filled a plate with some of his "everything" cookies. They were always a surprise. They could have any flavor of chips, any variety of nuts, oats, peanut butter, coconut, candy pieces, anything that could conceivably go into a cookie. They were different every time. Henrie tried to stay away from raisins and craisins, because Annie would chide him for fooling her into thinking it was chocolate.

Mem took the tray into the library, turned a lamp on low in the corner, poured a cup of mulled cider, and watched as Tom and Helen woke up, deep breaths accompanying each awakening.

Mem put on her innocent voice. "Did I wake you?"

"No," said Helen. "That smells wonderful."

"It just so happens I have extra cups."

Mem curled into a blanket and did what she did so well. Tom and Helen didn't even realize they were telling her their life stories.

The Inn was shattered by screams coming from the basement. Annie and Sis were the first to see JoJo pounding up the steps, screaming in an eerie falsetto, "Rat! Rat! Huge Rat! Mongo huge rat!"

Sis jumped and ran in the opposite direction. She ran to the library, saw scared people she didn't know, turned and ran to the back porch, saw animals in a cage, turned and ran to the foyer. She ran in circles until she found the stairway and went up.

The second floor was filled with cats, awakened suddenly and howling, along with Cyril. Sis kept going until she got to the third floor.

The apartment door was closed. She couldn't go anywhere but down, but down held all kinds of horrors. She jumped and paced on the landing, howling in fear.

Henrie and Annie stood at the bottom of the steps leading to the third floor. Henrie whispered, "We must keep calm. And we need to silence Cyril and the cats."

"I'll take them to the basement...no, the back porch...no...um...I'll take them somewhere and try to calm them down."

Henrie heard noises that sounded like Annie trying to herd cats. That wasn't going to work. But at least, they got quiet. He heard soft footsteps and a snuffle. Cyril.

This could be helpful.

Henrie reached to Cyril's head, stroking it softly.

"Do you know what to do? How to calm her?"

Cyril seemed to take a deep breath, and he walked slowly up the steps.

Carter thought he could do it now. He had to get on the boat before the cop got back.

Those people were napping. Snow did that to you. You didn't have to be busy. It was a kind of snow sickness. It tired people out.

Not him.

The sleet mixed into the snow pricked his skin while he made his way to Albert's boat. Darn. He would never be able to replicate the crazy pattern the police tape made. No problem. He was wearing gloves. No one would figure it was him.

Once in the cabin, he moved the flashlight back and forth. The body was still there.

Carter knew his way around a boat. No one could build a hiding place that he couldn't find. He found several.

In one cubby, he found a passport and fifty thousand dollars. In another, there was another passport and another fifty thousand. Eventually, he found a third set.

Three passports and one hundred fifty thousand dollars. That wasn't enough of a haul. He had to have more than that. Maybe the guy that killed him got some.

Then he looked at the body. There was one more place something could have been built. He used his foot to kick the body aside.

Cyril said, *"Sis, look at me."*

Sis howled, paced, turned, paced, howled again.

"Sis, JoJo didn't mean to scare you. She just saw Freddie. Freddie's a ferret, not a rat."

Sis paced, turned, paced, she no longer howled.

"It scared all of us, but we're calm now. You need to do the same."

Sis paced, turned, paced.

Cyril sat down, keeping his eyes on the frightened dog. *"I'm just going to stay right here until you're calm. Okay?"*

Cyril turned his head to see Henrie, joined once again by Annie. They sat on the middle step, only visible from the head. That was alright. Hopefully they would stay there.

Eventually, Sis tired. She lay heavily on the floor. Cyril waited a couple of minutes, then rose and went to her, licking her ears, her head. Sis allowed it, and when Annie walked slowly to her, she allowed herself to be stroked.

Soon, Annie led her downstairs, back to the kitchen, and settled her on the bed. She applied more petroleum jelly to her feet and motioned for Cyril to take the bean bag chair. Soon, the dogs were asleep, feet and faces curled together.

When they woke up, they found themselves without human supervision. They crept up to the second floor landing and joined the cats.

Cheryl had put a cot and some other furniture and lamps in the laundry room, making a semi-private bedroom for Carter. Carter was now used to the large Portuguese water dog and paid no attention when he followed.

He put the duffle bag, filled with what could be close to a million dollars, on the floor beside his cot. He pulled out the small computer notebook and opened it.

He was able to turn it on, and he located a guest wifi signal. He logged on. Now it was time to look around. There were no files. None. On the desktop was one link to files on the cloud. He tried to open it. No good. It was password protected.

He could wait. He had friends that knew how to crack codes. He would hold onto the notebook until he could get with those folks. He bet there was something there that would lead him to money. Lots of it. He wouldn't even need what his old lady had. Maybe he'd be able to do his sister a solid and let her have it all. Or not.

He put the notebook back into the pouch and pushed the bag underneath the cot.

17

Henrie met Laila and the kids as they came through the back door of the kitchen.

"I hate to be the bearer of bad tidings, but we had an incident."

"What happened?"

Henrie served hot chocolate to James, Ava and Carl as he continued. "I cannot say how it happened. I believe I know how, but...well...let me just tell you. Freddie has escaped."

Three youthful voices raised at once. "No!" "Where is he?" "We'll never find him!"

"Trust me, children, he is still in the house. He is, however, loose."

Laila sat heavily on a kitchen chair. Henrie put a cup of hot chocolate in front of her and touched her back gently. "Never fear. He will be found."

Laila said, "Kids, before you do anything else, go all through this house, top to bottom, and find that ferret."

Janet and the three girls climbed down from the street department truck. They had packed sparingly. The better to fit two bags and four females, three of which were women-sized, onto the bench seat of the truck. With a driver.

Pete had pulled his considerable strings to arrange for the ride from their suburban home to the Inn. Ginger, a freshman in college, grabbed the larger bag and the hand of her youngest sister, Tamara. Tamara stood and gazed in wonder at the wall of snow, three times higher than herself. She continued to look up as they walked through the passage to the Inn.

Clarice grabbed the smaller bag and followed her mother through the passage. Both waved their thanks to the driver. After two days at home, she was looking forward to seeing her friends James and Ava. If they were lucky, they wouldn't have to spend time with Tamara and Carl. Babies.

Janet smelled the cider and nearly cried. Heat. Food. Friends. They had nearly frozen into popsicles the night before. She didn't care if she had to sleep on a floor.

Annie met her in the foyer. "What happened?"

"The generator just didn't come on. We even tested it a couple of weeks ago, when that first storm hit."

"You're staying until the roads are clear. Any idea when Pete will be home?"

"He can't even find time for that murder. They're all busy getting to people that need shelter. He could be hours. Have you talked to Chris?"

"Not since this morning. He'll be here sometime tomorrow."

Annie and Janet had made it to the third floor. Janet, Pete and the kids would take the bedroom. Annie would sleep in her recliner with her cats.

"Really, Annie, we can sleep on the floor."

"We haven't run out of beds yet. Well, you might have the last one."

"I hope the kids don't mind."

"I was thinking…maybe Laila can come up and sleep on the couch, and the kids could have a slumber party on the porch."

"Good idea. I'll let mine know."

The landline rang. Annie answered.

"Hello. This is, well, my name is Terry. I'm over at your little house? I'm taking a break?"

"Yes, Terry. How can I help you?"

"Well, I almost hate to ask, but…well…I was hoping I might be able to get a bite to eat?"

"Henrie put lots of things in the refrigerator and freezer there, and he put canned goods in the cupboards also."

"Yes'm. Someone's been through it pretty good already."

"I wondered how long things would last. Come on over. We can make you a sandwich, heat up some soup."

"That sounds mighty good. Thank you for your kindness, and for leavin' this number here for us."

"Happy to do it. Anyway, come on over. I'll meet you at the door."

Sis smelled him as he came through the door. She crept, face and belly to the floor, to the rail of the landing. That was him. Her human. He was talking to that woman, but looking around. Looking for her.

She shuddered. She could smell the drugs.

He went to the dining room and maybe the kitchen. That woman was getting food for him or something.

Time was short.

She hissed to Cyril. *"My human is here. Where can I hide?"*

"Your human? Where is he?"

"He went with that woman to get food. But he's really here to find me."

Cyril roused Tiger Lily. *"Help me hide her!"*

Tiger Lily looked around and realized the best place would be behind the couch in the corner.

"Go back there, quick. Come on, kids. We have to help."

Sis crept behind the couch and eleven cats surrounded it, some on top, and some on the floor so no one could see underneath. Cyril lay down at the end. If anyone came to the second floor, he would sit up, keeping the crack between the back and wall invisible to human eyes.

They heard Annie talking to the man. He said he hated leaving his dog at home, and did she have dogs?

Annie was saying she didn't. She had cats.

"I thought I saw dogs when I came in."

"Oh. Those don't belong to me. They belong, well Cyril is the town police dog. Pete, the Chief, is staying here until the snow is cleared."

"The police chief?"

"Yes. He's a friend."

"Well, thanks for the soup and sandwich. I'm much obliged."

The dogs and cats breathed easier when they heard the door close.

Shorter had to go out on the last run. He was more than angry. That kid – well, George wasn't a kid, but he wasn't Coast Guard, either. Anyway, he didn't like being shown up by a volunteer.

And here came that darn reporter. Dan Fancy Tapper. Well, he needed to clear his head.

Shorter sat at his desk, opened the bottom drawer and took out a bottle of Listerine mouthwash. Except it wasn't. It was a regular-sized bottle, the kind you find in a medicine cabinet. It was full.

He took a drink, sat back, and took a deep breath. Something was wrong. What was it? He looked around the office. Took a drink. Looked through the windows into the communications room. Took another drink. What the heck. He took one more. The bottle was half empty.

He stood to meet the reporter. When he reached the reporter and shook his hand, it hit him. He looked through the windows to his office. The maintenance logs were gone.

He looked at the faces of everyone around the room. No one seemed to act awkward or guilty. Had he done something with the logs himself? No.

Dan Tapper was saying something. The cameras were rolling. Shorter tried to focus. "Um, sorry, could you repeat the question?"

In the kitchen, Annie walked around, pulling ingredients out of cupboards and the refrigerator. She had decided the kids should be rewarded for searching – albeit unsuccessfully – for Freddie the ferret, aka the mongo huge rat.

She made crusts, following a recipe she found online. She had found a passable Bisquick recipe, then, as Henrie would never keep a packaged baking mix on hand, she found a recipe to make the Bisquick in the first place.

She could do this.

She found a recipe for pizza sauce and added a bit more pepper. Crusts and sauce ready, she added pepperoni, olives, peppers, mushrooms, green peppers, bacon, pineapple and two kinds of cheese. On a fit of whimsy, she sprinkled the top with pistachios.

She remembered to pre-heat the oven – her mother would be proud – and finally, two large pizzas went into the oven to bake.

Annie trotted upstairs to put food in the cat and dog dishes, filled bowls with water, repaired her make-up, brushed her teeth, put a layer of clear polish on her nails, buffed her heels, put lotion on her feet, picked up some stray clothing items, made sure guest towels were in the bathroom, and stopped.

The dogs and cats were howling on the second floor landing. What was the problem? Had Freddie appeared again? Then she heard it. The smoke detector in the kitchen went off. She had forgotten to set the timer!

By the time Annie got downstairs, Mem and Martha were airing out the smoke, opening the doors to the wind, snow and sleet. Henrie had already tossed the pizzas in the trash. He was on a step ladder, reaching for the smoke detector.

Most of the household was now downstairs, milling around in the dining room, foyer and library. Little Fred cried loudly, yelling "Mamamamamamama!" Sis howled, afraid of the commotion, but Cyril seemed to stay by her side as a calming influence.

Henrie looked at Annie. She shouted over the commotion. "It was going to be so good, Henrie…"

"Pizza?"

"For the kids."

"I will find a suitable replacement. It is time, Annie, that we review our kitchen rules."

"I know. Rule number one. Annie stays out of it."

"Annie does not have to stay out of it. Annie does, however, have to keep her hands off the ingredients and the appliances."

Henrie finally got the detector down and ripped the batteries out. Silence.

Pete walked into the babble. He was tired. He was looking forward to seeing his wife and children. And Cyril.

Cyril was the first to greet him, hitting him hard in the chest with two front paws. It was as if he were saying, "Get me out of here!" Cyril was joined by another big dog. A big gray dog he had never seen before. This one wanted to go out, also. Not out. Away.

Smoke alarms blared, Little Fred cried, cats howled. Teenagers laughed and shouted over the sound of the smoke alarms. Adults came from every entrance and the stairway, asking if they needed to leave.

He had to force himself not to take out his sidearm and let off a shot in the air. It would have gone into someone's bedroom. Maybe into someone.

First things first. He would have to take a chance that this dog didn't need a leash. She couldn't get far, at any rate, and she could only go up and down narrow walkways and one-lane roads. He opened the door and followed the two dogs out.

The gray dog didn't move from the porch. Pete thought she seemed somehow surprised to find herself outside. Cyril turned and barked once. The dog followed, and they both trotted around the building, toward the basement door. Pete followed.

He watched as they each picked a spot and peed into the snow, and watched again as they padded around, sniffing. The gray dog looked up and back often, either to make sure he didn't get too close, or he didn't go back in without them.

The gray dog finished first. She walked to Pete and stood, looking up at him. Then she looked behind him and sat directly in front of him, looking up with what Pete thought was desperation.

"You have a very fancy collar on. I suppose when we get inside, someone will tell me your name." Pete crouched. It was hard, with his coat and equipment. The walkway behind the house was barely a person wide. He took the dog's face in his hands and stroked her cheeks. Then he looked down. "Man. Look at those paws. We need to get you inside."

He stood, called for Cyril, and led the way to the porch and back into the now-calmed-down mayhem. The gray dog nearly bolted through the door.

Randy cursed his luck. The dog was out, but she was with that chief of police. He took two pills out of the vial, thought about it and popped a third.

Sis saw him. He knew she saw him. It looked like she was hiding, putting that police officer's body in between them. She couldn't get into the house quickly enough.

He forgot he had taken three pills and popped two more.

Pete saw Henrie when they entered the foyer.

Henrie said, "Obviously, you met Sis. She went out without a leash. And returned."

"She needs a leash?"

"We do not know. Annie took her out earlier; Doctor Ralph suggested a leash, both for her safety and for her emotional well-being. Knowing that she would not be abandoned in the cold."

"I didn't know. It was a little loud when I arrived. What happened?"

"Annie attempted to make pizza."

"Oh. Don't you have rules about that?"

"We have reviewed the rules once again."

Pete was going to ask how Sis came to be at the house, but he was interrupted by hugs from a wife and three daughters. It was good to know they missed him. Then he spied Kullen and Barry. He should chat with them again.

Over Janet's head, he pointed to the two of them, letting them know he wanted to see them, and eventually, they found themselves in the kitchen.

Henrie busied himself around them, setting coffee and hot chocolate out, and replacing the dinner Annie had so lovingly tried to make for the teens. Kali followed them in, and once again, she rubbed the ankles of first Kullen, then Barry, over and over.

Pete looked at Kullen. "Did you keep your promise?"

"Which one? I haven't been to the lake…"

"You couldn't get there if your life depended on it. I mean the one about talking."

"Oh. Yes. I've not said anything to anyone. Not even Barry. But he was gone most of the day, anyway."

"Good. Let's keep our voices down. I don't want anyone else to hear what we're talking about." Pete looked at Barry, who had broken out in a sweat.

"Are you okay?"

"Yeah. Yeah. I'm fine. What's up?"

"I had a chat with Kullen earlier today. We had a murder here yesterday…"

"A murder?!"

"Keep your voice down, now. Yes. Over at The Marina. Sometime after you saw the couple walking in that direction."

"Did one of them…"

"No. As a matter of fact, they are guests here. Kullen has already seen and talked to them. I'm sure you will soon. Henrie's going to serve supper for everyone."

"So if they're okay…"

"Someone at The Marina is not. I'll need to interview them and another couple staying here, to see if they saw anything. For now, please tell me what you remember."

"Well, let me think." Barry took a deep breath and a drink of hot chocolate. Pete thought he looked calmer.

"Um, my idiot brother, here, was putting on his gear, and he did a kind of swing, and hit the guy in the butt with…" Barry looked at Kullen, wide-eyed.

"It's okay. We've already talked about it. He knows I went out."

Barry looked back at Pete, eyes still wide. He took another deep breath, another drink of hot chocolate. "Well, the guy went spastic, called Kullen some names. Kullen is like, 'I'm sorry, man,' and the guy is like, 'you bet your…' well, he said a bad word, and then Kullen is like, 'sorry,' and the guy said something, and they walked away."

"Did you see where they went?"

"Well, they were walking over to that boat place, the marina."

"Did you see them later?"

"Um, yeah. When Kullen first went into the water, I was still up on the walkway, and I looked around. They were coming off of one of those boats."

"Do you remember which one?"

"Which one?"

"Which boat? There are two in the harbor."

"Oh, yeah. It was the yellow one."

"Yellow?" Pete tried to remember which one was yellow. He had not seen them in daylight. At least not in daylight that wasn't visually hampered by snow.

"Do you remember if it was the one on the left or the one on the right?"

"Let me think." Barry seemed to concentrate. He moved his hands to the front of his body, wiggling first the right one, then the left. "It was the one on the left."

"Are you sure?"

"Pretty sure. It was yellow."

"What color was the other boat?"

"Blue. Or green. No. Blue."

"The yellow one on the left."

"Yes."

"Did they go from that boat to the other boat? The one on the right?"

"No. They walked in a straight line from that boat toward the entrance of the lot."

"Did they seem in a hurry? Worried? Angry?"

"I don't know, man. That's a long way away. If someone really put me on a stand or something, I don't know if I could swear it was the same two people. It was two people in dark coats. We saw a man and a woman…"

"And you assumed it was the same man and woman…"

"Yeah."

"But it could have been someone else. If someone were to put you on the stand."

"Yeah. But I didn't see anyone else. I saw two people go in that direction, a man and a woman in dark coats, and I saw two people get off a boat."

"Thanks. This has been helpful."

When Kullen and Barry left, Pete looked at Henrie. "I can make one call, to Ray, to find out which boat is yellow, and which is green or blue, but then, if it's the boat I think it is, I need to interview the alive guy and ask him why he lied."

"And I understand you still do not know which of the couples – if it was in fact one of our couples – exited the yellow boat, supposedly on the left."

"You got it."

Tiger Lily gathered her siblings to eat supper. They ran upstairs and through the cat door. They stopped suddenly. Someone had eaten most of their supper.

Tiger Lily turned on Ko. *"Why did you eat it all?"*

"I didn't! I swear!"

"You didn't come up here and eat our supper?"

Ko looked sheepish. *"Well, I came up once. Maybe twice."* She stood taller. *"But I didn't eat all of this!"*

Mo said, *"Trill!"*

Sassy Pants interpreted. *"I smells it, too, Mo. Someone else been eatin' our supper."*

The cats sniffed around. Several voices said, *"Freddie!"* *"That ferret was here!"* *"I'm gonna finds him an bites him!"* *"Trill!"*

Eventually, as they cleaned themselves following the meager supper, Kali shared what she had learned. *"That second couple that got here, Robert and Sue, they went to The Marina, but they went to the other boat. They didn't go on the dead guy's boat."*

"So they didn't kill him. It still could have been the first couple, Tom and Helen."

"It was kind of confusing, but I think Barry only saw Robert and Sue. So, yeah. They could be the murderers."

Randy realized he was done for. He couldn't get to Sis. He was sure she had seen him, but she didn't try to get to him. She was afraid of him.

These people would take care of her. She would be safe. But they would find that chip.

Driving conditions were dangerous, but he had no choice. He had to leave town now.

He got out of the truck, looking up and down the street. He traded license plates with a Ford Focus, got in, and headed east, the same direction as the storm.

Jock had long been jealous of Cyril. Cyril got all the glory as a police dog, while he, Jock, could only be a hero on occasion. Now, he saw his chance to be the one to "tell the humans something."

Ray and Carter were watching something on television. Cheryl was reading a book in the back bedroom. Jock took Cheryl's hand in his mouth gently and pulled.

Cheryl knew something was up. She got up and followed him to the laundry room. Jock lay down beside the cot and put his nose on the floor. Cheryl got down on her knees and saw the bag. One she hadn't seen before.

She looked back once, to be sure they were still alone, and she pulled out the bag. She unzipped it only a little bit and saw money. Lots of it. And a small computer notebook stuffed into a side pouch.

She gave Jock a pat on the head. "Good boy. We'll have to let Pete know somehow, but we'll have to be careful. This guy could be dangerous."

18

Annie longed for a sense of normalcy. She rounded up her usual suspects and got them upstairs to her dining room: all of her friends from The Avenue that happened to be under her roof, including a very tired Henrie and a very tired Pete.

They opened wine, grabbed lasagna from the freezer, made coffee and turned on some blues.

From the dining room windows, they could look over the dark town. From the kitchen, they could see one light glowing not-too-far-away. Ray and Cheryl were okay, still safe at The Marina, supposedly with their boarder.

They laughed. They talked. They made friends with Sis, who mingled with Cyril and the cats.

They huddled in blankets, throws and sweats, unable to throw off the feeling of being out in the snow.

Annie turned on the television in the dining room. It seemed people could never get enough of a disaster. They watched The Weather Channel and heard how bad it was in Chelsea. Not only in Chelsea. The blizzard stretched almost to New York. By tomorrow, the snow and sleet would be gone from here, but their struggles would remain. Electricity. Roads. Emergency services. They still had to dig out.

Henrie looked at his watch, picked up the remote, and switched to local news. Charles Veritone was on screen, behind his desk. His onsite reporter, Dan Tapper, stood beside the desk. They were looking at one another with earnest expressions.

Dan Tapper was saying, "...and you'll see in this clip, Charles, that ongoing issues on the lake continue to create harrowing experiences for our local Coast Guard."

Dan turned to face the camera. "This is my live, onsite report, from the Coast Guard Station earlier today."

The screen cut to video. Dan stood with Shorter, a microphone in his hand. Shorter looked...drunk? Well, Annie thought, he might have just come off a boat. That can lead to a disheveled appearance. She had never seen Chris give that appearance, though.

Shorter said, "...repeat the question?"

"Yes. A boat just came in, and it appears several people were rescued. Can you tell our viewers what happened?"

"Well, we were out, um, on the lake, and, um..." Shorter looked around the room. Annie thought he looked a little angry. Then she was sure of it. He leveled a glare at someone walking behind the cameras.

Dan tried to focus the interview. Annie wondered if he had an ulterior motive leaving this in. Like interviews in her past, he showed mostly warts, editing out the positive footage and leaving the negative.

"And, can you tell us what happened?"

"Oh. Yes." Shorter seemed a bit more focused. Did he slur that 's'?

"We had to go to Haverport. A barge was iced in, and we had to break up the ice. Much like the incident with the Governor's son..." Shorter found his stride and looked straight at the camera, face serious, "we had to effect a rescue. My men and I took four survivors onboard. We brought them back to the Station for medical attention."

The camera moved slightly, putting Dan back in center. Shorter could probably tell only the left side of his face was on camera. He moved closer. Dan moved away. The cameras followed and closed in, cutting Shorter out of the frame.

"We heard there was more heroic action out there today. Can you tell us about that?"

Shorter responded, but his face was only partially on-camera. "I don't know that anyone was particularly heroic. We just do the job we have to do."

"But I was told…"

"We don't talk about individual acts. The crew…my crew and I were heroic. All of us."

Dan looked into the camera and said, "And there you have it. I'm Dan Tapper, here at the Coast Guard Station in Chelsea, with an everyday hero. Back to you, Charles."

The screen showed Charles and Dan, again at the desk, looking earnestly into the camera. Charles then turned to Dan. "Did you receive additional information about that act of heroism?"

"I did, Charles. The heroic Coast Guard member is actually a volunteer. He refused to be interviewed on camera, but he said, and I quote, "It was a rush. It was a zip line rush, from our boat to theirs, and back again. If it weren't so blippin' cold, I'd do it again in a heartbeat. And let me make a shout-out to Candice!"

Annie caught her breath. George! She picked up her phone as her guests broke into peels of delight.

Candice picked up the phone. "Hey, Annie. Guess you saw the news."

"I did. Is he okay?"

"He's fine. Well, he's mad as heck, but he's fine."

"What happened?"

"Making a long story short, Shorter was going to wimp out and leave those guys on a boat that was going down. George and a few others put a rig together and got them off. Shorter told George he's going to put him on report."

"He's going to be fired as a volunteer?"

"If Shorter has his way. But George said he has a surprise for Shorter, too."

"What surprise?"

"Don't know. He fell asleep as he was talking."

"Tell George we're thinking about him."

"Who all is there?"

"Almost everyone from the other side of The Avenue. They don't have generators. We have emergency workers in the carriage house, Boone, Hilly and their crew, a few folks from town. And a partridge in a pear tree."

Before long, most of her guests had gone off to bed. Pete was asleep in the bedroom, but Mem asked Janet to stay a while. Henrie, Laila and Annie were still in the living room.

"I know there was a murder, and as usual, I know your guests have become suspects. I wanted to share the very interesting conversation I had with Tom and Helen."

Henrie and Annie were visibly interested.

Mem lowered her voice. "I know you can't say anything about the case, if you know anything, that is, but these folks have a sad story. If Pete is looking at them, he needs to hear this, Janet."

Mem began. "First of all, they both had privileged upbringings as single children of successful parents. They were able to attend a top university, and they married shortly after graduation. Tom got a high-paying job in a field he loved, and Helen went to work as a social worker. She wasn't going to work long. They planned to start a family, and she was going to be a stay-at-home mother. But then one disaster after another beat them down."

"What kind of disasters?"

"Well, first Tom's parents died in a car crash. And while losing his parents was an emotional blow, he learned they had more bills to pay than money to pay them. Tom, even though he didn't have to, absorbed one of those debts. A large one. They put off thoughts of children for a couple of years. Then Helen's parents became ill at the same time, different illnesses, I don't remember what they were, but they both needed extended nursing home care. They lingered for several years. Helen quit her job so she could spend more time with them."

"So, less income, more stress. Did she have to pay for nursing home care?"

"Eventually, her parents' assets were used, they went onto Medicaid. Tom and Helen paid for the extras that weren't covered, things like medical equipment that the government didn't think necessary. That kind of thing."

"And they put off children again."

"They did. They were in pretty serious financial trouble by this time. Because Tom got the job of his dreams so early, they over-extended on their home. Helen went back to work to help financially, putting off those children yet again. But life wasn't done with them."

"What more could happen?"

"Helen had to have a hysterectomy. There was cancer, they got all of it, and she's no longer sick, but she had to quit her job. She hadn't been there long enough to have sick or personal time. Tom's insurance was top-notch, and they didn't go significantly into debt over her illness, but their income was lessened. Then his company downsized. Here are two people, who thought they could live the American dream. They are now significantly in debt, unemployed and uninsured, and they can never be natural parents. They were out of work for months and their house went into foreclosure. They were evicted three months ago."

Henrie broke in. "I have seen her social media pages. She has posted photographs of the two of them vacationing almost everywhere."

"That's a façade, Henrie. Before they left their house, she enhanced background photos, adding cropped out pictures of themselves, dressed appropriately, into various locations. She scheduled those posts to go out every couple of weeks, so their friends, what few they still have, will believe they're on the road, enjoying the good life."

"How is it they can afford to live? If they have been doing this for some months, they have been paying for hotels or other lodging all this time."

"No, they haven't. They've been living in that camper. They've paid for minimal maintenance, gas and oil. They stayed on top of the weather situation, and they knew they couldn't survive in the camper any longer. So…they used what credit they had left for rooms here. And now I'm going to get to the sad part."

The group leaned in. Mem reached into her purse and brought out a pistol. "They planned for this to be their last stop. They've spent this week looking around, trying to find a place they could do it. You know. End it."

"You're kidding!" exclaimed Annie. "Here? In Chelsea? Where?"

"Well...they picked a spot, a secluded spot by Lake Scott. They were going to send Henrie a red herring, tell him they were going to ski at the state park again, then go, you know, to the spot they picked. They would do it and not be discovered until sometime after the snow melts."

"Why didn't they do it?"

"They found it Tuesday. They were going to go Wednesday, but Henrie said something that changed their minds."

Everyone turned to Henrie, who backed into his chair, surprised. "What did I say?"

"You let them know that you knew they were not skiing. They couldn't tell you they were going to ski in the state park. You would know they were lying. They couldn't give you a red herring, so they...chickened out."

"Chickened out?"

"That was one term they used. Helen also said that perhaps it was a sign that they needed to try to work it out. Make a different kind of life for themselves."

"How did you get the gun?"

"I asked for it."

Annie and Henrie looked at one another, then back to Mem. Annie asked, "Did you get permission to share the story?"

"No."

"So we can't talk to them about it."

"Not yet. I'll work on it tomorrow." Mem gave the pistol to Janet. "Pete might want this, if nothing else, to rule them out as killers."

The humans were so engrossed, they didn't notice Little Socks had listened to the story. She slipped out of the room without being seen.

19

The animals huddled close together, feeling, like the humans, a deep cold inside their bones. Sis especially. Several cats nestled into her chest, stomach and back to keep her warm.

"Does you feel like talking? Can you tells us who you is?"

"Well, I'm Sis."

Cyril looked at her. *"Don't you have a story? How did you get here? What's wrong with your human?"*

"Are you really interested?"

Several cats answered. *"Yes!" "Sure!" "Tell us." "We want to know."*

"Okay. Well, my human is Randy. We have a house, and I have a yard to run in. Sometimes we travel for his work. That's what we're doing now. He used to be a real nice guy."

"What happened?"

"He changed. He started to smell funny, act funny."

"Is he drinking?"

"No. He and his friends sometimes get together and drink, you know, like play poker and drink beer, or go out for beer. This is different. It's not beer. I can smell it, like, coming from his skin."

Cyril said, *"He's using drugs."*

"I think so. Anyway, he still has his job, and I still travel around with him, and he still takes care of me, but he's different. The last few days, he's been yelling a lot, and hitting the dashboard and the steering wheel, and then..."

"What did he do?"

"He hit me."

"No!"

"He said he was sorry, but he's still really angry, and he's still hitting other stuff. So when he let me out to pee, I ran. I used to like my human, but..."

"You can stay here. We'll find you another human. A nicer one."

"That might be okay...except...is it always this...exciting here?"

Sassy Pants answered. "No. You just caughts us on a bad day. We'ze usually pretty boring."

Several heads nodded in agreement.

Sis looked unconvinced.

Cyril asked, "What are you doing here in Chelsea?"

"Well, it's Randy's job. He's a marshal. You know, a federal marshal? He's kind of a policeman."

Cyril nodded.

"He works with these people he calls witnesses."

"I know that program. People – bad people, usually – say they'll testify against even worse people, and in exchange, they get money to start up a new life, with a new identity and everything."

"That's right. That's why we travel a lot. We go to lots of states and check in on these people. Then he started using drugs, and he started getting mean with these people, and they paid him, like, I don't know, hush money is what he called it. I don't know what kind of money that is."

"That's still money, but they pay it so he'll hush up about them. That's how it got the name."

"Oh. That makes sense. He doesn't always let me out of the truck when he talks to them, so I only hear what he says on the phone and stuff."

"So there's a witness here in Chelsea?"

"Yes. He's on a boat. Randy was looking for the boat for several weeks. He kept saying something about big money, and he was talking to this guy on the telephone, but only when the guy called him. He got madder and madder that this guy wouldn't tell him where he was."

"But he knew it was a boat?"

"Something this guy said. Something about Randy would have to swim out to him. That got Randy to looking at boats, and, well, you know this is his job, so he has lots of help looking for people. They just think he's trying to find his witness. They don't know anything about the hush money. At least, I don't think they know."

"You're probably right about that. He would have a lot of freedom of movement. And if a witness is really missing, the federal government would help him find the guy. They wouldn't know he was looking for money, too."

"It was supposed to be a lot of money."

"So Randy was here to find this guy and get the money."

"He was going to find the guy, get him to tell him where the money was, and then he was going to lie to his bosses and say he missed him."

"That makes sense," said Cyril. "I have to ask you some questions about this guy he was looking for. A man on a boat was killed yesterday."

"No! Was it the witness? Do you think Randy killed him?"

"It might have been the witness. His name was Albert. So far, the only suspects we have are two couples who are staying here at the Inn. Anyway, some people saw a silver pickup truck, and my friend Jock said he saw a dog in that truck. Was that you?"

"Are you talking about that handsome black dog? The one that lives at the boat place?"

Cyril huffed. *"That would be him. I didn't realize he had an opportunity to meet you."*

"We didn't meet, really. We just saw one another. He's cute."

Cyril huffed again. *"Let's get back to the guy. Who was he?"*

"His name was Gerald, but he took another name. I guess it might have been Albert. Anyway, this Gerald, he worked for a hedge fund manager somewhere on the east coast, and he put lots of money into banks in several different names. Millions."

"So…maybe your human found out where the money was and killed him, or maybe this guy wouldn't tell him where the money was, so he killed him."

"If he killed him. He never did anything like that before."

"But you said he was getting worse."

"Yeah."

"So, for whatever reason, Randy killed the guy on the boat, and he must have stayed in town to look for you."

Sis sighed. *"I wish he would just leave. I don't feel safe."*

Little Socks joined the group. *"Guess what? That bullet wasn't going to be used on that man. It was going to be used to commit suicide."*

She told them the story. *"So they weren't the murderers either."*

"*No, and guess what? We know who did it! Sis's human!*"

A low growl came from Mr. Bean. Everyone turned to look. Freddie the ferret was in the room, edging toward the cushions.

Tiger Lily said, "*It's okay, Mr. Bean. We have to talk to him, and he's had kind of a bad day.*"

Little Socks said, "*You've been out of your cage all day. Have you eaten anything besides our food?*"

"*No. I can't find anything low enough.*"

Sassy Pants asked, "*Where you been peeing?*"

"*There's this wagon on the back porch. It's private and everything. I can climb onto a chair and jump into it.*"

Voices came from all over the cushions. "*No!*" "*Dat's ours!*" "*Trill!*" "*You ruined it!*" "*It's not a potty!*"

Freddie backed up and was ready to turn and run until Tiger Lily said, "*Come on, guys. Give him a break. I'll show him where the litter pan is, if he'll promise not to use our wagon anymore.*"

Most of the cats nodded a grudging assent.

Tiger Lily walked Freddie to the litter pan, which he used, and walked him back.

"*You can sleep with us, but kind of stuff yourself between a couple of cushions so Mommy doesn't see you and throw you out.*"

Freddie climbed up, found a hole, and sighed.

Tiger Lily turned to go to sleep. "*You're gonna owe us for that wagon.*"

The highway truck pulled to a stop. The driver couldn't pull over. Roads were still one lane, at best. Which meant he wasn't going anywhere until this pick-up truck got out of the way.

He lay on the horn. Nothing. Again. Nothing.

He climbed down and walked to the front of the truck. He almost slipped and fell. Well, this is why the truck was pushed into the drift. The road was sheer ice underneath the top layer of snow.

He got to the front door and looked in the window. This guy wasn't going anywhere. The truck had hit something, looked like the cement abutment of a bridge, hidden in the snow. Glass was everywhere.

The guy never made it out. He may not have been severely injured, but if he'd been here for a while, he'd frozen to death.

He trudged back to his own truck and used his radio to call it in. State police were dispatched.

20

Henrie's breakfast was less sumptuous than most mornings. He needed to consider food conservation, in the event storm recovery took longer than planned.

He served only breakfast casserole, oatmeal with cranberries and almonds, a variety of breakfast meats, three types of bread for toasting and a variety of pastries from Mr. Bean's. His guests would just have to suffer.

The television played The Weather Channel. The anchor said, probably for the one hundredth time in two hours, "The storm is moving to the east, having buried the Great Lakes region in thirty inches of snow. The top layer is mixed with sleet. This formed a virtually impenetrable shell. And remember, that count does not include snow still on the ground from the early December storm."

Henrie barely listened as the announcer discussed Pennsylvania, now in the middle of the storm, and New York, which would be buried by this time tomorrow. The storm continued to build in intensity.

His ears perked when he heard, "Hundreds of thousands are without electricity this morning, and we can expect that number to climb as the storm moves east."

Henrie sighed and looked at the monitor. The generators were still on. He picked up the phone and called Felicity.

"Good morning."

"Hey, Henrie. Is everyone up already?"

"No. Only I. How is everything at the Café?"

"We've been busy. Those crews bunking at the Carriage House are well-fed. Hilly and Boone were over with their boys. We gave them breakfast on the house."

"Good. They were able to eat together?"

"The snow is gone. We still have wind, but all they have to do is keep ahead of the wind on the paths they've already carved out. Today should be relatively easy for them."

"I will call Boone and ask him to check on the generators. By now, certainly they need tending."

"He said something about it. Go ahead and call, but I'll bet he's already on it."

"Do you need anything?"

"No, we're good. We had enough staff stay over that Mo's and I are set. We're still good on food. Cookie and I will talk later today about Bon Vivant."

"Encourage him to take a weekend off."

"I will. He may try to open for one day, though. I guess our Christmas In Chelsea went belly up."

"I believe we can assume so. Call if you need anything."

Pete plodded in, eyes half open. At least he had a clean uniform today. Henrie poured coffee. "Will you be on rescue detail today?"

"Not right away. I called Marco. He's going to stay on that with our reserves, and I'm back on the murder."

"Do tell. Anything to do with the story Mem told us last night?"

"A little. I've at least crossed Tom and Helen off my list of suspects. The bullet the cats found is the same as the ones in the gun they had. Now I need to go back to The Marina. I need to have a chat with Carter."

"The alive guy."

"Yes. Him. Ray confirmed the boat on the left is yellow, so Barry was on the right track. Two people were seen leaving his boat. I assume it's this couple…um…"

"Robert and Sue."

"Them."

"I'll talk to them first. Maybe."

Henrie heard movement in the dining room. "Excuse me." He took the coffee pot.

"Good morning. You have remained in your room for nearly twenty-four hours. Can I interest you in anything around the house? Board games, books, movies, sporting events on television, chats with others?"

Robert said, "Oh, we've been watching TV in our room. It is boring, though."

Sue added, "I've watched The Weather Channel until it's all I can do to keep from screaming."

Pete, apparently shored up with a cup of coffee, entered the dining room. "Good morning. Robert and Sue, right?"

"Yes."

"I'm the Chief of Police. We met briefly yesterday. Mind if I sit?"

"Please do."

Henrie left, but sat at the kitchen table, where he could hear Pete and the couple.

Pete said, "I spent the evening before we met at The Marina, investigating a murder."

"Murder?"

"Yes. I wondered if you could tell me, please, who you were going to see the morning you arrived."

"Going to see? No one."

"I don't have a lot of patience at this point. I'll tell you what I know. I know you were in a hurry. I know you have been less than forthcoming about your reason for being in town. I know you went to The Marina. And I know a couple fitting your description was seen departing from a boat in the harbor. I suspect you did not care to talk to a police officer yesterday morning. Care to fill in the gaps?"

Henrie heard nothing for a few moments. He assumed Pete would not speak again until one or the other responded. He heard Sue.

"We came to see my brother."

Silence.

"My brother, Carter. A private investigator located him. Well, located a boat registered to him, and we just got word that it docked here for the winter."

"Why did you hire a private investigator?"

"Carter's been missing. Well, he left several years ago. A few decades ago. I was just a child. I didn't even know if I would recognize him, but I did. It was just luck, really. We were driving in here, to register, and he was walking down the sidewalk, toward the harbor. I ran up to our room to drop our bags, and, well, it was just luck again that we had a deck that looked out, and I watched long enough to see he was going there."

"So you left right away, and went to the harbor to talk to him."

"Yes."

"About?"

"What?"

"What was the purpose of your conversation? I assume you had it, you left, and you were ready to leave town right away. What was the conversation about?"

"Well, Momma passed away. I just wanted to tell him."

Silence.

Pete spoke slowly. He paused for emphasis after each phrase, formatting each as a statement until the final one. "He was gone for decades…apparently didn't care about your mother…and you paid a private investigator to find him…just to tell him your mother…for whom he didn't care…died?"

"Well…it was a little more complicated."

"How complicated?"

"Well…Robert?"

Robert said, "Sue and Carter are the sole heirs." He paused.

Silence.

Robert continued. "Well, he disappeared. He just disappeared. By all rights, everything should have gone to Sue, but…"

Sue picked it up. "He didn't disappear completely. Every year he sent Momma a card on her birthday, and she gave those to her attorney. The attorney had all of her mail forwarded to him, so…well, he got another card a couple of months ago and he said – again – that we can't have his half. He's still alive. Even if no one knows where he is, it's still his."

"He doesn't deserve a penny," added Robert. "He didn't help take care of her. He didn't even like her."

"So you hired a private detective, found him, and what were you going to do?"

"Convince him to sign over his half to us."

"And did he?"

Sue snapped, "He laughed in our faces! Laughed!"

Robert added, "And then he thanked us. Said he'd get with the attorney and claim his share. And then we left."

"So why did you have an issue with talking to a police officer?"

Silence.

Sue finally said, "I may have threatened to kill him."

"You may have?"

"I may have shot at him."

"Excuse me?"

"I may have taken a gun out of my purse and shot at him. There. I said it."

"Did you hit anything?"

"Not that I could tell."

"You didn't want to finish the job?"

"Robert grabbed my arm and hauled me off the boat."

"And then you went to lunch. And planned to leave town."

"Huh? You know we went to lunch? Well…we were both plenty shaken…and we needed to take some time to calm down…and then, yes, we were going to leave town. I couldn't believe I'd done it. He's a cad. But I still…I almost shot a man! My brother!"

"I see. Well, I'm going to have to see that gun."

"Why? I didn't hit anything."

"I don't know that. If you're telling me the truth, it's a long shot, but you may have hit the guy that died."

"What? He was nowhere near that boat!"

"But you shot a gun, and you don't know if you hit anything."

"I know I didn't hit a man!"

"A man was shot."

"They have ways of proving this. Ways of proving my gun didn't do it."

"They do, and we'll conduct those tests. But we have to get the bullet first."

"You don't have the bullet?"

"It's still in his head."

"They didn't take it out?"

"It's complicated. Please. I'll go with you and relieve you of that gun."

"Are you going to arrest me?"

"I don't know. For now…"

The voices faded away as they walked upstairs to the room. Henrie didn't know if he was overly tired, punch drunk or snow sick. He laughed so hard, tears were streaming down his face when Annie walked into the kitchen.

George sent a text. "Check FX hospital. Logs coming. UO me & Trev."

At the nurses' station, Janelle was given several pages of faxed data. She took the documents and two cups of really bad coffee to Chris's room, where they now sat, going over the information.

Chris's eyes were on the pages as he asked, "Where are the logs?"

"Sometime today they'll be back in the file where they belong."

"Who do we have to thank?"

"George."

Chris looked up. "George couldn't have gotten his hands on them. Who do we have to thank, Janelle?"

"Will that person be in trouble?"

"No. It's obvious we have a problem. That person will be commended for coming forward."

"Trevor."

"Huh. Good man. He stepped up to help a good woman."

Janelle met his eyes, smiled, and they went back to the paperwork. Until the door opened.

"Uh, oh. Sorry. I left the door unguarded."

The Governor stood in the doorway, flanked by two aides. "You're a hard man to get to. Protected as you are by this…woman. I'm sorry about that interview. I was flustered and didn't know quite how to correct my mistake on camera. I appreciate that you said or did nothing to illuminate the error."

"Not a problem," said Janelle. "We don't care to comment on air in most instances."

"Now, that's not completely true. I've seen the television reports coming from the Station in Chelsea. You have a vocal Officer In Charge."

Chris cleared his throat. "That would be me, Governor."

"That's what I thought. Until I saw the footage. Do you have some sort of a rebellion going on?"

"No, sir. I guess, until I return, Officer Shorter is temporarily in charge. I should have been back on duty yesterday. The hospital has been kind enough to stall my discharge until I can get home."

"Is the problem the roads?"

"Yes, sir."

"Our State Police are traveling now. Some of the roads are still one lane, but they manage. Could I offer you an escort?"

"I would hate to use state resources…"

"You wouldn't be using resources that didn't already need to be used. I understand there's been a murder in Chelsea. Our boys want to take a peek at that."

"A murder? I haven't heard…"

"They've kept it out of the news. All of the reporters are focused on rescue efforts, and I understand your local police department has been unable to get to the body. So no morgue. No report. Just that department and my Staties in the loop."

"May I ask, sir, who was murdered?"

"Some guy livin' on a boat. No one seems to know him, and they haven't got a hit on his given name."

Chris gave a sigh of relief. Annie's Inn wasn't involved. For once. He looked up at the Governor. "You sure it wouldn't be a problem?"

"I've been trying to thank you for a couple of days now. I understand your hesitation. You don't want me to come on strong, ask you to lay off my boy. I have no intention of doing that. I'm very happy he's alive and safe, but I hope to God someone will finally hold him accountable for his shiftless ways. I've been thinking you'll be just the person to get that done. Let me do this one thing for you, to say thank you, and you push forward with everything you need to do."

Chris and Janelle threw their few belongings into the trunk of the state police vehicle. The trip was slow. They couldn't get enough of the view. One lane. Walls of snow fifteen to twenty feet high. Hit an intersection, and pray no one was coming from the other direction. If someone did, one vehicle backed to the last intersection.

Finally, tired of the snow, they sat back. Chris asked, "What can you tell us about the murder? From what the Governor said, it had to be one of the boaters tied up at The Marina for the winter."

"You're right. Your police chief sent a copy of the boat registration with a name and address, a picture of the dead man and a set of fingerprints. Mighty curious. Can't find that man anywhere."

"Pete has resources that no one else has. He'll surprise you. He always does."

"We heard he was kind of a magic man. Solving cases that no one had any business solving. Like he has some kind of a sixth sense."

"Something like that. I've had the privilege of watching him turn a brash suspect into a quivering mass of jelly. Add that to…well, let's just say his sixth sense, and you're looking at the best investigator in a five-state area."

Pete looked at the information coming in. State Police reported a man dead in a one-car crash. Silver pick-up truck. No identification. License plates stolen, belong to a green Ford Focus registered in Chelsea. No time to search further until snow emergency lifts. Contact if you have information.

Pete wondered briefly if this was "his" silver pick-up truck. He looked up to see two uniformed state troopers entering the building.

"We're here to take a look at that murder."

"I've had the scene on deep freeze. Haven't had time to get to it, and I was just headed that way."

Pete told them everything he knew as they made their way to the boat. Before he let them walk on deck, he stopped. "I don't think this is recent, but someone has been here since me. Look at these tracks. He – or they – came on after the sleet started, and some of the indentation held."

The state troopers looked past Pete at the scene.

One asked, "Do you think it was the killer?"

"Could be. Very few people know about this. Us, and the folks here at The Marina, including the guy that found the body." He figured he didn't need to confuse the situation by mentioning Annie, Henrie and the surfer guys. And the woman who may have shot the victim. For now, keep it simple.

One of the officers asked, "Think we can get prints?"

"Not out here. Maybe inside. It's my own fault for leaving it so long. Let's take a look."

Pete remembered the night he had come onboard. It was cold, windy and snowing, but still, he thought he did a better job with the tape than this.

Inside the cabin, Pete saw immediately that the body had been moved. It was still upright and leaning against the bed, but the clothing was crooked, and his head was in a different position. He looked at the bed. Yep. He could swear the covers were indented in more than one place.

"Let me take some photos. We can compare them to the ones I took that night."

Soon, the three were kneeling by the man, Albert, and moving him about. "There has to be something behind him. Something someone wanted."

Pete found it. A cubby hole, covered in such a way as to make it completely invisible. Except it wasn't closed correctly. Pete reached all the way in and came away with a leather pouch. It contained a passport and fifty thousand dollars.

"There was room for a lot more in there. This was shoved to the back. Almost like someone got a lot of something from the front and didn't bother to reach all the way in."

One of the state troopers tipped a chair back and tore off a false bottom. One more pouch with a passport and fifty thousand. The two troopers tipped all the chairs but found nothing else.

Pete received a text from Cheryl. "Jock found $$ & computer. Come over."

Pete said, "I'll bet they got a lot of money from that hiding place."

"Why would you think that?"

"Oh, no reason. Money. And maybe a computer leading to even more. I'll just bet. And I think I know who did it. Come with me, and follow my lead."

"We've heard about you. I think we'll just learn from the master some people believe you to be."

Pete led them off the boat and over to the office. Inside, Cheryl feigned surprise and called Ray to the front. "Pete, are you cold? I have coffee."

Carter strolled out from the laundry room.

Pete said, "Carter, it's nice to see you safe and warm. When do you think you'll be back on the boat?"

"Oh, definitely by tomorrow. I'm not going anywhere, though. I'll be here all winter."

"That's good. Hey, these two are with the State Police. We have a few questions for you about that day. Maybe you've remembered more details?"

Cheryl put a carafe of coffee at the conference table, brought some cups, and backed away with Ray. Pete, the state troopers and Carter sat.

Jock stayed under the table where he could listen to everything being said. At the right moment, he would jump out and save the day.

Carter said, "I don't really remember anything more. I think I told you everything."

"Sometimes, details return. Let me ask you about that day again, see if anything else comes up."

Pete flipped through his notebook, and put on his most thoughtful tone. "You said a man and a woman asked for Albert, and you pointed them in his direction."

"Yes, sir."

Jock lapsed into a daydream. He would make fun of Cyril, who wasn't on duty when Pete needed him. But he, Jock the Wonderdog, was.

"Can you describe them? Black or white, other details, like what they were wearing?"

"White. Um, medium everything, height and weight. Coats, maybe black or dark brown. That's about it. I didn't really talk to them."

"Can you remember the time? You said mid-day, after breakfast and before the storm. Can you pinpoint that a little bit?"

Cyril would get red in the face, would huff, would try to downplay his absence. He, Jock, would sit tall and puff out his chest. The beautiful Fiamma would get stars in her eyes.

"Well...Albert and I had breakfast, but it was a late one. We had finished, we walked back, maybe, I don't know, ten thirty or eleven?"

"And did you go right down to your cabin?"

"No. I moved some things around on deck, to give them a little shelter from the wind. I did that for maybe five minutes. Maybe ten."

Jock wondered. When was the last time he'd seen the beautiful Fiamma? Maybe she and her human would be here for Christmas. Or New Year.

"And did they come onto your boat, or did they call to you from the dock?"

"Called from the dock."

"And you directed them to the other boat. Did they ask for Albert by name?"

"Yes."

"They asked for Albert. Did they have a last name?"

"Uh…I don't know. I guess I don't know his last name. I heard 'Albert' and just pointed."

"And then?"

"I was finished with my work. I went to the cabin."

"And you didn't see them either go on or come off Albert's boat."

"Right."

"And you didn't hear a shot."

"That's correct."

Jock's love-starved brain now fixated on Fiamma's face. The flirty way she tossed her dreadlocked and matted hair. The way she wagged her tail when she saw him.

"Were you surprised when I told you about the silencer? Because you seemed surprised."

"Well, it sounded like you said that woman...I mean either the man or the woman...shot him. They just didn't look the type to have a silencer."

"Did they look the type to have a gun?"

"You can never tell, these days. Lots of people have guns."

"You assume it was her that shot him?"

"No! I...either one could have done it."

"You said something about Albert hiding assets from his ex-wife."

In Jock's daydream, Fiamma looked at Cyril with disdain. She said, "Jock is my hero."

"I said that he said he was hiding assets. I assumed it was an ex-wife, and he kind of let me believe that. I don't know if it was that or something else. Someone else."

"But you didn't know what kind of assets he might have had."

"No idea."

"Can you think of anything else he might have said or done, in your presence, I mean, that could help us?"

"No." Carter shook his head, apparently disappointed he was being of no further help.

Jock saw Cyril, head hanging, eyes downcast, as he slowly turned and walked away, leaving Jock to be with the lovely Fiamma. Only Jock...and Fiamma...

"What about a computer. Ever see one of those?"

Carter's eyes went to the table. "No. Never saw one."

"You know, this is a small town. People think we cops in small towns don't know very much. But I need to tell you a little story."

Pete leaned back, poured coffee from the carafe, and took a deep breath. Carter's knee began to bounce up and down.

"I couldn't get any further in that storm the other night than the bed and breakfast up on the corner. I tumbled in there, cold, wet, confused – I think I was hypothermic, you know, kind of like you – and the next morning, I met a few people. Nice couple from someplace south, Georgia, maybe. Name of Tom and Helen. Another nice couple. And two brothers. They're kind of goofy. You know, they came here to surf."

Pete had been looking around the room as he talked. Now he looked at Carter. "You ever hear of that? Surfing a Great Lake in the winter?"

Carter shook his head. A bit nervous, thought Pete. He looked around the table. The state troopers were leaning back, legs crossed, enjoying their coffee.

Jock was sad. He hadn't meant to hurt his friend. Why was he always doing this? Teasing Cyril to the point their friendship was in danger?

"Anyway, these young men were getting ready to go out on the lake and get themselves killed, and they saw this couple. Saw them walking over here. One of those young men, he swears he saw those folks getting off the yellow boat on the left, and then they walked back toward the Inn."

Pete looked at Carter. "Isn't that your boat? The yellow one? On the left?"

"That's my boat, but you said it yourself. The guy is goofy. He must not have seen what he told you."

"Well, we talked about it long and hard. You see, I didn't know the colors of the boats. I saw them at night and during a snow storm. Didn't see them in the light of day. Until now, that is. You're sure about this? They didn't come down here to see you?"

"No. They didn't. They asked for Albert."

Fiamma wasn't worth it. No. She wasn't. She was cute, and flirty, and he liked it when she preferred him…but she wasn't worth losing his best friend.

"Albert. By name."

"Yes."

"Because we can't find anyone named Albert that was actually on that boat. We don't know what his name was."

"It wasn't Albert?"

"No. But I'll tell you something else. That other couple? Their names are Robert and Sue. They're from south Texas, and they drove two and a half days just to see and talk to her brother. Now you're going to enjoy this. His name is Carter. Just like yours."

Carter's eyes closed, and his head went down.

"What do you have to tell me now?"

Jock sighed. Loud enough that Pete looked down at him.

"I…well…I wasn't very kind to her. Actually, hadn't seen her since she was a kid. She had to tell me who she was." He leaned in with an earnest expression. "Even though I wasn't nice to her then, on the boat, I lied about seeing her because…well, because…"

"You thought she shot him."

Carter sat back, a look of surprise on his face.

"With that gun she had just purchased, that she didn't know how to use, and when she tried to shoot you, the shot went wild."

"Yeah."

Jock started to come up from his daydream. He was still here, at The Marina. He hadn't done anything stupid yet.

"And then I told you about the silencer, and you thought…"

"Thank God, it wasn't her."

"And…"

"And…maybe the guy really did have some assets."

"So when did you go back on the boat?"

"Yesterday."

"What did you find?"

"Nothing."

"Do you want to try that again?"

"I didn't find anything! Why would I lie to you?"

"Indeed. Oh. Looky here."

Pete rose and walked to Cheryl, who held a brown duffel bag, heavy with something. Pete took it from her, turned and smiled at Carter.

"Then you won't mind if we take a look at this bag, found on property owned by this couple."

Carter tried to jump to his feet. He looked down. Jock's teeth were firmly clamped onto his pants leg. He slumped back into his chair. Pete handed the bag to one of the state troopers as he reached to the back of his belt for handcuffs.

"I didn't kill him," said Carter. "That wasn't me." He kicked a bit. Jock growled, but held onto the pants leg.

21

Cyril was happy to be left behind again today. It was cold out there! He and Sis talked with the cats about their problem. How to let Pete know about Randy and the guy in the boat.

Annie left the apartment door open for them, because there were too many people and not enough places. The companions gathered in her dining room.

Freddie stayed in the cushions, having established a shaky friendship with the companions. He didn't join in the conversation, but he didn't leave the comfort of the room.

Tiger Lily wrapped up the conversation they'd been having. *"No one stayed here, so we can't find clues to give them. I don't know how to write 'Sis's human killed the man on the boat,' and we haven't come up with another way of saying it."*

"That sounds about right."

Speckles asked, *"So, that's it, then? This is what you great and glorious detectives do? You solve a mystery, then give up on doing anything about it?"*

"No!" "It's not like that…" "We'ze good tectives!" "Trill!"

Tiger Lily asked for quiet. *"She's right. We can't give up. Who else has an idea? What can we do?"*

Mr. Bean asked, *"Do we have a boat? Could we find a boat and give it to Pete? Then maybe he could ask the yes/no questions."*

Little Socks said, *"Mommy has some books with pictures. Maybe we could find a picture."*

"What about a picture of a gun?"

"And a truck, the kind that Randy drives?"

"Or, wait, if we can combine pictures with some words that you know, Tiger Lily…"

"…yeah, and we could put them in order somehow."

Tiger Lily said, *"First, we have to find pictures. It would take forever to go through Mommy's books. We'd have to push them to the floor, one by one."*

"What about all those magazines? The ones all over the house?"

"Yeah! Some of those are boat ones!"

"And there are car ones! I bet they have trucks!"

"And guns? Do we have any with guns?"

"Go get some. Bring them here. We'll figure it out."

The town was still dark. No electricity, and no guestimate of when the power would come back on. Annie's neighbors – now her guests at the Inn – stayed busy in ways they could help.

Ben kept the sidewalks in front of Annie's businesses cleared of blowing snow. JoJo stayed on laundry detail. She didn't believe that rat was actually a friendly ferret. She kept Henrie's ball bat with her at all times.

Diana worked in the kitchen at the Café which was continually busy with emergency crews. Mem and Laila did prep work for Diana and the other cooks.

Guests, for the most part, were keeping their own rooms clean, but Hilly saw to the upkeep of the carriage house throughout the day, as crews left and before a new batch arrived.

Carlos had extra help, with his wife, mother and sisters captive on The Avenue. Teresa waited tables at the Café; Clara made a mess of things at Mo's Tap.

Holly and Jolly kept busy with the kinds of things no one else could master. Holly tended to minor repair on the generator, which blinked a couple of times, and Jolly unclogged a couple of over-used toilets.

Martha tended to Little Fred while Georgia went to work.

Annie decided to play matchmaker. Of a sort. The dining room was seriously over-capacity, so…this was something she needed to do. Or so she reasoned.

She knocked on the doors of both couples at the same time and stood back in the hallway. When they opened their doors, almost at the same time, she looked from one to the other and said, "I'm serving lunch on the landing. We have too many people for the dining room, so please, come join me."

Three women looked at one another. Annie in the hallway, Helen and Sue from their respective doorways.

Sue finally said, "We had a big breakfast."

Helen nodded ascent.

"It's light. Soup and salad. You'll want to try it. The salad is mixed greens with almonds, mandarin oranges, feta cheese and a light balsamic dressing. The soup is pure comfort. Chicken and dumplings."

Robert's head appeared in the doorway. "Chicken and dumplings? Let's go."

Annie led them to the feast, laid out on a coffee table surrounded by comfortable chairs. She handed each guest a tray table and ladled chicken and dumplings into deep bowls. As she worked, she chatted, apparently in an aimless fashion, eyes on the food, not on the guests.

"I haven't had time to get to know any of you. Strange, since we've been locked in together for a while. But...you know...I've been busy. I'm looking forward to seeing a friend this afternoon. Someone that was caught on the lake. You know. Being a hero. Rescuing the Governor's son."

"You know him? He's been all over the news."

"Yes. He's been stuck at that hospital, out of town."

"How's he getting here? Aren't the roads closed?"

By now, Annie was seated, facing her guests. "Well, he has a new friend. The Governor, finding that his State Police need to be in town, arranged a ride."

"The Governor! My. He moves in great circles."

"Not really. I think this is a one-time thing. Kind of a thank-you. Anyway, I've missed him because of this weather. What about all of you? What are you missing out on, being stuck here?"

And just like that, two couples began to talk amongst themselves. Annie joined in on occasion, but soon, she excused herself and left. The better to let them get to know one another. They deserved to wait out this emergency with friends, not sequestered in their private miseries.

By noon, the sun had started to make an appearance. Every now and then, the snow sparkled like diamonds.

Since snow was the only thing visible from any window, the effect was mesmerizing.

Henrie served lunch for the teens in the dining room. Boone and his crew ate at the back table in the dining room in shifts. Martha made lunch for Little Fred and took her into the library to look at the snow.

Kullen and Barry looked at the teenagers, full plates in hand, and seemed pleased when Henrie invited them to the kitchen.

As they settled with their plates, Henrie fixed a plate and joined them. "May I ask, does the inability to do what you do for a day or two impact you seriously?"

They looked at one another. Kullen answered. "Well, there's two parts to it. One is where we make money, so yeah, not being able to do it for a couple of days can hurt. But also, other people can cut you out of the action. If we aren't online, someone else is, and, well, we could lose business that way."

"That would be distressing. Are you able to work from our computers here? Have you tried?"

Barry looked at his plate. Kullen took a deep breath. "We don't want anyone to get the IP address from here."

"Why on earth would that be a problem?"

"Well, for all the good things about my brother, here, including his willingness to keep me alive, well, he did something…"

Henrie remained silent, taking a page from the Book Of Pete's Interviewing Skills.

Eventually, Kullen continued. "Apparently we owe some guys some serious money."

"How serious."

"Serious enough that they'll probably try to collect. Soon."

"How will they do that?"

"I think they have what they call leg breakers. They might try to break a leg. Or something."

"And they will come to Chelsea to do that?"

"We're closer to them here than we are when we're home. Barry thinks – based on a little online argument – that they might be coming."

"How would they get here? We are under a state of emergency. No one is to be on the roads unless, well, there is an emergency."

"They'll probably be clear soon. Maybe by tomorrow. We thought we'd leave as soon as the emergency is lifted. If we aren't here, they won't have anything to break."

"But you evidenced concern about something called an IP address?"

Barry said, "They would have it from the cyber café, and they asked for the name of the place. I told them. But they don't have it for here. They wouldn't come here."

"Why would they think you could stay there? Would they not look for a hotel, motel or B&B?"

"I probably shouldn't have done it. That Mem is a real nice lady. I told them we were staying there. She had rooms."

"Why on earth would you tell them how to find you?"

Barry started, "They said they wanted a face-to-face. I knew what that meant. It meant…"

Kullen finished the sentence, "…legs breaking."

"Well. That does present a problem. Perhaps I should call Pete."

"Oh, that dude hates us already."

"That 'dude' is the best protection you could have. Tell me, would your leg breakers potentially ignore the emergency situation and be on the road as we speak?"

"Potentially."

Henrie moved to the telephone and called Pete.

Annie and Henrie got into their safe space. The kitchen. Certainly, people other than they would be there on occasion, but generally not without an invitation.

They sat. They had hot chocolate heavily flavored with coffee. They shared news of the household. They watched the early afternoon news.

Dan Tapper was on. Annie dropped her head to the table. And then she heard his voice. Chris. She sat up.

Chris was saying, "…let me repeat, the Coast Guard will have no comment. Thank you." He turned and walked away from the camera.

Dan Tapper quickly regained his composure and centered himself in the camera's view. "And there you have it. No comment on the biggest story of the day. A staff shake-up following a series of heroic actions. Back to you, Charles."

Charles Veritone said only, "Thank you, Dan," and was off to other news stories.

"Staff shake-up? Did you hear…?"

"No. I did not."

"He must have done it. Accepted that promotion."

"You do not know that for certain."

Annie would not be placated. Tears streaming down her face, she ran for the stairs. There, even with tears, she couldn't help but see the bits of paper strewn about.

Angry, stressed, overwhelmed by people, she picked up every piece. By the time she reached the second level, where her guests still sat, her emotions were under control. She had several pieces of what appeared to be magazines in her pockets and wondered who would be so rude as to rip them up and drop them.

She smiled, nodded, and continued to the third floor, still picking pieces from almost every step.

22

The companions looked at the cacophony of magazines on the floor, in various states of dishevelment. Cats were never particularly concerned about dishevelment.

Tiger Lily said, *"Okay. Let's all look for pictures."*

For the most part, they all tore into the magazines, looking in their own haphazard ways for pictures to tell the story. Sis backed into a corner and watched the furor.

Cyril was the first to find one. *"Here's a boat!"* He grabbed the page by his teeth and ripped. Half of the picture of a luxury liner came with him; the other half remained on the page. He leaned into it and got the second half.

"What do I do with it?"

"Put the pictures on the windowsill. That's out of the way, and we can line them up there."

Mr. Bean came up with a silver car. *"How about this?"*

"That's a car. Is there a truck?"

Sassy Pants tore most of a page out that had a bottle of wine. *"Where I puts dis?"*

Tiger Lily looked at it. *"How does that help us with this story?"*

"Mommy likes wine when stuff is goin' on." Sassy Pants took the picture to the windowsill.

Tiger Lily rolled her eyes and watched as others turned pages, with varying degrees of success. She ran the list of pictures through her mind. Boat, truck, gun, maybe a picture of a dog – that would be Sis – and what else?

Kali and Ko said together, *"We have a truck!" "A truck!"* In their haste to get the picture – a child's bright yellow toy truck – it came out in three pieces.

Daryll and Speckles worked together. They found a picture of a police officer. *"What about this? We could let this be Sis's human."*

Tiger Lily agreed.

The two young cats seemed to work well together. Daryll sat on half of the magazine, holding it solid, while Speckles carefully ripped the page out. She got all but the feet of the police officer. It was a man who looked like a dog, or a dog who looked like a man, with a big gold badge on a black vest.

Tiger Lily watched in amazement. "Watch these guys. They know how to tear out pages."

Sassy Pants came close and watched. She looked at Mr. Bean. *"We could works togeder."*

Tiger Lily jumped to the top of the table. She looked at the windowsill and the pictures already gathered. *"We still need a gun and a dog."*

Mo said *"Trill!"*

Kali ran over. *"Gun! He has a gun!"*

Gleefully, Mo pulled on the page with the picture of a machine gun, coming away with the tip of the barrel. He walked regally to the windowsill with the partial photo.

Kali remained with the rest of the picture. *"Mo, come back here. We need to get the rest of it."*

Mo, satisfied he had exercised enough for the day, ambled over to Sis and lay down, cuddled into her soft hind quarters.

Kali sighed. Ko appeared at her side, and together, they got the rest of the picture in two tries.

Tiger Lily looked carefully at the pictures and announced, *"I'm going to try to put them in order. We still need a dog."*

Cyril stood at the windowsill, looking at the pictures with her. *"What comes first?"*

"I think the policeman."

"You're right. And next, a dog."

"And then the gun."

"Next, the boat."

"Where do we put the truck?"

"I don't know. What about a dead man? Can we find a picture of a dead man?"

Tiger Lily put the question to the group. *"Can you find a dead man?"*

Fat Cat and Scaredy Cat had been very quiet. Now, they looked at one another and flipped as quickly as they could through their most recent magazine. They found it. A picture of a man on the floor, bullet hole through the head, and a man leaning next to him, facing up to the camera.

"We have it!" said Fat Cat. The two worked together very carefully and pulled out the entire page, mostly intact.

"Great! Put it here on this side." Tiger Lily pointed to the right side of the windowsill.

Mr. Bean cried, *"We have a dog! A big dog!"*

Sassy Pants added, *"She's dark, like Sis!"*

They worked together, Mr. Bean sitting on the magazine while Sassy Pants tore. Incredibly, they delivered, intact, the picture of a dark gray giant schnauzer.

Tiger Lily and Cyril had just succeeded in getting the pictures in order when Annie came into the room.

Pete arrived as Annie's ankles disappeared up the stairs. He went to the kitchen and found Henrie, preparing the next meal.

"So tell me again. What did our boys do?"

"It appears they have been consorting with the wrong sort online, and that they owe money to someone. Leg breakers."

"Leg breakers." Pete shook his head. "Where are they?"

"I requested they wait for you in the library."

"Where's Cyril?"

"I believe he is upstairs with the cats. And the new dog."

"What about that dog, Henrie? Any idea where she came from?"

"I am certain she was well-loved. She is recently trimmed. She was not overly hungry. Given the condition of her paws, it is likely she was on her own for no more than a day."

"I've asked around. No one has put up a notice. Generally, folks at the Café hear if someone is missing a pet, and they've heard nothing. They want to meet her, though."

"I am certain they will have a chance. We will take her to Doctor Ralph as soon as we can travel. Hopefully, she has a chip, and we can locate her owner."

"Well…guess I'd better go talk to our boys."

Pete walked toward the library to find out what he could about the leg breakers.

He didn't make it. Reverberating through The Avenue, in between the buildings and careening off the hard surface of high snows covered by ice, came the sounds of multiple gunshots. And the sounds just kept coming.

Wisely, Pete did not emerge from the Inn until the sounds subsided. When he got outside, he heard, but could not see over the walls of snow, a car screeching away, past the police station and out to the highway.

Cyril and Tiger Lily leapt up, looking over the snow from the third floor, to see the men shooting at the buildings across The Avenue. They shot through every window in every storefront.

Cyril barked and paced the windows until he saw Pete leave the Inn and cross to the other side.

"I've got to help Pete!" He ran out the apartment, down the steps and slid into the front door. He jumped, barked and howled to be let out.

Henrie pulled at his collar and held him as Annie opened and squeezed through the door. Henrie was able to get out, letting go of the collar just in time to shut the door firmly behind him.

Cyril howled in protest, but realized he was not going anywhere. He ran back to the apartment, the only floor with a vantage point to see across the street.

Tiger Lily, who had not left the windowsill, turned to the rest of the cats. *"How are we going to explain this to them?"*

Annie hit the floor, coming up only after the echoes of gunfire died away. As she stood, she heard the car careen away. She saw Pete looking around the corner of the wall of snow on the north side of The Avenue.

Annie did what many other humans did at that moment. She ran downstairs to go outside, heedless of cumbersome winter outerwear. Cyril was already at the front door, howling to go out. She and Henrie, somehow, managed to get outside, leaving him to howl on the inside.

The Avenue still had one access point from north to south, the one leading from the Inn to The Drug Store and The Clinic. Annie and Henrie were the first to reach it, followed by Jolly. Others were beginning to come from where they were spending their day, until Pete nearly had a mob on his hands.

Pete surveyed the damage, starting at the church. Annie quickly realized everyone was safe with the possible exception of the sisters. She ran to The Clinic. Henrie followed.

They opened the door to find Jennifer, sobbing, over the prone figure of Marie.

Annie cried, "Jennifer! Jennifer! How bad is it?"

"I don't know!"

Henrie kneeled by Marie while Annie pulled Jennifer away. He touched Marie tenderly, moving his hands, searching for injuries.

Annie watched as he seemed to find no wounds on the front of her body. He gingerly picked up her shoulder, below which pooled more blood than she cared to see.

He turned around. "Jennifer, please, get control of yourself. You are the only one who can help her now. We need to stop the bleeding."

Annie held Jennifer as she took a deep breath, then another. Jennifer gathered herself and kneeled next to Henrie on the floor.

Annie turned to see Pete come in the door. He turned quickly to block the entry of anyone else. Annie said, "I'll keep them out. Please help them."

Chris drove onto the one accessible lane of The Avenue to find it crowded with people. He backed up and out of the way as the siren from the ambulance turned on.

He watched Jennifer pass, grim-faced, and his stomach clenched. He got out of the car, looked down the street, and saw that spaces had been cleared for cars on the other end of the street. He got back in and drove slowly, careful not to hit any of the gawkers. Gawking at…broken windows? He realized the gawkers were his friends. Business owners surveying the damage from…? What?

He parked in the first space he reached, not far from the one walkway he could see from north to south. The snow was at least fifteen feet high, cleared from the one lane and a few feet of sidewalk. Annie was there. At the doorway to The Clinic. With Henrie and Pete.

Chris walked to her slowly, watching her as she watched him approach. Her face was tear-stained, her mouth set in a grim expression.

He reached her and opened his arms. She sank into him and lapsed into sobs. She was cold. She didn't have on a coat, gloves, hat or scarf. He looked around. No one did. Everyone on the street, with the exception of Pete, was without outerwear.

Chris walked slowly, pulling the sobbing Annie with him, until he reached Henrie, who stood, stunned, staring up the street, the way the ambulance had gone. He put his hand on Henrie's shoulder.

"Henrie, let's get everyone inside. You'll all freeze."

Henrie stared at him.

"Henrie! Tell everyone to get in!"

Henrie seemed to come to. He turned and walked up the street, taking people by the shoulders and turning them toward that one opening in the snow. Slowly, everyone turned and walked toward the opening. Some, like Laila and her children, walked stoically, facing front. Others, like Clara and Mem, walked backwards. Still others, like Teresa and Jolly, walked forward, but kept looking back.

Chris stood, arms around Annie, warming her as he could, until everyone but Henrie and Pete had gone through the pathway. He handed Annie off to Henrie and joined Pete, who continued to survey the damage.

Chris watched as Henrie and Annie went through the snow channel, then asked, "What happened here, Pete?"

Pete was staring at bullet holes in the walls and shattered windows. "Leg breakers."

Little Socks said, *"Chris is here! We have to help him and Sis get together!"*

Sassy Pants jumped to the windowsill to look out. *"How we do dat?"*

Mr. Bean and Mo said together, *"She has to flirt."* *"Trill!"*

Kali and Ko said together, *"Yes, flirt!"* *"Make google eyes at him!"*

Sis was confused. *"Who is Chris, and why would I flirt with him?"*

Tiger Lily said, *"You need a home. And Chris needs a dog."*

"Why does he need a dog? And who is he?"

Fat Cat said, *"He needs a dog so the dog can help us detectives when we're detecting and stuff."*

Scaredy Cat added, *"He's real nice. He's a good friend of Annie, and he stays here sometimes."*

Even Speckles and Daryll got in on the excitement. *"You would have a fur-ever home!"* *"We would see you lots!"*

Sis looked at the floor. *"I don't know how well I can flirt. I'm pretty shy with new people. Would he...is he...would he be a good human?"*

Cyril answered. *"The best. I stayed with him for several days one time. It was last winter. I wasn't very nice to him, because I thought Pete deserted me. But he didn't get mad or anything. He was really good to me."*

Tiger Lily added a little spice. *"You'd be able to meet Jock, that handsome dog from The Marina."*

Sis smiled.

Cyril huffed. Then he said, *"Let's go down. They're coming inside."*

Freddie followed.

23

As the crowd milled around, waiting for Pete, Tiger Lily ran to Henrie and tapped him on the leg. He didn't respond. She tapped again, harder. When he still did not respond, she bit his leg.

Henrie's head snapped down. She trotted to the kitchen turning to see if he followed. He did.

She jumped to the counter and sat in front of the cabinet that held the monitor for the street cameras. Henrie just looked at her.

She turned and tapped the door.

Henrie smiled. "You are one smart girl."

In the foyer, Pete was confronted with people. Lots of people. People recovering from shock to become angry. With anxious cats, a couple of prowling dogs, and…was that a ferret scooting under a table?

Annie had the telephone in her hand. She hung up and turned to Pete. "Boone believes the road is open to their warehouse. His crew can start cleaning immediately while he picks up plywood to cover the windows. If it's alright with you, that is."

"Sure. It will be dark soon enough, and the street lights still aren't working."

Teresa asked, "How is Marie?"

"She was conscious when Jennifer took off. And stable. Diana went with them."

It seemed everyone talked at once. Pete made out a few sentences. "Who was it?" "Why did this happen?" "Will you catch them?" "The insurance company isn't going to believe this!"

He raised his hands and pushed the air down, asking for silence. "We'll get the answers you need. For now, I want each of you to go to your places and take a quick look around. We need to be quick. It will be dark soon enough, and we have no power."

Pete turned to look out the window. It was already half dark. He turned back. "Touch nothing if a bullet has lodged or struck it. I need to gather that evidence. Take a quick look. Quick. Look. Come back here. We'll talk when you get back."

As the business owners hurried out, this time with coats, hats and gloves, Pete stood back. His eyes were on Kullen and Barry, standing at the doorway to the library.

When the last person left, he closed the door and walked toward them. They backed up, slowly, until they reached a sofa. They sat down, perfectly in sync, slowly, eyes trained on that angry face.

Pete sat opposite. "Leg breakers?"

Kullen and Barry spoke quickly, one after the other.

"Really, sir, we didn't expect this."

"Maybe they aren't the same guys?"

"Maybe it was a gang?"

"Maybe..."

Pete held his hand up to stop them. "Let's not play games. Let's assume these are the guys. Tell me everything."

The brothers took synchronized deep breaths. Kullen opened his mouth, and Pete heard, "Pete! You have to come upstairs!"

"Do. Not. Leave."

Annie stood on the bottom step, watching as her friends got coats, hats and gloves and walked quickly out the door. Soon, the only person left in the foyer was Chris.

Eleven cats and two dogs milled around, anxious and afraid. And…was that the ferret? Whatever it was disappeared under a chair.

They were alone. With the companions. And maybe a ferret.

Annie couldn't breathe. She wanted to make sure he was okay. She wanted to slap him. She wanted to hold him. She wanted to get Henrie's ball bat and create a new hole in his head. She wanted him to run to her and put his arms around her.

He didn't run. He walked. Slowly, deliberately. He joined her on the bottom step and put his arms around her. She leaned in and sobbed into his shoulder.

When she could finally talk, she said, "You're leaving."

He put his hands on her shoulders and pressed her away, so he could look into her eyes. "No, I'm not."

"There's a shake-up…"

"I fired Shorter for cause."

"You…"

"Fired Shorter for cause. Then I called my commander and told him I would not take the promotion."

"What does that mean?"

"I think it means I'm out of a job."

"What?"

"We have a lot to discuss. Let's go upstairs."

"Oh! Upstairs! The kids have a message for us! Pete! You have to come upstairs!"

Chris took a deep breath. He couldn't be surprised. Not where Annie and her cats were concerned. He followed Pete and Annie up the stairs.

Cyril and Tiger Lily ran ahead; the other companions walked more sedately. Mo walked with a regal step, tail held high, keeping pace with Pete.

Chris felt something at his hand. He looked down, surprised, as a large gray dog gazed up at him. She paced herself and stayed with him into the apartment's dining room.

Chris hung back as Annie walked to the windowsill. Pete followed. The two looked down and paced. Something was on the windowsill. Tiger Lily jumped and sat on the far left side. Cyril sat on the floor in front of her.

The dog, a schnauzer, thought Chris, wore a pretty rainbow-colored scarf around her neck as a collar. She gazed up at him. He stroked her head, then kneeled in front of her to use both hands. He stroked her cheeks, her neck, her back. He looked down. Her feet seemed to be healing from frostbite.

He sat in one of the dining room chairs. The dog inserted herself in between his legs and sat. She put a foreleg on his thigh and leaned in. With one hand on her head, Chris watched Annie and Pete. Little Socks jumped to his other thigh, and, surprised that she would come to him, he cupped her body with his other hand. She curled into a ball, sighed and purred herself to sleep.

He didn't notice when Freddie slipped in, under his chair and close to Sis's right haunch.

Annie hated to ignore Chris, but the curious set of magazine pages on the windowsill seemed to have some importance.

Pete said, "What is this?"

"Magazine pictures."

"I can see that. Why am I looking at them?"

"Cyril and the cats put them here. I think we have to look past the, um, creativity, and look at them like the kids did."

"Like the kids did?"

Annie looked at Tiger Lily. "Is this supposed to tell us a story?"

Tiger Lily blinked once.

She looked back. "Okay. Let's decipher this, one picture at a time. On the left, we have a ripped up Tonka truck."

"I think it's ripped because our friends don't have thumbs."

"Okay, so a Tonka truck."

"Or just a truck. Why a truck?"

"You said something about a truck at The Marina."

Pete looked at Cyril. "Is this supposed to be the truck from The Marina? The one Ray saw?"

Cyril moved close enough to touch Pete's right foot.

"Okay. Looks like we're on the right track. What's this next picture?"

"Deputy Dawg?"

"Or a policeman. Is it a policeman, Cyril?"

Cyril looked at Tiger Lily, who looked back. They both turned to look at Pete, but made no move to touch a foot or blink."

Pete looked at Cyril. "Not a policeman, but something like a policeman?"

Cyril touched his right foot.

"Okay." He looked at Cyril again. "Does this person, who could be something like a policeman, drive this truck?"

Cyril touched his right foot.

"Okay. Let's move on. This one is easy. It's a gray schnauzer. Is this Sis?"

Cyril barked happily and jumped up. He came down and touched Pete's foot one time.

Pete turned to look at Sis. "Did you help with this?"

Sis looked at Cyril and up to Chris. She huddled closer to Chris.

Pete looked back at Cyril. "Does Sis belong to this man? The man that drives the truck?"

Cyril touched his right foot.

Annie was looking at the next picture, two halves of a luxury liner. "Is this supposed to be the boat where the guy was killed?"

Tiger Lily blinked once.

"And this, does it mean he was killed with a gun?" Annie was in front of the three pieces of a machine gun.

Tiger Lily blinked once, and Cyril jumped around again.

"Because this is him, right? This dead man?"

Tiger Lily blinked several times.

Pete looked at Cyril. "This dog, Sis, belongs to a man who is some kind of a policeman, who drives a truck, who took a gun and killed that man on the boat at The Marina."

Cyril barked happily, and Tiger Lily jumped down, job done.

Sassy Pants had jumped to the far right side of the windowsill. Tiger Lily had neglected to remove the picture of the bottle of wine. Sassy Pants touched it.

"Yes, Sassy. Now we deserve a glass of wine. Thank you."

Pete crouched in front of Cyril and gave him a hug. "Thank you. Now I have an idea."

"What idea, Pete?"

"We couldn't get a firm identity of the dead man – Albert – based on the information he gave Ray. It's possible this something-like-a-policeman is a federal marshal, and it's possible the guy is in witness protection. It's something to check, anyway, and if that gets us nowhere, I'll think it through again."

"How hard will it be to find the marshal?"

"We might get lucky. A silver truck ran into a bridge in the middle of the night. They haven't had time to identify the body. The truck had license plates stolen from Chelsea."

"Oh, no. I hate that…but if he killed a man…." Annie looked over at Sis. "We'll take Sis to the vet. If she has a chip, that might confirm everything."

"I think you can get through tomorrow. The highway is clear now, and the storm is gone."

"She'll need a new home. Well, I can't get ahead of myself. Identify the man, maybe it will be the marshal… then we'll know for sure."

"Tell me as soon as you get the name."

"I will. Pete, do you know what's amazing?"

"What's that?"

"We didn't even question their intentions or our own reasoning for following this line of thinking."

"They're training us."

They turned as Henrie entered the apartment. "Pete, Boone kept the cameras clear of snow. We have excellent footage of the men and their vehicle."

24

The Inn was full. Annie wanted to console her friends. She needed to talk to Chris. Without a word, she put on her coat and motioned to him. He followed her. Out the front door, to the narrow sidewalk, and down to the shoveled walkway that led to the Winery.

They entered to the smell of mulled sangria. And an empty room. Except for Jet, at the bar, and a table of people who looked vaguely familiar.

Jet smiled. "Good evening, and welcome to Sassy P's," he said.

"Is this it? All of the customers you've had today?"

"This is it."

"Did you send Jesus and Minnie home?"

Jet motioned with his head to the table of vaguely-familiar people. "They're taking the night off. I assured them I could handle the evening crowd without supervision."

"Please set us up. A bottle of your finest dry red and two glasses. Put it on the most private table."

"Yes, ma'am."

"And don't ma'am me."

"Yes, ma'am."

Chris was already at the table of vaguely-familiar people, shaking the hand of a handsome, friendly guy. As she walked to the table, she heard Chris say, "Thank you, George. For everything. And for the record, I've done a thorough investigation. You will not be put on report."

"Thanks, Skipper. Want to join us?"

"No, thanks. I need to catch up on some missed conversations."

Annie smiled at the group. Some of her finest. Felicity and Trudie, George and Candice, Jerry and Cookie, Carlos and Isabel, Jesus and Minnie.

Felicity asked, "Have you heard how Marie is?"

"Diana called. She'll be fine. We'll be without an ambulance until sometime tomorrow. Jennifer refuses to leave."

"What do you know?"

"I don't know anything, but Boone is the hero. He kept the cameras clear of snow, and they lasted on battery power. Pete has clear photos of the men who did it and their car."

George said, "What's this we hear about a murder at The Marina?"

"That's leaking out?"

"Can't keep something like that quiet for too long."

"Well, Pete still has an active crime scene. It's frozen, I think. He'll clear the scene tomorrow."

"Anyone we know?"

"I know the guy was at the Café a couple of times, don't know if he came into other places. We'll have a photo soon. Probably tomorrow. Speaking of tomorrow, we might be halfway back to normal by then."

Cookie put a thumbs up. "We'll have a relaxed Bon Vivant. You'll love it."

Chris and Annie had begun to back away. They turned and walked to their table in a private corner of the back dining room.

Chris held the tall chair so Annie could get in, then moved the café table for her comfort. He sat directly opposite her, so he could look her in the eyes, poured the wine, and took one of her hands in his.

Annie opened her mouth, but he silenced her. "Just let me talk."

And he talked. He talked about Thanksgiving weekend. The argument he had with both of his parents. The telephone calls from the Senator from his home state. The conversations with his commander. The ultimatum, probably given under pressure from the Senator, who was under pressure from one of his most significant donors.

Take the promotion, or retire. Decide by…Chris gave her today's date.

He had no choice of posting. It would be to a major city in his home state, on a lake hundreds of miles from this one.

Annie said nothing until he finished. Finally, she asked, "Why did you turn it down? It was more money, a better pension, a chance for something more."

"Would you move?"

"I would be tempted…but, no."

"I wouldn't expect you to. Which meant I had to make that choice. The choice my mother insisted she would not force me to make. Only she flipped it. It would look like I was choosing between you and my career. Not you and her."

"We could try something long distance…"

"Do you want that?"

"No…"

"Neither do I."

Annie said nothing. She looked at her hand, entwined with his. "It's just that…um…" She looked up. "It took you a long time."

"It did. I thought the decision would be easy. I wanted the Coast Guard all of my life. I couldn't imagine life without it. But I couldn't imagine life without you. I decided I could replicate the Coast Guard. I can't replicate you." He smiled. "And I'm not that young anymore. I can't do what Janelle does. What George did."

"You did a great deal…"

"And I nearly died."

"Anyone would have."

"Anyway, I'm ashamed it took me this long to decide. And I'm ashamed I didn't talk to you right away. I hope you can forgive me."

"Forgive you? What for?"

"For…not choosing you right away."

"Chris, didn't you just ask me if I would move?" He nodded. "And what did I say?"

"You said you probably wouldn't."

"If you forced me to choose, I would think about it. Probably for a long time. Probably longer than a few weeks."

"You just admitted to some angst about the length of time I took to decide."

"Well, you convinced me it was necessary."

Chris squeezed her hand and took a sip. "So, what else is bothering you?"

"Not bothering, really. But…would you like a dog?"

Simon Finnegan and Oscar McMurphy found their way to Holly and Jolly's room. Jet wasn't home from work yet, so they went to sleep on his sofa.

Speckles and Daryll were missing their girl. They crept onto Little Fred's bed, careful not to wake her, and curled into her sides. Her little hands closed around their tails.

Cyril lay in bed between Pete and Janet, sound asleep. No amount of trying on the part of either of the humans could get him to move, so they left him where he was and held hands over his midsection.

Freddie the ferret slithered to the back porch and into his cage. James heard the sound and latched the cage door.

Laila offered the sofa to Chris, but he declined the offer. Instead, he accepted Henrie's offer of the couch in his apartment. Sis followed him downstairs. When he got to the apartment, he looked down at her. She gazed into his eyes with an unreadable expression.

"Okay. Come on, Sis." She slept on the floor in front of the couch, his hand on her head. He was surprised when Little Socks jumped onto his chest. She kneaded it for several seconds, turned around two times, pushed her right shoulder into his face, and purred herself to sleep

Annie settled into her reclining chair and waited for the rest of her cats to find a place to sleep on or around her. It only took ten minutes. They were too tired to fight with one another.

Henrie walked around, checking on everyone who had a make-shift room. The teens slept peacefully, iPads and telephones in their hands, on the back porch. Clara and Teresa were sound asleep in the front half of the library, Mem in the back. He turned to look for Diana, but remembered she would still be at the hospital.

He heard nothing from the second floor and could see no lights in the carriage house. He went to his apartment, careful not to wake Chris, Sis and what was Little Socks doing here?

He didn't realize it, but as he dropped off to sleep, the electric crews finished their recovery efforts. The lights of Chelsea were on once again.

25

On Saturday morning, Henrie busied himself with his last large storm-survivor meal. The morning news was tuned to WQVX. The anchor reminded his audience every ten minutes that New York was now in the crosshairs of the storm, but saints be praised, regional power had been restored.

Most people, suffering in their homes through the worst of it, would already know the power was on. At the Inn, the only indication was the red light on their monitor. The generators were off.

Felicity called. "Henrie, is Annie up yet?"

"I have not seen her. Can I help you?"

"Well, we decided last night that Cookie will open tonight, but it will be a little different. Really relaxed. A celebration that we made it through the storm. I put it out on all of our social media sites, but I wondered if she could get something on TV."

"It is too late for an advertisement. Allow me to think about it. We might be able to do something."

"I hope so. If you can do it, we're having a buffet with prime rib, cooked to order, main dishes to suit nearly every preferred diet, a couple of soups, and Carlos has promised a surprise dessert selection. And we'll have entertainment."

"Come again?"

"Entertainment. We're going to incorporate some of the things that got cancelled, you know, the Christmas In Chelsea stuff."

"Very interesting. I may have an idea. Are you still busy with emergency workers?"

"We're feeding the last bunch now. Those guys from Indiana are leaving town. They may have to go to Pennsylvania next. They asked me to thank you for the hospitality. They think they're the last to leave the carriage house."

"That is good to know. We will be ready for our scheduled guests next week."

"Are you busy over there?"

"There is movement from those who are preparing to return to their homes here in town. Our typical guests will dine shortly after the neighbors' departure. I have what you would call a steady, but not overly busy morning."

Henrie replaced the receiver and continued his preparations. Another light morning. A few bacon, egg and cheese casseroles, a variety of breakfast meats, oatmeal with cranberries and almonds, quinoa, and, horrors, he could find only white, wheat and rye breads for toasting.

Chris wandered into the kitchen, Sis at his heals. "Does she need a leash to go out?"

"Pete did not use one. However, if you plan to walk her around town, you may want to start with something."

Henrie reached into a drawer and pulled out a cat's harness and leash. "See if you can do something with this."

Chris unhooked the leash from the harness and fastened it around the scarf. "I'll walk up toward the Café. Can I bring anything back?"

Henrie thought for a moment. "You might see what Carlos has in the order of breakfast breads."

Two teenagers wandered into the kitchen. James said, "Good news, Henrie. Freddie came back."

Ginger added, "You've got a problem on the porch, Henrie. It smells like a sewer in there."

The Inn was silent. Local humans and cats, a dog and a menagerie that included the ferret were gone. Guests had eaten breakfast and now lounged in the library. Tired of television – in particular The Weather Channel – they read books and magazines.

Robert and Sue chatted with Tom and Helen from time to time. Kullen and Barry were engrossed in magazines about guns, cars, computers, decorating and fashion.

Kali sat on the top of the sofa in between Barry and Kullen. They seemed not to notice her.

Some roads were clear, but the emergency had not been lifted by the State Police. They had been advised to wait until Sunday morning to leave.

Most of the cats and Sis lounged in the apartment, on the cushions near the dining room windows. Sis tended to her paws.

"They're almost healed. That's good. I need to get in a good run tomorrow. I wonder if anyone will take me out."

Tiger Lily said, *"Chris will take you out. He was good about letting Cyril run last year."*

"He took me on a walk this morning Do you think he will keep me?"

"I bet he does. I heard him tell Mommy he'd take you to see Doctor Ralph today."

"I don't understand why I have to see a doctor."

"He's going to check you for bugs and stuff."

"Bugs? I don't have bugs!"

"I know. Humans are silly like that, though. They just have to check."

"Will it hurt?"

"No. Probably not. They want to look for a chip, too."

"What's that?"

"I'm not sure. I think sometimes people put something inside us, and then the doctor shoots you with a gun and they know who your human is."

"Guns like the one that killed that man?"

"No, like when you go to a grocery store, and you go to the counter to pay, and they shoot the stuff and figure out how much the humans owe. That kind of gun."

"That will hurt."

"No, it won't. You won't even feel it. It's like rays of light or something."

"Well, okay. Maybe I won't hide. Chris was nice this morning. I got to meet lots of people."

"Who?"

"Well, I went to this place that serves lots of food, and a woman named Trudie gave me a treat..."

"That was my place! That's Tiger Lily's Café. Starting next week, I'll be back at work there every day. Did you go anywhere else?"

"We went to a bakery. It smelled really good. They had special kinds of treats, and a nice woman gave me two. I think

her name was Isabel. I met a dog there. I can't remember her name."

"That was Tillie. She's there every day. Well, every day but Sunday."

"She was very nice. She wanted me to tell you all that she missed you this week and can't wait to see you all again."

"Yeah. We missed her, too. She unlocks doors for us. Cool stuff like that."

"Where do you think Chris went?"

"He had to go home. He's been out of town for a few days, and he needed clean clothes. And then he was going to the Coast Guard Station, and then he's coming back here, to take you to see Doctor Ralph."

"Okay. I really want him to like me, but I'm still kind of scared about going. What you said, about finding out who my human is. They think Randy is the man that died in that accident. If it was someone else…if my human, Randy, is still alive…will they make me go live with him?"

"No. It sounded like Pete will try to find him and arrest him. He would be in prison. They can't make you go there."

"I guess you're right. I feel bad for him, if he's dead or if he goes to prison. He really was a good human. Until recently."

"Once they go bad, you have to get rid of them."

"That sounds heartless."

"No more heartless than I hear some humans can be to us."

26

Henrie was pleased the wind had abated. Still, he bundled for the cold. He approached Justin. "I have a job for you."

"Sure. What can I do?"

Henrie reached into his coat pocket and brought out two cans of spray paint, one red and one purple. "I need you to vandalize the building again."

"What?"

"I need you to take this paint and write these things." Henrie gave Justin a tablet. "One statement on one building, then another on another, until you finish."

"I can't do that!"

"You can, and you must do it quickly. I called in a news tip. Cameras are coming to film the most recent debacle."

"What?"

"Do not question me. Just do it."

Justin took the tablet and the purple paint and sprayed. Henrie followed. When the purple was gone, he gave Justin the red. He finished a minute before the news van stopped at the corner. Henrie pocketed the paint; Justin grabbed his shovel and continued to move snow.

Dan Tapper stepped out of the van. He saw Henrie and walked in his direction. "What happened this time?"

"Vandals shot the windows of every storefront in the building."

"Another Muslim scare?"

Henrie could not help himself. His eyes closed and he took a deep breath. "The individual who draws your attention is Hindu, but no, we have no reason to believe her business was targeted in particular."

"Not in particular. Well, what, then, would you say?"

Henrie ignored the question and instead made a suggestion. "Perhaps your crew can take long shots from one end of the building to the other?"

"Oh, sure." Dan turned to his crew. "Set up, take some long shots. Make sure you get all of the graffiti."

"But..."

"Just get it. Do I have to do everything for you?"

"Yes, sir."

"Who can I interview?"

"Allow me to bring business owners to you. Your cameras can use the building as a backdrop. Your viewers will keep the travesty in mind."

Henrie knocked on the door of Soul's Harbor. Pastor Teresa stepped out wearing her Sunday morning regalia. She was careful to stand where viewers could read the words on the building behind her. She made a brief statement and returned to the church.

In short order, Henrie led Dan and the cameras down the street as one business owner after another stepped out, made a brief statement, and ceded camera time to the next. Henrie ended the segment with a brief interview of his own in front of The Drug Store.

Dan was ecstatic. "This is the first time an interview on this street went as planned. Thank you!"

"You are most welcome. Please call if you need additional information."

He walked to the camera man and someone who appeared to be an editor or producer. Each nodded and slipped something into a pocket as he passed.

Chris huddled with his most trusted staff. They needed to plan for the immediate future, while they waited on a replacement.

He, Janelle, Trevor and the communications chief drank coffee and ate donuts – just like cops, thought Chris – in the staff lounge. Over the intercom, he heard, "Skipper, wanted on the main floor."

Chris stood to go, but was stopped in his tracks. His Commander, posted hundreds of miles away, strode into the room. Chairs went back, bodies straightened, and salutes were given.

"At ease. Let's talk in private."

Chris led his commander to his office, where they sat. And talked. And talked. His crew glanced through the windows from time to time, nervous.

Eventually, Chris came to the door and said, "Janelle, please call Annie. I'm not going to be able to take that dog to the vet, and he'll close pretty soon."

"Yes, sir."

Annie got off the telephone and went to the dining room. She looked at her pile of cats and a dog and said, "Well, Sis, we're having a bit of a bad start. Your maybe Daddy is held up at work. I'll have to take you to the vet. Doctor Ralph closes at noon today."

Sis seemed to understand her. She hid her head underneath her paws.

Annie watched as Tiger Lily, Mr. Bean and Kali leaned in, licking her and purring things into her ear. Eventually, Sis rose.

Annie hooked the leash to the rainbow scarf and led Sis from the Inn to one of the vehicles. She wasn't sure if Sis would know what to do, but she seemed to handle herself well. She jumped into the driver's seat and crossed quickly to the passenger side, turning to face front.

"Okay. You know how to ride. Let's see how you do with the vet."

Pete went to the Inn and looked into the library. There they were. Kullen and Barry. He couldn't understand why he liked these guys so much.

They looked up as he entered, got "that look" on their faces, looked at one another, then rose, slowly and in sync, to follow him to the kitchen.

Henrie wasn't there. Pete had passed him on The Avenue, doing something outrageous with Dan Tapper's news crew.

Cyril stuck with Pete. He wanted to hear what the two goofy guys had to say. Kali followed and settled into Cyril's side.

Pete put a file on the table and opened it to the security footage photos. "Tell me what you know about these guys."

Kullen picked one photograph out of the pile and looked at it. Pointing, he said to Barry, "This is Crank, isn't it?"

"Yeah. Crank. And that one is Spaz."

"I don't know the other two. Do you?"

"Nope. Never saw them."

Pete said, "Who are Crank and Spaz?"

Barry answered. "They're the number one and two of their group. He's the one that lays down the bets and..." Barry looked at the table.

Pete said, "Bets? That's how you lost money? You're gambling?"

Kullen looked at the table now. "I didn't know he was doing it. Not until recently. He did it when I wasn't there."

Barry still looked at the table. "Way to throw me under the bus, man."

Kullen's eyes didn't leave the table. "No, I'm not doing that. I just thought you were a better gamer when I wasn't around, so I started leaving you alone more. I thought these guys had a gaming crew."

Pete asked, "So what were you doing when he was gambling? Something else illegal?"

"I was...um...well...I met this girl...."

Barry looked up at Kullen. "You spent all your time with her? You didn't say, man!"

"I didn't...well...I've been thinking I need to get a real job. I, um, well...I just need to do this, Barry."

Pete shook his head. "This is really sweet. But tell me about Crank and Spaz."

"Oh. Well, they work as, like, regional guys, enforcers, kind of, for this sport site."

"What's the name?"

Barry told Pete everything he knew. Kullen looked at the table. Cyril yawned, having learned more than he ever wanted to know about online gambling and leg breaking.

Pete finally asked, "Why would they shoot up the entire street?"

Barry looked at him, confused. "It's not like we can figure this town out, ya know. And if we can't, I mean, we aren't dummies, how do you expect other people to do it?"

"I don't understand..."

Kullen said, "You need to put up signs in this place, man! Annie figured it out. She has signs on her places, but just look around. You can't tell the cyber place from the flower shop."

Barry continued, "You have to say 'the blue one on the south side of the street, or the yellow one next to the green one...'"

"Or the orange one next to the purple one..."

"Or go straight across from the Inn, turn right and count three doors."

"Signs, man. Signs."

By now, Pete was laughing too hard to explain the sign problem. He rose to leave, then asked, "Hey, Kullen. What's your girl's name?"

"What? Oh. Um. Toni."

"When's the last time you talked to her?"

"Before we left."

"You'd better be giving her a call. She might wonder why she hasn't heard from you."

Kali said to Cyril, *"If he ignores her like he ignores me, she'll drop him for some other guy."*

Annie rushed home with Sis. She had to be there on time. Henrie filled the buffet with a light lunch, finishing it just in time.

He switched on the television and caught the beginning of the noon news. Charles Veritone's face filled the screen.

"Welcome! You're tuned to WQVX, the Lake Region's good news station." He continued with news of the storm recovery, cutting to Felix with up to date weather information. After an interminable commercial break, Charles was back on screen, Dan Tapper beside him.

"I understand there was another shoot-out in Chelsea, Dan. What do you have to tell us?"

Dan looked at Charles with an earnest expression. "Well, Charles, once again, the Muslim neighborhood on Sunset Avenue has met with tragedy. Tragedy in the form of people who cannot accept people of a different religion."

It looked to Annie as if Charles had swallowed a cotton ball.

Dan continued. "I'll let this video tell the story."

The screen cut to video. It was a long shot of the building, windows boarded up, with what looked to be red and purple graffiti on the walls.

Close-up of Pastor Teresa outside Soul's Harbor. "It was tragic to hear the gunshots. Most of us were staying in a community shelter during the storm. Being without

power, we were not home or at work on this side of the
street. Then shots rang out, and you can see the result."

The camera moved in for a close-up of the graffiti, then
moved to Mem outside CyberHealth. "The shots rang out.
We huddled in place, too frightened to leave our shelter.
And then, we heard car doors slam, and the sound of a car
careening away from The Avenue." Once again, a close-up
of the graffiti preceded the next speaker.

Laila stood, solemn and dressed in her signature
Pakistani clothing, in front of Babar Foods. Dan moved
close, the better to show he was standing proud beside this
Muslim woman. In a sad voice, she said, "We all suffered
damage to the exterior and interior of our stores. We
thank God that only the first floor was hit and that more
people were not injured or killed."

Close up on graffiti, then the cameras focused on a
wretched-looking Holly, shivering in her wheelchair and
without a coat in front of DoubleGood. "They didn't care
who was hurt, who would suffer, from their senseless act
of violence."

Close up of graffiti, then the cameras moved to Clara at
Bloomin' Crazy. There she was. A sad excuse for a sassy,
vibrant woman. No flower in her hair. No make-up. Tears
streaming down her face. Sniffling, and with a tissue to her
nose, she said, "I had intended to send my dear mother all
of my profits from Christmas sales. This ludicrous assault
on humanity will make that impossible."

Another close up. Finally, the camera moved to Henrie,
in between The Drug Store and The Clinic. The camera
moved back obligingly, to show graffiti on both sides. As
Henrie spoke, they closed in on first one, then the second

set of graffiti. Henrie said, "Most tragic, our dear friend, and a friend to everyone in the region, a nurse practitioner, on duty during the storm, was injured in the attack. She is recovering at the hospital."

Dan turned to Charles Veritone. "There you have it, Charles. Another tragedy in Chelsea."

Charles, face red, mouth contorted in what looked like choked-back laughter, looked down at his notes. He read, "Downtown Chelsea Rocks tonight five to midnight. Buffet for all at Bon Vivant Grille. Special sales downtown all night. Santa Claus, Madrigal Singers, Jazz Quintet. Desserts and treats to die for. Celebrate the end of the storm! More information on our social media sites."

Dan, expression still earnest, said, "What?"

Charles broke into laughter. He managed to say, "Felix, what's the weather like?"

Annie and Henrie laughed so hard they couldn't speak for several minutes. Finally, Annie asked, "What did you give his crew?"

"Complementary meals for two, drinks included, at Bon Vivant, good until the end of the year."

"We won't be able to do that again."

"I fear not. But it was fun the first and only time."

Annie stopped in the dining room before going upstairs. All of their guests were there, chatting amiably and laughing about the more dramatic instances of their visit.

"You've endured a lot here," she said.

"But what fun!" said Helen.

"I'm glad you enjoyed it. We want to make up for the little incidents, you know, what we would consider out-of-character. The ferret, the fire alarm, the gunshots...you know. The kinds of things you don't want to find at a resort."

"They weren't a problem, really," said Sue.

"But just because…" Annie handed each of them a ticket for a meal on-the-house, drinks included, to Bon Vivant. "Downtown Chelsea Rocks starts at five o'clock and goes until midnight. There will be shopping, food and drink specials, music at Mo's Tap and Sassy P's Wine & Cheese. It's a real celebration."

Kullen and Barry dressed for cold weather. They were determined to see the rest of the town. Or at least, the rest of The Avenue. The side that had signs.

They reached the door but were stopped by Henrie.

"I dare say, you will have time to enjoy the town, but first.…" Henrie gave Kullen a bucket filled with chemicals and brushes. He gave Barry a bucket with warm, soapy water.

"If you have need of more water, let me know, or make use of the snow."

Kullen asked, "What are we doin' here, Henrie?"

Henrie walked them to the front porch and pointed to a red wagon with a top. It was made of resin. He opened the lid and pointed down.

Kullen and Barry jumped back, holding their noses.

"What's this?" "Cripes!"

"Do you remember our conversation on the back porch? The one in which you, shall I say, fiddled with the latches to some animal cages?"

"Oh, yeah. That rabbit almost got out."

"Almost. Unlike the ferret. He was out of his cage for two days and a night. He fashioned his own toilet."

"Oh."

"Yes. Oh. I was certain you would offer to clean it, if only you knew."

"Um...well, yes, Henrie. If only I knew, and now I do, so yes. Let me offer to clean it."

"Thank you. And please enjoy the rest of your stay at the KaliKo Inn."

27

Henrie moved to the front door to meet his "date." Martha came in with Little Fred, Speckles and Daryll running in behind her.

JoJo came to the foyer behind Henrie. "Come here, Little Fred. We're going to have fun tonight!" She looked at Henrie and Martha. "Stay out as long as you like. I'm taking her with me to my room in the basement."

Ray and Cheryl stopped at the Inn to pick up Chris and Annie and to drop off Jock. Pete and Janet got out of their car at the same time. Cyril bounced out happily.

The dogs had not seen one another in several days. They had a lot of catching up to do. Cyril wanted to hear about Carter's interview. He heard Pete tell Janet how Jock had kept the man from getting up to run. Jock wanted to meet Sis, the girl dog he had seen in the truck. Cyril had kept her to himself.

The crowd in the foyer grew as Clara walked in, Ramon on her arm. He and the band had made it as far as Chelsea. The roads in Minnesota opened a day before the roads leading to Chelsea. At last, they were free to travel, but their next gig, on the eastern edge of Ohio, was canceled due to snow. They found a welcome shelter in Chelsea.

The rest of the band was already settled at the Inn. Jules and Noelle, the trumpet and cello of the quintet, and married to one another, were in the room recently vacated by Holly and Jolly. Manny, a heartbreaker and the drummer of the group, bunked with BeeBop, the guitarist whom no woman would have, in the upstairs room of the carriage house.

Cyril and Jock stopped sharing stories with one another long enough to gape. There she was. The beautiful Fiamma. A Bergamasco. Face and eyes covered by matted and dreadlocked hair. Well, entire body covered with matted and dreadlocked hair, but it was the hair over her face and eyes that she so fetchingly tossed whenever a boy dog was in the room.

Cyril and Jock stood, mouths open, tongues out, drool running to the floor, while Fiamma glanced around the room.

She smiled and winked at the boys, but she walked to the back of the foyer, where a shy, scared giant schnauzer stood, shaking at the commotion, with a phalanx of cats surrounding her. Keeping her steady.

Fiamma approached and sat. *"Hello. I'm Fiamma. We're going to be great friends."*

It was Saturday night. And what a night. The roads were clear. Kind of. Piles of snow that looked a mile high were in the median and in the middle of most intersections around town. It was still dangerous to drive. One had to drive slowly and check from all sides before turning or proceeding. The state was enforcing an "every intersection is a four-way-stop" rule.

Christmas In Chelsea specials were in abundance. So were shoppers. The combination of the news story, which started trending immediately, and information on social media sites brought families from around the region in droves.

Spotlights shone on the building on the other side of The Avenue, although you had to actually be on that side of the street to see it. Justin had continued his vandalism. In red paint, he scrawled the name of each business to the left of each door, perpendicular and against the frame.

The windows, still covered with plywood, had been festooned with strings of holiday lights. Inside the businesses, dark due to the lack of windows, and each suffering some degree of damage, bright holiday decorations added to the atmosphere: five foot high snowmen, seven foot tall candles, rotund Santa Clauses, and multi-colored inflatable Christmas trees.

All of the businesses would be open until midnight, and they would be staffed by trusted employees. They needed extra cash having been forced not to work for several days, and the owners planned to party on the other side of The Avenue.

Santa Claus – really, it was Greg, a local realtor and president of the Rotary Club – met children inside the yoga studio. Bright lights shining through the windows showed the way. An eight foot tree had been hastily raised, festooned with bows and ribbons and lighted with lightshow projectors.

The holiday music that played outside came from the studio. An entertainment system with amazing speakers was an early Christmas gift from Annie to Henrie. He loved to listen to classical music, blues, jazz, hip-hop, country, bluegrass, gospel, contemporary Christian and, well, everything. He kept the level low, but this system would allow soft tones to emanate from every corner of his apartment. Now, they blared in the yoga studio, and Jolly had added outdoor speakers, including some that worked through a wireless connection on the other side of the snow barrier.

Annie and Chris walked arm-in-arm, which was rare. Generally, they kept a certain amount of physical distance in public. Tonight, they didn't. They could get back to normal later.

Tonight, they planned to dine with their friends at the Bon Vivant Grille, then move to Mo's Tap where they would sample flights of artisan beers and listen to madrigal singers. Before making their last stop, they would pick up breakfast treats, perhaps a pie or cookies, and at least one box of truffles from Mr. Bean's Confectionary. Yes, even the bakery was open until midnight.

They would end the evening at Sassy P's Wine & Cheese. Ramon's band, the jazz quintet Bergamasco, would play until midnight. Or longer.

Christmas In Chelsea would not be a complete bust. They wouldn't make as much as they had planned, but Saturday evening sales all through town were greater than they had dreamed.

At the Inn, since even the guests planned to spend the evening on the town, Annie left the apartment door open. The big dogs had free run of the house, just like the cats.

As the humans left, the rest of The Avenue's companions came on a dead run. Simon Finnegan and Oscar McMurphy, who loved making the run through the snow tunnel from one side of the street to the other, and Tillie. Tillie was at the Inn for the first time in several days, certainly for the first time since the snow started, and she had missed all of her friends. They all talked, one after the other, as they caught up on town news and gossip.

"We missed you, Tillie. We needed to get the doors unlocked, and you're still the only one that can do that."

"But you got outside somehow, and rescued Sis."

"Mommy forgot that basement door again."

"I think she's doing it on purpose now."

"I think you're right. Anyway, we were really lucky that Justin kept the stairway clear, so we could open it."

"He was in the bakery several times this week, getting coffee and something to eat. I like him now. He used to be mean and scary."

"I heard him tell Darryl and Donnie that he has a five-year plan."

"What's that?"

"A plan where you start something now, and end it in five years."

"What's he gonna do?"

"Well, he's going to work hard, keep going to school, get a degree…"

"What's that?"

Cyril said, *"That's a college education."*

"Oh. Okay. What else?"

"And then he hopes he can get a place of his own, and a good job. He wants to get a job here in town, but he doesn't know if he can."

"Why not?"

"He has what you call a bad reputation, and he doesn't know if five years is enough."

"But Boone doesn't care."

"No, he doesn't. And Ian, too. Ian has been spending time with him."

"That's good, but what does he do with Ian?"

"I think he'll be helping with festivals and sports things and stuff. You know, the things that Ian does with most of his time."

"But he doesn't get paid for."

"Yeah."

"So what else is happening?"

Cyril brought everyone up-to-date with the police end of it. *"Pete thinks he found your human, Sis. He's pretty sure he's the guy that was found in the truck."*

Sis looked at the floor. *"That's too bad. I really never wished that kind of bad luck to him."*

"But it helps you. It means you are free to go with someone else."

"Yeah. Like Chris."

"He hasn't said for sure that he will take me."

"He's been busy. Tomorrow's Sunday. Everything slows down on Sunday. I'll bet he says it then."

"Well, maybe. But what else about Randy, my human?"

"They found a gun, and Pete has what they call a silencer, something that keeps the bullets silent. They'll test the bullets and see if that's the gun that was used. That way, he doesn't have to tell anyone about what we did."

"*You mean the clues.*"

"*We gived good clues. Why don't Pete wants to give us credit?*"

"*Because it's not something he can take into court.*"

"*We could go to court with him!*"

"*And do what? Those people don't understand us, and they would think Pete was crazy or something.*"

"*Oh.*"

"*What about that Carter guy?*"

"*He's in our holding tank right now. He'll probably be going to jail for a long time.*"

"*I heard Sue say something about seeing him.*"

"*Yeah. She and Robert went in to see him. Pete told her that he lied to protect her, and she wanted to thank him.*"

Jock said, "*I was there, you weren't. I was a hero.*"

"*Oh stuff it.*"

"*I was!*"

"*I'm glad, but don't rub it in. I can't be ten places at one time. I was busy doing other things.*"

"*Well…you're right. You did other stuff.*"

Speckles said, "*Tell us what's happening with the goofy guys!*"

A tear slid down Kali's nose, and she curled into a ball. Ko lay down beside her, arms around her in comfort.

Tiger Lily said, "*They're okay. They're goofy, but they didn't really do anything wrong. The one guy, Barry, he's going to have to probably go to court for the gambling.*"

"*Pete doesn't think he'll have to go to jail or anything.*"

"*That's good. I saw the other one, Kullen, talking to a girl on his cell phone. He was using that camera thing, showing her all over the Inn, all of the rooms and things. He told her he would show her all of the places he goes tonight.*"

Kali sat up. "*He has a girl?*"

"*Yeah,*" said Mr. Bean. "*Tory or Toni or Toby. Something like that.*"

"*Maybe that's why he wouldn't look at me. Maybe she would be jealous if he did.*"

Speckles and Daryll laughed. Tiger Lily shushed them.

"*So what about the other folks? The ones that wanted to kill themselves?*"

"*They've gotten really friendly with Robert and Sue, and they've been talking business. Robert said he could use a guy like Tom, because he's taking his company somewhere.*"

"*International.*"

"*Yeah. International. Where's that?*"

Cyril answered. "*That means he's going to expand his business in places outside the United States. He could open up in Canada or Mexico, or further away, in Europe or something.*"

"*Wow. That would be fun! Maybe Mommy could go international!*"

"*I don't know how she would do that...*"

"*She could. I know she could.*"

"*But...*"

"*But nothing. We could go to Paris!*"

"*Rome!*"

"*I heard about a place called Belgium where they make really good chocolate.*"

"*Or Italy. Dey makes good wine dere.*"

"*Give it a rest! Anyway, since they don't have anything to worry about, no house or family or anything, they're going to follow Robert and Sue home to somewhere in Texas, and it sounds like everything will work out for them.*"

"*Now all Pete has to do is find the leg breakers.*"

"*I duzn't understand. Why does leg breakers shoot at tings? Why duzn't dey just break legs?*"

Cyril answered again. "*I think that is what you call an industry term. There is an underworld of criminals, and people who are called leg breakers are also called enforcers. They can be mean and...well, mean.*

"*Will he be able to catch them?*"

"*Yeah. He told those state troopers and gave them pictures. They already know who the two are, Crank and Spaz. They were real happy to get those pictures. They'll be able to put them in prison for a long, long time.*"

Tiger Lily asked, "*Why is it that Pete gets along so well with those state guys? Didn't he used to have trouble with them?*"

"*That was before he started really listening to us. Now that he listens to us, and doesn't let them know that's what he's doing, they think he's some kind of magician. They were saying he has a sixth sense.*"

"*What's that?*"

"I think the definition is that he has a sense that other people don't. Everybody has some senses, like hearing and seeing, but this sixth sense, it's like a really good intuition."

"What's that?"

"It's an ability to understand something right away that nobody else can."

"Does Pete have that?"

"No. He has us. We tell him what he needs to know, and what nobody else can see."

"But in a way, it is a sixth sense. Only him and Mommy and Henrie..."

"...and Chris..."

"...and Ray..."

"Yeah. Only those folks. We're their sixth sense."

Fiamma sighed. *"I love hearing your stories. I wish I could be here sometime when all of this stuff happens. I feel like such an outsider."*

Jock looked at her in a moony, dreamy way, and his tongue dropped out of his mouth, dropping a little dog drool on the floor in the process.

28

Sunday morning dawned with a clear sky and sunshine. The wind was a breezy five miles per hour and warming across the lake. Now the messy part would begin.

Piles of snow would begin to melt as the day wore on, and water from the melt would become ice underfoot when the sun started its descent.

Annie complained to Henrie and Chris, "I want it to snow from December first through February, then magically melt away. None of this thawing and freezing over and over again."

Henrie merely smiled as he listened. He glanced down briefly. Little Socks was on top of Chris's thigh under the table, eyes closed, a soft purr the only evidence she was awake.

He took fresh breakfast items from the kitchen into the dining room. Eight guests gathered at the table. Two in the carriage house had not made an appearance. Kali and Ko were on hand at their stations. Ko sat up and watched as everyone ate. Kali stared at Kullen and Barry and seemed…sad.

Noelle was saying, "…and I saw most of you on the dance floor last night. Why didn't you get up, Kullen?"

"I was dancing in my heart. Believe me. I was with a date…"

Barry cut in. "He had his girlfriend on camera phone almost all night. I was ready to ditch him and find someone that would talk to me."

"Seems like you found someone. Trudie is one of my favorite people."

Barry laughed. "She wanted to make someone jealous, and I needed, well, I was getting pretty bored. There were only two of us at the table, and I was still a third wheel."

Jules laughed. "She's working on Manny, our drummer. He has a thing for her, but only when we're in Chelsea. She has started an 'I don't care' campaign, to pique his interest."

Noelle said, "It's beginning to work."

Henrie had finished stocking breakfast items and went back to the kitchen. The animals had a snack of bacon earlier, and he wondered if he should try to locate them. Certainly they were fine.

Chris was saying, "…I'll do that after church. Then maybe you could bring her over this afternoon."

"That will work. I might bring Little Socks. She seems glued to you this weekend."

"It's been nice, having her close."

The purr machine revved a bit.

"I wonder if Little Socks, or at least one of the cats, should stay with her for a day or two, so she feels at home."

"I don't think so. Henrie, what do you think?"

Henrie turned from the stove to face them. "I believe she will transition well. I have done some reading on the breed. She will react well to the solitude of one dog, one human."

"I guess I may as well use my new-found can-do-no-wrong status and start taking her to work with me."

Henrie sat at the table with a cup of coffee. "Please tell me about that. We have been so busy I have not had an opportunity to hear about your status."

"I thought I lost my job when I turned down the promotion. I was coming up with ideas for how to spend my time. But after a visit from the Commander, that's all changed."

"How has it changed?"

"Well…I get the promotion, but I get to stay right here in Chelsea. It will be a title-less promotion, and I'll get more pay."

"What occurred to change your situation?"

"I fired Shorter. He was in charge of overseeing maintenance, and he'd been negligent. After our little adventure in Bayless, he realized he needed to doctor the logs – again – but I got them before he could do anything. And then, well, where there is smoke, there is fire."

"What had Shorter been doing?"

"I was alerted to a drinking problem, an on-the-job problem, and when he lost his job, some folks came forward at the Commander's office. Some people had been feeding him false information about my performance. Information they received from Shorter."

"Do tell."

"And the rest of it involves the Governor."

"He did something for you?"

"I didn't ask him to do anything. On his own, he called to commend my efforts on behalf of his son, and in the course of the conversation, they talked about my silence with him and the media, and his appreciation. He let it be known that having me in this state was an asset."

"And the Commander was not aware of this?"

"He thought I was an asset, but he heard those rumors. He saw a way to mitigate the situation by acquiescing to the demands of a Senator in my home state. When things started to tumble together, he came here to discuss it with me personally."

"And you were able to convince him…"

"…that I would be a much better asset here than there."

Annie looked at the clock. "Oh! We'll be late!" She stood, but was stopped in her tracks by several cats and a big dog.

"I was just coming to get you. It's time for church."

Henrie went to the front porch to get the wagon. Annie and the cats waited in the foyer.

"Jump in, kids."

They didn't jump in.

Henrie looked at Annie. She looked back. Henrie thought, why not. They probably know about the problem. And he spoke to the cats.

"I'm sure you are aware your wagon was used for an unintended purpose. Our guests, Kullen and Barry, took it upon themselves to clean the wagon. I dare say you will find it in perfect order."

Tiger Lily looked up at Henrie, then back at the cats. Tentatively, she rose to look inside. She sniffed. Apparently, she found nothing objectionable. She jumped in, and the others followed. Except for Kali.

Henrie looked around the corner. Kali still sat on the buffet, looking listlessly at Kullen and Barry. Henrie picked her up and carried her into the foyer, placing her gently in the wagon. She didn't seem to care. Ko hissed.

Annie, unfashionable outwear in place, grabbed the handle of the wagon and left, Henrie, Chris and Sis following.

Pastor Teresa had a subdued crowd. The windows were still covered in plywood and holiday lights; tall outdoor decorations added a bit of light to the dim interior.

She gave up on her sermon, as no one seemed the least bit interested, and said, "Let's end with a song. I love this one. It's a gospel song, written by Mosie Lister. 'Till The Storm Passes By.'"

She sang in her strong mezzo-soprano while the congregation joined in.

In the dark of the midnight have I oft hid my face; while the storm howls above me, and there's no hiding place; 'mid the crash of the thunder, precious Lord, hear my cry; "Keep me safe 'til the storm passes by.

'Til the storm passes over, 'til the thunder sounds no more; 'til the clouds roll forever from the sky, hold me fast, let me stand, in the hollow of Thy hand; keep me safe 'til the storm passes by.

When the long night has ended, and the storms come no more, let me stand in Thy presence on that bright, peaceful shore. In that land where the tempest never comes, Lord may I dwell with Thee when the storm passes by.

Hold me fast, let me stand, in the hollow of Thy
hand; keep me safe 'til the storm passes by.

As always, Annie thought Teresa spoke to her heart.

After church, it seemed everyone from Chelsea wanted
to meet Sis. Most of the folks from The Avenue had met
her and knew most of her story. Others had heard only
rumors.

Annie, Chris and Henrie were peppered with questions,
and Sis was surrounded by well-wishers who wanted to
touch her, pet her. Sis, with good reason, got scared.

Chris didn't know how to calm her, but Pete came to
the rescue. He walked over with Cyril, and in his Police
Chief voice, he said, "Sit!"

Cyril and Sis sat and looked to him for more
commands. Pete reached into his pocket and brought out
two treats. He gave one to each of the dogs. It worked.

"If you plan on adding to your family, keep a pocket full
of treats at all times."

Henrie checked the rooms. The members of
Bergamasco would stay on another day, but everyone else
was gone by the time they returned from church. The
rooms seemed to be in order and ready for Hilly to clean
the next day.

Kali ran into Kullen and Barry's room, looked all
around, and left, head down and tail dragging the floor
behind her.

He put together a light lunch for himself and Annie,
one of the rare times they were alone recently.

Annie picked out a ham salad sandwich and helped herself to potato salad and fruit salad.

"What a week. I'm glad it's over."

"I believe we ended on a happy note. I understand Tom and Helen will follow Robert and Sue to south Texas. He will go to work for their company."

"I heard. It was a good thing you did, Henrie, confronting them when you did. You stopped a tragedy."

"I do not believe their hearts were in the deed."

"You're right, but still…. And what about the brothers? Do you know what's in store for them?"

"I believe Barry will have to return to face some legal music, and Kullen has requested use of the honeymoon suite for New Year's weekend."

"No."

"Yes. He talked to Pastor Teresa, who will perform the nuptials."

"I can't wait to meet this woman."

"Indeed. She is in for a ride. I trust she is up to it."

"Well, we have to get past Christmas. Have you thought any more about my offer?"

Henrie sighed. Earlier in the month, Annie had suggested that he visit his family in…well, had he actually told her where his family lived? No. Not yet. Maybe soon.

"You say this with the greatest sincerity, Annie, but I have not reached the point that I am comfortable making that trip."

"Okay. So here we are with no plans for Christmas. My family is headed in other directions, Chris is, well, I don't

think he wants to see his mother face-to-face. And you
don't want to visit your family. What do you suggest?"

"We have only a moderate number of guests. We could
decorate the house and plan two days of feasting."

"Christmas eve oyster stew."

"With pizza. I investigated the carnage from earlier this
week. Your toppings were unique. I will try to replicate
it."

"Perfect. At home, if we didn't have oyster stew, we had
pizza. This will be the best of both worlds. Did your family
have a Christmas Eve favorite?"

"Not necessarily for Christmas Eve, but a favorite dish
in my household was Ndole. It is made with spinach and
bitter leaves, but we can stick with spinach, also peanuts,
beef and shrimp, garlic and other spices. "

"Sounds wonderful. Maybe we can ask Chris if he
would like to add anything."

"And for Christmas day, chicken poulet and sese
plantains, perhaps some kwakoko bible."

"What are they?"

"Allow me to made a traditional meal from my home
country, and as we eat, just you, Chris and I, I will tell you
about my hometown and about my family. On Christmas
day. Not before. And now, it is time for you to take Sis to
her new home."

The companions introduced Sis to the detective agency.
They had spent little time in it during the past week, but
had done so much detecting, it hardly seemed useful. But it
was still a comfortable place.

The cats picked seats on the cushions, and Tiger Lily showed Sis how Cyril would lie, outside the agency, with his head under the tablecloth.

She tried it.

"You need to ask Henrie to put a long cushion here. It would be more comfortable."

"That's a good idea. I'll have to work on that."

"So what do you do in here?"

"We detect things."

"What kind of things."

"Likes da kindsa tings dat we did wit da pitchers."

"You mean telling your humans about my human?"

"Yeah. Like that. We sit in here and cogitate…"

"What's that?" asked Mr. Bean. *"We've been cogitating, and I don't even know what it is?"*

"That means we think about things, and talk about them, and turn them over and over until we understand them."

Sis asked, *"What you were talking about, about being the sixth sense for your humans, will I do that with Chris?"*

"Trill!"

"I hope so, too."

"You understood that?"

"Of course. It's just a different language, is all. I think most dogs can understand it."

"But Mo's a cat, and I can't understand him."

"You duzn't work at it," said Sassy Pants.

"You don't, either. You just read his mind."

"I reads everbody's minds."

318

Sis looked at Sassy Pants with awe. *"You do? Did you read my mind?"*

"Not at first. I have to get to know you first, and then I can. I can now, but I couldn't until we'd been around each other for a couple of days. Now, I can see your human and the truck and everything. I couldn't, in the beginning."

"That's a good skill to have."

Little Socks huffed.

"We're going to need your help in the future. Like Cyril helps with Pete and Jock helps with Ray. You'll have to listen to Chris and everything he says to help us detect things. If we're lucky, he'll take you to work, and you'll hear everything that goes on at the Coast Guard Station."

"That sounds exciting. Do you think he'll take me on the boats?"

"Can you swim?"

"Not yet, but I bet I can learn."

"You wouldn't want to swim in cold weather, so hopefully, Chris won't take you out until it gets warm, and you learn in warmer water."

"I hope you're right. He seems like a nice person. I haven't smelled any drugs on him."

"You won't."

"Cept maybe aspirins," said Sassy Pants. *"I tink I seeze him take aspirins one time."*

"Aspirin is okay. It's the harder stuff that isn't."

Little Socks said, *"It will be really important that you tell us if Chris ever says he might leave us. We don't want him to leave us."*

"I can't imagine he would do that, Little Socks," said Tiger Lily. *"He likes us too much."*

"But he almost left."

"No, I think someone wanted him to leave, and he said he would quit his job before he did that."

"And be poor?"

"I don't think he would be poor...."

Tiger Lily looked over at Kali. She had not said a word. Her fur looked shabby. A tear trickled down her nose.

"What's up, Kali?"

Ko answered. *"Those goofy guys never looked at her. Not once."*

"Were they that important?"

"She kind of liked that Kullen. But he never looked at her. Never touched her."

"Henrie said he would be back over New Year, with that girl.

"Bummer. I hope she's over him by then."

The cats and Sis came to attention when Annie came into the dining room. She lifted the tablecloth and said, "Come on, Little Socks. Come with Sis and me to see Chris."

Little Socks jumped up and trotted after Annie. Very un-Little-Socks-like.

Annie and Sis got out of the car. Annie opened her arms for Little Socks, who was too small to see over the snowbanks surrounding the sidewalk.

Little Socks spoke to Sis. *"There's more room out here. Chris's condo looks out at the beach, and the snow moved around more. It's not nearly as high as it is on The Avenue. You'll have a big place to run."*

"It looks nice. What does it look like without snow?"

"I think it looks like the beach at our house. You didn't see it. It's on the back side and it's a whole bunch of white sand."

"Oh. I saw that from my human's truck. Kind of. It was before the storm. There was already snow on the ground, but in some places, the sand was showing through."

"It will look like that, but all sand."

By now, Annie and the girls had reached the door. Chris stood there, holding it open. He stood back and motioned with his hand. Annie hung back, to see what Sis would do.

Sis looked up at Little Socks, who nodded. She then took one more look at Chris's face, and walked in.

It was very nice. It was clean and cozy. Most of the colors were brown and beige, very soothing. In a nook by a chair and a fireplace was a big dog bed. Sis walked to it and sniffed. New store smell. That was okay. She'd gotten things from Randy with new store smell before.

She stepped in and tried it out, moving her feet a few times until she figured out the best way to lie down. It was perfect.

She sat up and looked around. There were some dog toys here and there. Were they from a former dog? She got up and walked to a chew toy. Smelled. New store smell. No. She was a first dog. That was just fine.

She walked into the kitchen. It had a table and chairs, and there was another dog bed. She sniffed. New store smell. This was getting better and better.

Sis explored the entire house. She wondered – once – where Little Socks was, but she was too interested in exploring to look.

Here was a bedroom, and another dog bed. That was silly. She wouldn't sleep in a dog bed in this room. She would sleep in the bed with Chris. She would have to train him.

There were more toys. This would turn out to be alright. She had made the right decision to run away. It was frightening, but…all in all…it was a good thing.

Sis went back to the fireplace cushion and lay down. Chris and Annie were there, comfortable on a sofa, and there was Little Socks, curled into Chris's lap.

Annie pulled Chris to the sofa. "Give her time to explore." Little Socks went straight to his lap, where she curled up and purred herself to sleep.

"All this time she never came to me, and now look. She wants to be with me all the time."

"She loves you. I think they knew something was wrong. Well, silly me. They understand everything we say, and they have a deeper understand of human nature than we do. Of course she knew something was wrong. I'm glad you're here for her. And for Sis. I think she's going to like it here."

"Are you sure? She didn't stay in the bed very long."

"She has to explore."

"She's smelling everything. Should I have gone somewhere and gotten used things?"

"No, I think what you did is perfect. She's probably making sure she's the first dog."

"I don't want to look. Where is she now?"

"She's in the kitchen. Take a deep breath, Chris. She'll be fine."

They sat in silence for a minute or two.

"Where is she now?"

"She might be going to the bedroom."

"What if I do the wrong thing?"

"What could you possibly do wrong? You kept Cyril here for several days. Did you make mistakes then?"

"I'm sure I did."

"But Cyril still seems to like you. It couldn't have been too bad."

"I'm just nervous. I've never had a dog before."

"Not even when you were little?"

"Especially not then."

Annie shook her head. No one's childhood is perfect, but hers was more perfect than most. She had parents that loved her for who she was. She knew Chris was loved by his parents, but they put more emphasis on what other people would think.

Sis had returned to the living room. She was in her bed now, and looked to be headed off to sleep.

"See? She wouldn't go to sleep if she was nervous."

"Well, I'm nervous."

"Don't be afraid, Chris. She's a beautiful, apparently well-trained dog."

"That's not what's making me nervous."

Annie looked at him. He was nervous. "What is it?"

"I have something to show you."

He picked Little Socks up and put her on the sofa, rose, and took Annie by the hand. He walked her to a closet.

"You're nervous about a closet?"

"Not a closet. What's in the closet."

"Okay...."

Chris opened the door and pulled out a box of photographs. "Please put these on the table. We'll look at them in a minute."

Annie did, and returned. Chris had pulled out several watercolors. All were of her. Next, he pulled out pen and ink drawings, charcoal sketches, and charcoal sketches done in his more recent style, adding a pop of color to one element.

Annie took her time looking at them. He had caught her in repose, sitting in rocking or Adirondack chairs, walking on the beach, walking down The Avenue, talking to customers at the Café, sitting at a café table at the Winery, leaning on the counter at Mr. Bean's, drinking a beer at Mo's Tap, laughing with Henrie on the porch of the Inn, even holding the hero – Virasana – pose at the yoga studio.

She laughed. "You didn't see me doing that."

"You're right. You said your dad thought you could use a little yoga. I'm just following his thought process."

She walked to the table and looked at the photographs, all taken when she was unaware of the camera, perhaps unaware of his presence.

"Why have you never shown these to me?"

"I was afraid you would be overwhelmed."

"By the art?"

"By the feelings behind the art."

"I think I'm finally ready."

29

Ian had assigned decorating tasks to his students. They weren't his students, really, but he trained them for the sporting events that were held around Chelsea, and he had a great relationship with them. Sometimes. When he wasn't being a mean coach.

All of his students were, according to Ian, above average. They were good students, involved in some kind of volunteer activity, and athletically inclined. Some of them had been involved in heroic events. Last summer, Brendan and Renee, in their summer lifeguard jobs, pulled two local teenagers out of a rip current. That same week, Alena brought down a criminal, using some wicked moves with her bicycle tools.

Tonight, they would be heroes of another sort. Annie and her staff and all the business owners on The Avenue continually hosted block parties at the end of the month, every two months. The New Year's Eve party generally required the most attention.

Tonight, Ian planned to give them a breather. With the promise of an Olympic-quality shell boat and oars, his nine students would assist in decorating, hosting and cleaning after the party. They would help with everything but the serving of alcohol.

While they set up, Ian could hear the argument, over and over again, and with different students, of "who would be the coxswain."

He sat in the catering venue of the Café with his head in his hands when George arrived with coolers of artisan beer. "What's up, man?"

"I've created a monster."

"Hey. What else is new? This has got to be easier than dealing with women."

"How do you know? You're married."

"I've seen you with your women. Sometimes you, you know, forget and double book."

"Those days are over. I'm too old."

"Yeah. Anyway, the kids are gonna love it."

This year, the party had a casino night theme, with poker, blackjack, craps, roulette, and bingo tables. George and Boone's sons had again teamed up to construct a ball drop, and Pastor Teresa wanted to make her new year's resolution bonfire a tradition.

Both would be difficult with the snow, but the set-up, relegated to adults, had been done. Boone removed snow from behind Annie's buildings, an area large enough for both events.

Each block party focused on a different charity. The gift from this party would go to the One Acre Fund, a fund for East African small farmers.

Alena, one of Ian's students, was given the responsibility of managing the fund raising. She set up a table with farm scenes, built to look like an East African community. She was familiar with the 4-H farm scene projects. Instead of a typical Midwest farm scene, her table showed human labor instead of expensive equipment, and her storage facilities were grass huts, wooden sheds, urns and baskets.

The crops she displayed were potatoes, bananas, plantains, sugar, groundnuts and coffee. She wanted to do grains, but with only one table, she had to stop somewhere.

Every two feet on the edge of the table were hand-printed signs that listed typical difficulties faced by farmers in this region. Erratic weather patterns, climate change, the use of one type of soil to produce two or three crops, soil erosion and declining soil fertility, and agricultural processes that have not progressed with the increased population.

Ian was impressed with her effort and the finished product. Attendees would be able to drop contributions into African urns placed around the room.

Harry, the representative from the rental agency, had placed eight gaming stations around the room: two each of poker, blackjack and craps, one roulette and one bingo. Names of the remaining eight students went into a basket, and Alena drew names for assignments.

Brendan and Eddy got poker. Carol and Traci got blackjack. Jessie and Eric got craps. Renee got roulette, and Bill got bingo.

Games would be played with funny money, Styrofoam dice or plastic rainbow-colored chips. Winners would choose their prizes at the end of the evening from a "prize store." Such marvelous prizes as one ounce bubbles (without a wand or pipe), eight-count used crayons, ten-count (mostly broken) colored chalks, animal face coin purses, barrel slime, and glow glasses. Losers would not be disappointed.

Trudie, Carlos and Cookie teamed up to make traditional African dishes for the buffet line. They served chicken Marrakesh, shakshouka, Moroccan peach roasted chicken, lamb tangine, Ethiopian beets and potatoes, Moroccan Fish, Tunisian vegetable couscous, Peri Peri African chicken, and a flaky meat pastry called sambusa. For desserts, they had a milk tart with cinnamon, malva pudding, guava ice cream, and koeksisters, a twisted honey-soaked pastry.

Jesus found wines from Tanzania and had a selection of dries to sweets, reds and whites. Besides beer, George had real and virgin selections of mixed drinks: snake eyes apple martinis, jackpot margaritas, high roller vodka and cranberry juice, face card rum and pineapple, double down bourbon and soda, and wild card shots.

While the party was in full-swing, adults, teens, toddlers and babies enjoying the evening, the companions got together on a bank of cushions.

Cyril said, *"This pile gets bigger with every party."*

"You're right," said Tiger Lily.

The dogs present were Cyril, Jock, Tillie, Fiamma and Sis. Sis grabbed a cushion at the rear of the pile. Her back was to a wall, and she was surrounded by everyone else. She was still a little unsteady with all of the hoopla in this town.

Along with Annie's seven cats were Fat Cat and Scaredy Cat, Speckles and Daryll, and Frank's haughty antique store cat, Claire. As a rule, Claire didn't like cats. But she enjoyed Mo's company. Unless The Dreaded Uncle Honey Bear was present. Blissfully, for Mo, he was not. Mo canoodled to his heart's content.

Sis asked, *"Did Chris show you the picture he just finished?"*

"Yes." "He did!" "Trill!" "It was brilliant!"

His gray, brown and dark blue watercolor had finally been finished and now hung in Annie's dining room, along with another piece he had done some time ago. When he finished this one, he added just a little bit of color here and there.

A rainbow-colored scarf on a patch of dark gray fur in the lower right corner. A slender hand with a multi-colored ring reaching in from the middle left. And in the bottom left, a bright green eye inside black fur that could have been the face of a cat.

The title of the picture was "Home."

Kullen and his wife, Toni, came to the party. They sat next to Pete at a poker table. Pete looked at the young croupier and said, "Set them up. I understand Kullen might have some gambling skills."

"Now, Chief, that's my brother, not me. This is my new blushing bride, Toni. Toni, this is Pete, the Chief of Police. And a good guy, I guess.

Pete laughed. "I am a good guy, and yes, I guess it was your brother. This young dealer is Brendan. He's not only a good croupier, he helped pull a couple of teens out of the lake last summer. One of them was my daughter. I kinda like him."

"If he deals me a winning hand, I'll like him, too!"

Before the couple left the table, they were down. A lot. Kullen said, "It's a good thing we're playing with funny money. Otherwise, we'd start married life flat broke."

They wandered to the farm display and chatted with the young fundraiser. "I'm Alena. Can I tell you about farming in East Africa?"

"What would you do if we said no?"

"I'd tell you anyway." And she did.

Kullen made a sizeable donation.

Henrie spotted them as he picked up a glass of champagne. "Have you celebrated with champagne yet?"

"Oh, yes. A couple of times," answered Toni.

"Are you enjoying yourselves?"

They both nodded, but Kullen was taken by the sight of someone. "Excuse us, Henrie, but I have to introduce Toni to someone special."

Kali came to attention. She knew Kullen was at the Inn, in the honeymoon suite, but she rarely went to the rooms at the carriage house. She could pretend he wasn't there, for as much as he didn't see her.

But now, here he was, walking toward the cushions. She sat up straight. He was walking right to her!

Kullen took Toni's hand, looked between Kali and Toni and said, "More than anyone else, there was one person that took care of me. When I arrived, when I was sick, when I was being questioned, and when I was just being. That was this cat, Kali. Isn't she pretty?"

Toni bent down and picked Kali from the cushions. Kali allowed herself to be held by this stranger, which was totally unusual. Toni whispered into her ear, "I want to thank you. Because of you, he's going to get allergy medicine so I can have a cat just like you."

She kissed Kali on the cheek and put her back on the cushions. As they walked away, the heads of the companions turned to watch the ball come down outside the windows.

It was a new year, and Kali's heart was full.

Thank You For Reading!

The family of cats and the author hope you enjoyed reading this book as much as we enjoyed writing it!

About The Author

Kathleen Thompson was raised on a small family farm in Indiana. She has an undergraduate degree in Sociology from Manchester College (now Manchester University) and an MBA from Indiana University South Bend.

In a variety of towns and circumstances, she served as a probation officer, parole agent and juvenile residential counselor before moving into administrative, marketing and fund raising positions in human service organizations. Ms. Thompson took a break from human services for seven years to own and operate a bar and restaurant. Let's be honest; that's another type of human service.

While making plans to return to her rural roots, Kathi and her mother discovered an injured kitten at the family farm. The kitten, whose face was a mass of injuries, decided to make Kathi her guardian. She wrapped herself around an ankle, purred like a V8 engine, and wouldn't let go.

Against the advice of her mother, Kathi took the kitten home and to a veterinarian. The vet diagnosed road burn serious enough to take all the fur from the left side of her face, and the kitten – Tiger Lily – eventually healed and took a huge piece of Kathi's heart.

Tiger Lily was joined by the rest, rescue kitties, all: Little Socks (thank you, Aunt Mary); Kali, Ko and Mo (thank you, Connie); Sassy Pants (thank you, Ant Sherwy); and Mr. Bean (thank you, Pulaski Animal Center). Recent arrivals Speckles (thank you, Tennille) and Moriah (thank you again, Pulaski Animal Center) have joined the cast but will not live at the Inn.

Tiger Lily's Café rattled around in Kathi's brain – there isn't much else up there – for all of the years since, sometimes as an actual café and sometimes as a book. It was less expensive to write the book.

Connect with Kathi and her family of cats at their website: www.tigerlilyscafe.com, or find them on Facebook: www.facebook.com/tigerlilyscafemysteries.

Find us on the web: www.tigerlilyscafe.com

Find us on Facebook: Tiger Lily's Café, A Mystery Series by Kathleen Thompson

Text to join: Emails are sent every two weeks. You can opt out at any time. LILYSCAFE to 22828 (You may also sign up for the emails from the website.)

Kathleen Thompson